A CHANGE OF FAITH

Roger Kazanowski

To my wonderful daughters Katelyn and Ali,
Thank you for your continuous support
You're the very best!
Love you!
-Poppy

To Alex Foster,
For your support an help constructing this book.
Thank you very much!

Prologue

Ruth Anderson, the first female priest in the history of the Catholic Church, glanced fervently in her rearview mirror, now certain she was being followed. Trailing in the distance behind her was a black truck with tinted windows, its headlights bouncing with each pothole in the road. It was just far enough away so as to be inconspicuous, Ruth having left St. Joseph's Church half an hour ago. But the deeper she drove into the backwoods of Indiana, the more unlikely it became that the truck would take all the same turns. Yet, it did.

Fear welled up in her chest, making it hard to breathe. Tiny needles poked her lungs, and her stomach felt full of dancing butterflies. She wondered if it was the associate of the man who had called her at church earlier. It must be.

Dusk was casting a midnight bluish hue over the soybean fields as she turned back the conversation in her head. She'd been sweeping the pews when she heard the phone ringing in the office. It was five p.m., a bit late for a phone call. Nevertheless, she had set down the broom, went into the office and answered the phone.

"St. Joseph's."

There was a brief silence on the other end of the line. "Vicar Anderson?"

The caller had an accent, but Ruth couldn't place it. A

mix between French and Italian perhaps. Frowning, she said, "This is she.

The tone of the caller was insistent. "My dear, I am calling with regard to a subject of the utmost importance and discretion. Your very career might be at stake."

"Oh my," said Ruth, alarmed. "Is it about the rumors?" She was referring to a strange batch of rumors that had sprung up weeks after her appointment to the priesthood. The gossip circulated around her and a male member of the congregation, suggesting she had broken her vows. They were totally unfounded, of course, but the damage had been done. Being the first female vicar, ever, her reputation had suffered in the wake of the accusations. Some of the damage had been irrevocable—that of public opinion. But now, months later, few people believed in the lies, and those who did made little fuss. Until today, she thought it was water under the bridge.

"I'm afraid so," said the foreign voice. "But fear not, I may have discovered the culprits, as well as what they intend to do next. We must act fast and bring this information to the diocese before it is too late."

"Of course," said Ruth. "I'll phone Bishop Lewis right away."

"No, my dear," the voice interrupted quickly. "Not yet. I have files you must give him. They explain everything."

"Fine," said Ruth. "Can you deliver them here to the church? I'll wait as long as it takes."

"I'm afraid not. My presence, even in a small town like Landler, would bring far more media attention than would be beneficial. I have sent my associate to deliver the files to you personally. However, meeting in a public place such as the church is ill-advised. The men behind this wicked plot will stop at nothing to see you expunged. They have eyes and ears everywhere, even in Landler. I feel it best you meet in the country. There's a town nearby, Waterville, do you know it?"

"I do," said Ruth.

"Excellent. My associate will meet you near the abandoned fire station. After you read and return the files, I'll call again."

"How will I know it's him?"

A Change of Faith

Ruth could detect a warm smile in his voice when he answered. "You'll know, my dear. Now remember, treat this with the utmost discretion. Tell no one, not even fellow members of the congregation or people you trust. First we must get word of this to those of the highest order who can make a difference, before the media gets involved. Understand?"

"Yes, perfectly. Thank you so much."

"Very good."

"Who are you, by the way?" asked Ruth.

Again, there was a brief silence. "A friend of the Church," said the man at last. Then the line went dead.

Ruth was taking deep, calming breaths in her small Sedan, telling herself that the truck behind her must be the man's associate. It made sense, wanting to meet away from the prying eyes of the townsfolk. She was happy to be assigned to a small town like Landler after living in the hustle and bustle of New York most of her life, but small towns meant small town gossip...and there was plenty to be had concerning her of late.

About a quarter-mile before the fire station, the truck flashed its headlights. Ruth slowed to a stop on the side of the road and waited. The truck parked behind her. A door opened and out came a tall man dressed in a dark suit and dress shoes. His gold hair was buzzed military short. In the rearview, she saw him smile and wave her over. He glanced around to make sure no one was watching. They were parked next to a soybean field with not a house or farm in sight. Dying orange sunlight splintered through a copse of trees past the field, settling on them.

Ruth got out and walked toward the man, feeling better with each passing step. He was handsome—mid-30s, slim, with a boyish face and bright blue eyes. "Hiya Ruth," he declared, extending a hand. "Richard Moore. Sorry for all the secrecy here. We just didn't want this information getting in the wrong hands before being able to do something about it. These guys have worked real hard to save their hides. It was a heckuva job to find them."

"Hi Richard," said Ruth, shaking his hand. "Thanks for going through the trouble. Now, what have you got for me?"

"This here." Richard reached in the cab, pulled out a manila folder, and handed it to her. "Give 'er a read once you get back to St. Joseph's. Everything you need is in there. I'm glad to say you won't be having such troubles anymore."

Ruth leafed through the folder absentmindedly, quickly running her eyes over a bunch of printed words in what looked like a report. She snapped it shut and smiled. "I can't thank you enough."

"'Give thanks to the Lord, for He is good; His love endures forever.'"

"Chronicles, 16:34," said Ruth.

"Yes, ma'am." Richard nodded proudly.

"Well, thank you again. I look forward to the call from your...boss?"

"That's right. He'll call you before too long. Have yourself a good night, Ruth."

"Take care," she said, and they parted ways. Richard climbed back in his truck, turned around and drove down the road in the gathering darkness. He disappeared up ahead. Ruth got in her car and did the same, setting the file on the passenger's seat. She drove a few miles until she got to a valley, then ascended along its steep mountain walls, night stars twinkling. Lights of a small town far below.

Curiosity got the better of her. She flicked on one of the interior lights and grabbed the manila folder. Letting off the gas, her eyes flitting from road to file, she read the words.

Wait a minute, she frowned. This must be a mistake. He gave me the wrong file.

The file was composed of random printouts of classic literature. She recognized a passage from Moby Dick. "Consider the subtleness of the sea; how its most dreaded creatures glide under water, unapparent for the most part, and treacherously hidden beneath the loveliest tints of azure."

Behind her, a pair of headlights flashed to life and she could hear a vehicle accelerating. She dropped the folder and grabbed the wheel but it was too late; within moments, a black truck had sidled up beside her and she watched in mute horror as it rammed into the side of her car. She lost control, fumbling with the wheel as the car veered to the right, smashing through a guardrail and plunging headfirst into the dark valley below.

20 minutes later, Cardinal Montross received a call in Rome. He answered in an accented voice.

A Change of Faith

"It's taken care of," said the voice on the other end of the line.

Montross gave the caller the information to a safety deposit box located in New York City. Then he hung up the phone and glanced at the other two cardinals seated around a table in his stately room. He said nothing at first. All he did was nod grimly. Both cardinals breathed a sigh of relief as Montross reached for the decanter and poured three glasses of wine. He handed them out.

"I'm pleased to say," he began at last, lifting his glass in toast, "that order, my friends, has been restored. May we sleep soundly tonight, content in knowing our Father's work has not been in vain; that we fulfill it with our actions and our piety, though no man may know what we have done. Amen."

"Amen," echoed the cardinals.

They brought the wine to their lips and drank.

I

John Adams awoke early in his loft apartment overlooking the Eastern Market in downtown Detroit. Shafts of pink and orange sunlight streamed through the curtainless windows, setting a quiet fire to the canvases strewn haphazardly around the studio. Littered around the room were baked bean tins filled with various brushes, and palette cheese trays dappled with bright colors. Assorted tubes of paint lay piled on an old wooden table, all of it working together to give a collective sense of creative disorder.

Standing beside the full-length window in a denim jacket and dusty overalls, John sipped black coffee from an enamel mug and watched the scene below him, his fingers flecked with paint. Vendors were setting out local vegetables and imported fruit. Already in the predawn light there were Morel mushrooms, crates of freshly-picked apples from nearby orchards, and boxes of russet potatoes. Pretty soon shoppers would flood the market, and like on all Saturdays, John would muster up the will to head down and visit his friends working their fresh produce booths, farmers who would drive in the middle of the night from many miles away to set up.

It was a crisp fall day. Scattered maple leaves blew with the breeze, and folks popped their collars and pulled on their caps to ward off the cold. John smiled, remembering a fall day years ago just like this one, when he had first met Charlotte, the woman of his dreams. If only dreams were real, he thought.

Setting his mug on the windowsill, he walked up to

inspect his latest painting. The piece was large, 4' X 6' with a rugged masculine composition of hard lines and colors. In the middle was a dark, freeform amebic cross with a red dot in the center. Looking at it, he wasn't sure if it was a painting he could be proud of or a piece to be used in the fireplace to warm up his loft come Christmas. He was critical of his paintings, and though outwardly he was quite casual, John was very serious with his brushes in hand; his brows furrowed, lines creasing his face like pressure cracks in a leather belt. Was the painting too symmetrical? Were the colors too cold?

Criticism aside, John enjoyed working on his art. He'd better—he had given up a promising career as an automotive designer at the Ford Motor Company to pursue this passion, which most of his family and friends thought was insane. A creative automotive designer at one of the major auto companies was considered a very sought-after career, only available to a limited number of graduating designers.

John's father had been a bar owner for over 30 years (recently retired), and married to the love of his life, Bernice, for 46 years. During that time, John Sr. worked six days a week and 12 hours a day to support his four sons and wife. He set responsible yet simple goals for his boys: work hard, work honest, and work with respect.

Though John received his undergraduate degree from Wayne State University and a graduate degree from the Art Center in Pasadena, he was at Ford for just a short period of time when it became obvious that his heart wasn't in it. He didn't enjoy the constricted corporate environment. One day when the designer working in the same car studio told John that in only 12 years he could retire and then enjoy life, John realized it would be at least another 30 years before he himself could do the same. He couldn't imagine waiting that long, doing something he didn't really enjoy.

On his return home from work one day, John Sr., a wise and discerning man, asked his son to have a brief talk in the kitchen. It was obvious that John wasn't happy working in the corporate world. John Sr. knew the high status it was being a designer at Ford, but he also noticed the dissatisfaction in his son's eyes whenever he saw him. "John," said his father, "your mother and I have been doing some talking. We understand your frustration with your job. We know you have the passion of an artist…"

"Dad, I—"

"Hang on, son," said John Sr. "Let me finish. I'm not castigating you. Look, you're unhappy. It's obvious. We see it every day. You're never excited to go to work and when you get home you look totally discontented. Your mother and I want you to follow your dreams, whatever they are, but I know you think you'd be letting us down if you did. Well, maybe a few years ago that would be true, seeing as how we contributed to your schooling. But I'm getting older and maybe a little wiser, if you can believe it, and I'm realizing in my old age that if you're not happy doing something, well… then it's not worth the doing. You understand what I mean?"

John nodded, fighting the urge to frown. He'd never in a million years heard his dad speak like this. "My only request?" said John Sr., looking seriously at his son. "Just continue to work hard, and never forget where you come from. You have our support and we know you'll work hard at whatever it is you choose to do. I guess what I'm trying to say is, if you'd like to leave your position at Ford, we will support that decision."

Those words had meant the world to John, and he quickly set two goals in place. First, he would follow his dream of becoming an artist. Second, he would never let his parents down. Which translated to: make them proud and make myself proud. And for five years, that's exactly what he'd been doing. Or trying to do. The truth was, being an artist wasn't easy.

The sun full up now, blasting light into the studio, John went and flicked on his old rabbit-ear T.V. set. He scrolled through the channels until CNN came on, then he grabbed his coffee and sat on a wooden box in front of the screen to watch the news for a few minutes before going down to the market.

"…and there's some more unfortunate news here today, folks," said the newsroom broadcaster, a middle-aged man in a frumpy suit. On the screen was a helicopter feed of a crumpled car at the base of a steep mountain in a rural area. The vehicle was so damaged it looked like a giant had reached down and crushed the car like a ball of tinfoil. Also on the screen was a livestream of a woman in a dark blouse holding a microphone. "Now I'll hand you over to Sally Jenkins, live at the scene."

"Thanks, Chip," said the reporter. "Vicar Ruth

Anderson of the Catholic Church passed away last night in what appears to be a tragic accident just off Route 181. Details of the investigation are still underway, but it is assumed that Ms. Anderson lost control of her vehicle right up there—" the camera zoomed in on the mountainside, where gashes in the dirt showed the trajectory of the vehicle as well as a busted guardrail at the top, "—on a very dangerous and precipitous curve. Without offering any solid evidence, I'm being told indications point to human error as the cause of the accident.

"Listeners might recall damning allegations against Ms. Anderson some months ago, when she was publicly accused of having had sexual relations with a member of her church. The allegations have since been dropped, but there are lingering questions. I'm afraid the answers won't ever see the light of day. Our hearts go out to Ms. Anderson and her family. What a truly inspiring woman. We'll have updates as the investigation progresses. Back to you, Chip."

John stared at the screen, a lone tear forming in the corner of his eye.

Again, he thought of Charlotte.

It was five years ago on a day just like this one when John had met Charlotte Kotlinski at the Eastern Market outside his home. The market was a fun respite for an aspiring artist, a warm environment with many smiles and people greeting each other at every booth. The market originated in 1891, back when it was the central hub for hay and wood sales. At that time, moguls like the Dodge family aggressively lumbered large areas of pristine great white pines from Northern Michigan and wholesaled the stripped wood at the market.

During prohibition, groups like the notorious Purple Gang used the market as their legitimate cover to distribute whiskey smuggled in from across the Detroit river from Windsor, Canada just two miles away. Then, from the 50s through the 70s, the mafia actively ran their businesses through various locations in the market. Today, the 43-acre bazaar is the largest open-air flower market in the U.S. Some 150 businesses, many of whom have been there since World War Two, are still in operation, passed along through generations. It has been one of the inspiring venues sparking a resurgence in downtown Detroit.

That evening, John had friends coming over for dinner. He wanted to prepare a chicken marsala dish, so he had to walk down and purchase a few items. The market was bustling with activity, which was normal for a Saturday morning in autumn as bold colors, vibrant smells, and fresh produce came together to give the space a magical appearance; a much-appreciated dash of life just before the snows of winter came to whitewash the city.

John, discerning as ever, spent ample time selecting the perfect vegetables that would complement the dish; this included stops at the poultry market and the wine store. The perfect definition of a starving artist, John worked on a tight budget, which was another reason why he was so selective. However, his financial status didn't deter him from hosting great dinners for his friends, which over the years had become a competition amongst them to see who could prepare the best meal with the least spent per head. Needless to say, once the wine flowed and the dinner hit the table, few of them were ever able to keep track.

Approaching a booth full of fresh Northern Michigan asparagus, a woman stepped next to him, slowly picking out a bundle for herself. She had brown hair and green eyes, and she wore a plain gray peacoat with a flannel scarf wrapped around her soft, milky skin. John wasn't much for small talk; he was friendly, but being more of a thinker than a talker, he usually kept to himself. Yet something inspired him to talk to this woman, to say a few passing words. Without much thought, he commented on the nice weather and the warm atmosphere. The woman turned, facing him with a beautiful tulip-pink smile.

"While barred clouds bloom the soft-dying day, and touch the stubble-plains with rosy hue."

John was quietly taken aback. He frowned a little. "Is that a poem?"

"It is," she said, quickly glancing back at the asparagus. "By John Keats. It's called, 'To Autumn.' I like to rehearse it in my head as I walk to the market during the season. You interrupted me before I could finish, so you had to hear it."

John laughed. "Well, please pardon the interruption.

A Change of Faith

But I'm glad you shared it."

She was approximately the same age as John, early 30s. A sense of internal warmth emanated from her, like there was a furnace burning inside. She was pretty, but not beautiful. Her green eyes were alert and compassionate like the eyes of someone who cared and would listen without just waiting for her turn to speak.

They struck up a casual conversation about the resurgence of the city and how nice it was to see so many people driving down to the market. Then they paid for their asparagus and wished each other a good day and went on their way. John didn't know it at the time, but she turned and gave him a quick smile as he walked away.

John himself left smiling, wondering if he would ever see her again. He worked his way back through the market, completed his shopping, and headed home. There, he reviewed his painting, realizing there was something very wrong with it, but he couldn't pinpoint what it was. He just couldn't quite figure out the proper direction the piece should take. Leaving it alone for the rest of the day, he began to prepare dinner for his four friends.

Dinner would be chicken marsala with fresh oregano and Grand Dam Sherry ($9.85 a bottle) and Mondavi wine; grilled, wrapped asparagus sautéed with fresh onions and garlic, and whipped potatoes with light onion and fresh ground pepper. Having been brought up in the kitchen, where he watched and prepared meals alongside his mother, John enjoyed cooking. It was another artform, pairing this food with that, like mixing colors on a palette.

The group of friends met once a month. There were three men and two women, all of whom had known each other since high school. They enjoyed giving each other grief since none were married and only two involved in serious relationships. Secrets within the group were hard to keep and anyone in attendance had better have a thick skin when it came to dating.

His friends were also the toughest critics of his artwork. On more than one occasion he had buried his head while listening to them give their "constructive" criticism. Sometimes he felt it'd be more productive to give them a putty knife and demand they turn the painting into ribbons, because essentially what they were saying was, "It's got potential, but you don't want potential, you want perfection."

He expected the same criticism tonight. They may be tough on him, he mused, but they loved each other like brothers and sisters. Thank goodness he'd bought four bottles of his favorite $12 wine and wasn't driving. He was ready for any criticism that came his way, and he had even hidden the putty knife.

At six o'clock sharp, they began flooding into his apartment. As expected, they immediately launched into an impromptu review of his latest piece.

"God, can we at least have our first glass of wine before this starts?" said John.   Michael, also known as "Lumpy," crossed his arms and pinched his bottom lip, beginning his critique with the usual "Hmm... interesting." For an artist, to hear someone say "interesting" is like the kiss of death. Already you know the work is a failure. Michael continued, carving motions in the air, "Bright red diagonal streaks leading from the upper right to the lower left side of the canvas. What is the significance?"

Truth was, John didn't quite know the significance, and he told Michael this. Like a writer who wrote by the seat of his pants, John often put his tool to paper and progressed organically with little foresight or planning. Michael wasn't so thrilled about that answer. It only went downhill from there, but his friends knew not to push too hard as it could lead to a severe bout of artist's depression.

Michael and Scott took turns on the artistic review while Cindy and Diane helped prepare dinner in the small but functional kitchen. Michael was John's best friend. He was in the automotive supply business, the executive vice president of sales of a very large rubber company. The go-to guy for most employees in his office when things went sideways, his skills in the industry were well-respected. He was, however, someone with whom John and the rest of the boys had burnt many brain cells. Avid sailors both in the Great Lakes and down in the British Virgin Islands, there weren't many bars that hadn't been christened with some sort of tee shirt or other form of clothing tacked to a ceiling indicating the boys had been there. The group credo: wherever Michael went, the rum wasn't far away.

Later, the beautiful dinner served and the wine decanted, they brought up the latest gossip and teased anyone who mustered up the courage to admit a new crush. They were surprised when John casually mentioned the woman he had met earlier in the day. John was private about relationships, especially ones that hadn't yet taken form and probably never would. He kept those thoughts to himself. But once he mentioned the woman, there was no going back, even if he wanted to.

"So who was she?" asked Cindy, smiling eagerly.

"Don't know," said John, twirling his wine. "Never seen her before."

"Well?" said Cindy. "Does she have a name? Maybe one of us knows her."

John realized he hadn't asked for her name. The look of shock that came over his face was not lost on his friends.

"You old dope," said Michael, chuckling with a mouth full of chicken. "This girl flawlessly recites Keats to you and you don't even think to ask her name? Sometimes you surprise even me, and I think we can all agree that's saying something."

"I don't know," said John, his face reddening. "It all happened so fast. And I was feeling pretty withdrawn, in my own head."

"You asked for her number?" offered Scott, hopeful.

John shook his head. "Nope. Not this time. Maybe it's best this way. Next time I see her, we'll have some rapport and I can talk with her about something other than Keats and the weather. I can ask her to dinner or something."

"Maybe, buddy," said Michael. "But like we say down in the Islands, 'There are plenty of fish in the sea. The rarer, the better.' Just keep your eyes open."

John grew quiet while the topic fell on the backburner and his friends talked about future vacations. He didn't seem to hear them. He sat at the table, sipping wine, turning back his memories of the mysterious woman and hoping he'd see her again.

As the night progressed, the friends finished the wine and settled down in the living room with some Glenlivet scotch. The conversation took on a life of its own, needing little direction and even less lucidity. They discussed the future: no imminent weddings were taking place, and no one was expecting a baby. For that they crossed themselves and thanked the good Lord. Again, John felt himself drifting off into some warm space in his mind with thoughts of the woman at the asparagus stand. What was her name?

Who was she? What did she do for a living? He constructed fantasies. Maybe she was a young baroness who had grown up in America. Or a poet. Perhaps a children's book author. She could be anything, he thought. If only he had asked.

Buzzed or not, Cindy and Diane sensed John had something on his mind and it wasn't his artwork. But they were polite, choosing not to bring it up since they had already witnessed the abuse he took with his paintings, and the conversation about the woman hadn't exactly seemed to fill him with hope. A man could only take so much. Conveying so much to each other with their eyes, they sat on either end of John on the couch and started asking him about his parents, knowing it to be a happy subject.

After the dishes were cleaned, the wine and scotch all consumed, it was time to head out. By the group's standards it was still an early night—1:00 a.m. But some of them had work in the morning, so after the customary hugs and "love yous," John sat quietly in his favorite lounge chair in front of his latest painting, twirling the last bit of scotch and wondering what the piece was missing.

His last fleeting thoughts were of the woman—a slow motion scene of the wind ruffling her brown hair, a smile spreading slow and warm across her pretty face. Then his eyes drooped and he fell into a deep sleep peppered with the dust of dreams.

Over the next few months, John didn't see the mysterious woman again. He continued to work on his paintings, placing some pieces in local galleries. All pieces were on consignment and none were shown much interest or purchased. Even if they were selling, the sum left over after the galleries' commission wasn't going to support him for any significant length of time. Was it a mistake leaving his position at Ford, where he had a steady income and little pressure? He began wondering more often.

One cool spring day in Detroit, he sat quietly at home, feeling withdrawn. He wasn't interested in seeing or talking to anyone, not even his best friends, who were beginning to grow concerned for him. They'd started noticing his happy presence wasn't there, and when he tried, it was artificial. Sitting in front of his latest piece with a glass of old scotch, John felt lost. What am I doing with my work? he thought. I have no direction. Should I consider finding a job? What kind?

The next morning during his second cup of coffee he decided to walk down to the market to get some fresh air. It was a wonderful May morning, cool and crisp but still sunny. He enjoyed the market on those mornings, and that day was spring flower day, where floral vendors from all over the state came to sell their summer flowers. The market was full of color and excitement. Strolling up and down the aisles and greeting vendors he'd met over the past two years, John noticed the smile of someone familiar.

It was her, the woman from last fall.

In a yellow floral sundress and a wide-brimmed hat, she stood looking over flats of freshly-potted geraniums. John moved swiftly through the crowd, a silly expectant smile plastered on his face. He couldn't help but shake a few hands on his way until he stood next to her, breathless. "Hey, remember me from last fall?" he asked, hopeful. "We shared our asparagus together?"

The woman looked at him, her lips parting in a kind smile. "Oh, yes, how could I forget? It's nice to see you again. Did you have a good winter?"

No. The winter was long and cold and dreadful because I didn't even know your name. "It was all right." John glanced around. "Beautiful day, isn't it? My name's John, by the way." He reached out his hand before she could disappear again. "John Adams."

"Charlotte Kotlinski," she accepted his hand.

"Have any spring poems today?"

"There's one," she said.

"May I hear it?"

Charlotte cleared her throat and smiled. "From you have I been absent in the spring. When proud-pied April dressed in all his trim, hath put a spirit of youth in everything, that heavy Saturn laughed and leapt with him."

John cracked a smile. "I'm guessing that's not Keats."

"Shakespeare. Sonnet 98."

This time, John wasn't going to let her get away without some effort. "I haven't had my morning coffee yet. Want to join me after you finish your shopping?'

"I'd like that very much."

John helped Charlotte load her flowers into her car, and they walked in the brilliant sunshine to the market's eclectic coffee shop. The shop was one of those places where no two chairs matched, a hole in the wall full of warmth and fun. Sitting down, John felt himself in a rare and uncomfortable mood. It was not often he felt this way around a woman.

"Quite honestly," said Charlotte, "I was hoping to meet you again one day, John. You seem to have a unique personality—what do you do for a living? I bet it's not a normal nine to five."

John was surprised by her comment. How did she know he wasn't a normal nine-to-fiver? Probably his curious gait as he made his way through the market with no groceries, he thought. Casually, he went over his family background, his career path, his schooling and brief stint as a car designer. Then he moved into his current career as a fine artist and remarked briefly on how it was developing. Charlotte detected a sense of unease in his voice when he began describing his career. There was a lack of confidence there; a lingering word left unsaid.

The café was busy that day. Lots of customers streamed in and out of the shop, but John and Charlotte remained, sipping their coffee and eyeing each other from across the small checkered table. "You live around here?" Charlotte asked.

"As a matter of fact, I do," said John proudly. He gestured with his hand. "Just beyond the market there, in a loft apartment."

Her eyes flicked with interest. "That close, huh? Well, I'd sure love to see some of your pieces." She waited expectantly.

John hesitated. He hadn't wanted to admit it, but he'd been in a slump for months now. His artwork had not been serving him creatively as it should be. It was as if each time he picked up a brush, he knew in advance the canvas would become a messy waste of good paint. Expensive paint, too. He'd found himself growing doubtful of his decision to leave the Ford Motor Company, and always in the back of his mind was the mysterious woman from the market whose name he forgot to ask. He couldn't let her go this time, nervous as he was.

"Charlotte, can I be frank with you?"

A Change of Faith

She crossed her arms, interested to hear what would come next. "Of course."

John spoke without meeting her eye. "My work hasn't been accepted by collectors. I haven't been able to sell any. I'm struggling. Quite honestly, I'm considering giving up my career as an artist."

Charlotte was nonplussed. "Well, before you cave in and get back into the corporate environment, could I at least see what you've been working on? I'm not a connoisseur, but my art friends say I have good taste. Maybe I could offer some insight?"

John thought a moment. Then he clapped his hands together. "All right," he said. "You talked me into it. You're quite persistent aren't you?"

Charlotte smiled. "Guilty."

Finishing their coffee, they walked across the market to an oddly-designed building constructed many years ago—a building with character, people would say. As they walked up the stairs, John remembered his loft was a mess and became embarrassed. "My house is a disaster. Maybe you could go on a quick walk around the block and I—"

"Nonsense, where I come from, your house will look like it belongs to a Rockefeller. Come on, let's see some art."

Grinning, he opened the door, and suddenly he felt like Charlotte had been there before. A quiet sense of comfort settled in amongst them, even though the place had clothes and dishes and random knick-knacks lying around everywhere. Charlotte laughed. "This," she said, "is exactly what I was expecting. You are an artist." The loft had 20-foot ceilings with a large skylight directing natural light throughout the unit. It was a wide-open design with the kitchen and bedroom all in one room. In the largest part was John's work—a handful of canvases propped up on easels with five more pieces leaning together in the corner. The floors were old oak and in some places covered with splattered paint.

Charlotte gestured to the paintings. "Mind if I take a look?"

John's heart was thumping in his chest. This was a mistake, he thought frantically. He shouldn't have brought her here. His mind reeled with excuses. Maybe he could tell her he was feeling sick all of a sudden, but that'd be too thin. Fake a phone call? It was too late, anyway—Charlotte was already moving toward the paintings.

"I only ask one thing of you," said John. "Just give me your honest opinion. My friends do regularly." The last line came out sourly.

Slowly and meticulously, Charlotte inspected each painting. She was frowning slightly, heavily concentrating. She looked as though she were uncertain, like she had some bad news but didn't know how to put it in words.

"Each of your paintings has a certain sadness," she said, pinching her lip as she inspected the last one. "Even though you're incorporating vibrant colors and strong brushstrokes, they seem... sad. What I'm sensing is an artist who is a bit lost. It's like you have so much pressure to perform that you're unable to create what you really feel inside. You know what I mean? You need to get yourself to relax and truly enjoy what you're painting. I believe if you can let go of whatever's holding you back, you have wonderful work waiting at your door. Truly, truly wonderful work. I can tell just by glancing at these."

John felt an immense weight lifted from his shoulders as he realized she was right. He hadn't been relaxed or having fun while painting. For months, he'd been suffering from the mental anguish so intrinsic to the life of an artist—his work sucked. He didn't enjoy it. There was something missing, but try as he might, he just couldn't put his finger on it. Then, this mysterious woman walks back into his life, takes one look at his paintings, and delivers him a single profound statement that brings it all home. He'd been too hard on himself, pushing himself to do great work without really willing it. Forcing brush strokes at times when he should have been letting the brush lead him.

John leaned against the wall, placing his hands on his face and letting his emotions go. Charlotte placed a tender hand on his shoulder, and he looked up with watery eyes.

"Hey, it's all right," she said gently. "What's the matter?"

"Nothing," he said. "Nothing's the matter. You're absolutely right. I've placed too much pressure on myself and I need to let go, be myself, and paint what I want to paint, not what I think others would like." He shook his head. "Charlotte, how in the world did you know this?"

Charlotte shrugged her slim shoulders. "You have a very soothing demeanor. I barely know you, but I can tell you're a very warm, caring man who wants to make everyone happy. I could tell the first moment I looked into those gentle eyes. But it's that same empathy that might obstruct your personal goals. When you create, you just have to do it for yourself; for you and no one else, John. Others may appreciate your work. They might glean some remarkable lesson from it. But you don't do it for them, do you? You do it for you."

Now John was smiling.

"What is it?" she said, squaring her feet like a boxer. "What are you smiling at?"

"I'm just thinking that if I'd asked your name months ago, back when we first met, maybe you'd have come in here and said what you said just now, and my entire winter would have been productive instead of a drag."

"Hey, you said it was a good winter."

"It wasn't. But it's over now."

"Well, everything happens for a reason, right?"

"That's what they say," said John. He stood up with a warm smile. "Know what I realized? I've told you about me and my past. You've been invited into my house and looked at my artwork, which is like being granted a glimpse of my soul. And you've offered a strong, honest, and much appreciated opinion. Thank you. But I realize I know almost nothing about you. So, I have to ask: Who is Charlotte Kotlinski?"

"It's my turn?" she asked.

John nodded. "I'm afraid so. Some more coffee?"

"Please," she said. "This might take a while."

John fetched his pigeon-egg percolator and grabbed a couple of mugs. He scooped coffee into the percolator, then filled it with water and switched on the stove burner. They sat at his rustic kitchen table.

"I'm second-generation Polish ancestry," said Charlotte. "All four of my grandparents were immigrants who came to America at the turn of the 20th century. They never learned to speak English, but each one appreciated their new country and only wanted to start over with their families.

"My mother was the oldest of six children, and because of an alcoholic father and depression, she had to quit school as a girl and work cleaning houses for two dollars a week. My father was one of three boys and a sister. His father came to Detroit when Ford offered five bucks a day to work. He put himself through school and is now a practicing dentist. I have one sister, Shawne, who's in IT marketing for a private company. Like you, we were raised to work hard. I was lucky enough to attend Michigan State and received a degree in business accounting; now I'm a registered CPA. I worked for one of the major accounting firms as an auditor for three years before deciding I needed to do more for myself and the community. My folks weren't excited with my decision to leave my job, but they understood with time. Now I work for the Catholic Archdiocese of Detroit and am assigned at The Sweetest Heart of Mary Cathedral."

John was floored. "You work at the church? What's your position there?"

"I'm in community affairs. We have two problems: cash and attendance. I was placed in a no-win position, but I absolutely love it."

Upon learning she wasn't a practicing nun, John's relief was immeasurable. For hours, their conversation wound itself in many directions. They talked about their siblings and parents, their schools, their equal urge to get out and do something different; to see the world. More than once, John found himself laughing, holding his stomach, a reflex he'd had ever since undergoing a hernia repair surgery years before. And on one or two occasions, he caught himself gazing at the curve of her lips, the rise of her breasts through her shirt, and the twirling constellation of freckles on the side of her neck. A sense of longing was growing within him. A sense of passionate wonderment.

Both realized there weren't many people you could meet and talk to for hours without glancing furtively at the clock. When the time came for her to leave, John invited Charlotte to meet again for a glass of wine in the near-future, and this time he got her phone number. No date was set but a mutual agreement was in place. They would meet again.

After Charlotte left, John sat in front of his paintings

for a long time, thinking about her words. She was right—he had to let loose and create for himself. From that point forward, he decided, he would create for John and no one else. The two years of previous work would be destroyed and forgotten. John was moving on.

And he was falling in love.

II

John didn't need to call Charlotte, because the very next day, she called him.

"John," she said, "I'd like to see you again. How about tonight? I'll bring over a bottle of wine?"

"Sorry," John said, fighting a smile, "I'm terribly busy hanging out with this gal tonight. She's a real hardass when it comes to art, but I like her all right."

"That so?" she said flirtatiously.

"Yup."

"Well, in that case, I'll drop by at six."

"Six it is," he said.

John was in his blue painter's overalls, covered in paint. He had a brush in his hand and was standing in front of a half-complete canvas with a silly smile spread across his face. After what Charlotte had said the day before, he'd gotten a surge of artistic inspiration and set to work immediately. He'd worked straight through the night. His hands were not his hands—they were like strange but fascinating new appendages blessed with the ability to perform miracles. He didn't even think, he simply painted. The colors poured onto the canvas with fervor. Almost sweating from working so hard, John analyzed his work. It had a unique composition, a flow none of his previous pieces had. There was a subtle intensity to the painting, he realized, something he hadn't seen in his work before. The colors and the curves sprang to life with varying emotions. Gazing at the canvas, he felt something. But what was it? He didn't know. Not yet.

Even though he'd been working all night, he didn't feel the slightest bit tired. In fact, he felt rejuvenated and ready to take on the world. But even the greats needed to eat, he reasoned. If he had any intention of becoming one of them, he'd need some breakfast.

In the kitchen, he put on an old Woody Guthrie record and set about frying bacon and eggs in a cast iron skillet. He whistled with the music, flipping the egg over easy and dancing a little jig with a hand towel over his shoulder. As he sat at the creaky table to eat his breakfast, he made a list of groceries to buy for dinner. What did Charlotte like? He cursed himself as he realized he hadn't asked. Maybe he could call her back quickly, but wouldn't he seem clingy if he did? No, she had called him, surely he could call and ask? Again, he had no idea. He knew next to nothing about this woman and had only truly met her last night, so he didn't know her quirks, allergies, boundaries, anything. I'll just make something so delicious she can't possibly say no. He jotted down ingredients for veal scallopini, but instead of veal he would use beef tenderloin. He didn't know what Charlotte's take was on eating baby lamb and didn't want to find out the hard way.

After breakfast, he wandered the market with a basket over his arm, collecting everything he'd need. He bought a bottle of fine chardonnay for the sauce, as well as garlic, capers, local cremini mushrooms, and a quarter-pound of bright yellow butter fresh off the farm and wrapped in wax paper. He then purchased a bunch of fresh parsley and a small container of homemade black truffle oil that set him back 20 bucks. He felt like an idiot when he said, "Hey, you sure this is the correct price?"

The seller had a blank expression. "Sir, it's truffles."

"All right, all right." John bought the oil.

He knew Charlotte was bringing the wine, but he couldn't help himself; he had to get his favorite bottle of cab to complement the scallopini. Plus, he figured she'd love it if she was a wine-drinker. After the foray to the market, unloading the groceries from his basket, he realized he'd gotten the most expensive dinner fixings he'd probably ever bought. But it was worth it. Charlotte was worth every penny.

The food safely put away in the fridge, he glanced up at the clock—almost noon. Six hours. He slumped against the fridge as a wave of exhaustion hit him. Jeeze, he thought. I'd better get some sleep. He fell on his bed with a thump. Within moments, he was snoring.

John didn't awake to the first knock at the door. He didn't wake up to the second knock either, or even the third. He didn't wake until the fourth was pounding like an anvil in his dreams, and then he got up startled and disarrayed.

"What?" he muttered. Still half-asleep, he called out, "Who...who is it?"

"Charlotte," came the muffled reply through the door. His first thought: he could not believe that a knock that loud could come from a woman as small as her.

John glanced at the clock. It was 6:05.

"Shit!" He sprang to his feet.

"Something the matter?"

"Nope!" he said, taking off his shirt and pants from this morning and searching frantically for a clean change of clothes. "Everything's fine. Be right there!"

"If you say so," came the response.

He threw on a nice shirt, thrust its tails into his slacks. Searched in vain for a belt. Slicked back his hair with pomade in the mirror with one hand while buttoning his shirt with the other. He made it to the door in under a minute. Charlotte looked stunning. She was wearing a casual dress and sweater, earrings, no lipstick. Her hair was in a French braid and she had in her hand a bottle of fine cab. She gave him a playful smile. "Did I wake you?"

John was breathless. "Course not."

She raised an eyebrow. "You sure about that?"

His face reddened. His shoulders dropped. "All right... what gave it away?"

Without looking, she pointed down at his crotch area. His pants were unbuttoned and unzipped, and one of his shirttails was hanging over his pants. "You forgot something," she giggled.

John quickly remedied the situation. But despite his embarrassment, he felt a surge of happiness at the sight of her. "I was up all night painting," he said.

"And...?"

John tried to fight the smile, but it won. "And... I think I did all right. I think."

Not saying a word, Charlotte handed John the bottle of wine and stepped past him into the room. She went straight for his studio. John tried to stop her. "Hang on a second, shouldn't we have a glass of wine or something first...?"

"I want to see this." She stood in front of the half-finished painting on the easel. If one were to draw comparisons, they could say it was the marriage between Van Gogh's Wheatfield with Crows and a more linear Jackson Pollock. In perfect artistic irony, it looked as if the artist had no idea what he was doing when he began but had managed to created a beautiful masterpiece. The colors were dark, smeared, smooth; they were bright, sharp, and haunting. Shady regions in the abstract painting seemed to harbor some predatory intensity—a black panther hiding in the shadows, poised to pounce faster than a moving shadow.

"Wow," said Charlotte, mesmerized. "I don't know what it is, but I've never seen anything like it. It's so... different."

John stood at her elbow with his arms crossed. He was shifting his shoulders nervously. He felt like a giddy child, but he had to ask: "Do you like it?"

"John," Charlotte said seriously, her eyes wide. "This is incredible."

"Really?"

"Yes!" She was laughing now, and the sound of it filled John's stomach with longing. Again, that feeling from last night; it washed over him like a warm rain. For the first time in years, he felt like he was exactly where he was supposed to be and doing exactly what he was supposed to be doing. For centuries, writers had tried to capture this feeling in words. Painters strove to instill their art with it. Musicians tuned their instruments to it. Meaning. Purpose. Truth. Beauty. It was the convergence of all these things; it was one's destiny showing its face for the very first time, and suddenly, John Adams felt whole.

"Hell, I didn't really expect that reaction," he said, trying to make light of it. "But it's good. I like your reaction."

Charlotte barely seemed to hear him. She was still

staring at the painting, following its lines and curves with her eyes. Frowning with curiosity. "What are you going to call it?"

"The Convergence of Light and Shadow," said John. "That was the line that came into my mind when I finally stepped away after hours of working. When I stood in front of it and really looked at it."

"The Convergence of Light and Shadow. What does it mean to you?"

John shrugged. "I guess it's the middle point. You know, the middle path. There's good and evil, light and dark, love and hate. This is the very center of all that. It's like a place of emotional and existential limbo. When I was a kid, I used to dream up this place where only I could go. It was a big room with windows on all sides. Through each window I could see the whole world, anything I wanted to, anywhere. When I went into this room, all time stopped. People paused in their tracks. Animals, trees. Wars and storms and big natural disasters. It all froze in an instant, and there I was sitting in that quiet room with the windows, watching it all. So, when I look at this painting, that's what I think of."

Charlotte hung on his every word. Silence filled the room as she looked at him. John turned to her, and the moment he did, their lips met like two trains coming together. His heart thundered in his chest. He felt like he'd slipped into a dream. But this wasn't a dream. Charlotte was kissing him, her lips sweet and hungry for his. He wrapped his arms around her tightly and brought her close to him, exploring her back and sides with his hands. She melted into him.

Neither spoke as they stumbled toward the bed, tripping over laundry, painter's overalls and books. Laughing. They fell into the bed as one, holding onto each other and utterly refusing to let go. Passion swirled in John's stomach, his chest, his loins. He felt like his heart was the universe, expanding infinitely.

Time slipped away, and all at once they were in John's old room. Not his bedroom, but his Room of Exploration, as he called it, where he used to sit silently and watch the world and its stillness. Their clothes came off, and they explored each other's bodies like children granted access to some mystical kingdom.

An hour later, nude except for John's button-down, Charlotte walked barefoot across the hardwood floor, the sunset pouring through the skylight and casting fading rays against the shadowed room.

"Where do you think you're going?" asked John, curled up in the blankets.

"It's a surprise," she said.

But it wasn't. Not really. John could hear her fumbling around in the kitchen, then the sound of a wine bottle being uncorked. "I'm beside myself with anticipation," he said.

"You better be. This is the good stuff."

She strode back into the room with a bottle in one hand and two wine glasses in the other. She paused, standing there looking at John. She was smiling slightly, dimples pressed in her cheeks as she gazed down at him.

"What is it?" he asked, sitting up.

"Nothing," she said. "Everything."

The next three weeks were unparalleled bliss. John produced his best work, and each week it got better. Charlotte dropped by his apartment almost every night. They made dinner, laughed, made love. They went on long walks around the city, at times getting completely lost. But they didn't really care; they didn't feel lost at all.

John had loved girls before. He'd felt that fluttering in his chest, that warm comfort of being; of knowing that no matter what happened, good or bad, someone was there with him to share in it. But with Charlotte, it was vastly different. Where before he'd felt heart flutters, now he felt like the mere sight of her would make his heart explode and kill him on the spot. It was dangerous, how much he was falling in love with her. He couldn't stop thinking about her unless he was painting, and even when he was painting she was in his unconscious mind, her undeniable presence moving his very brushstrokes. He couldn't help it. Nor did he want to.

His friends noticed the stark difference in his painting style. Analyzing his newest canvases one day, Michael slowly shook his head. A surge of fear coursed through John's body. "What?" he said nervously. "Something wrong?"

"This woman, Charlotte. She's turning you into a goddamn Picasso." He turned to John, a toothpick in the corner of his mouth. "She have a sister?"

All John's friends wanted to meet the mystery woman, so he made party plans. He invited the usual group on a Saturday evening, plus Charlotte. Nothing extravagant—he didn't want to make the poor girl any more nervous than she had to be. John's friends weren't the easiest folks to get along with, after all. They never shied away from calling out the elephant in the room.

It was a potluck. Everyone showed up at seven with a different dinner. Scott brought a Stromboli, Cindy made green bean casserole, Diane baked fresh bread and Michael had put together a potato dish, along with ribs. John himself had made a huge salad. His friends gossiped and drank wine in the kitchen while setting the table. They prodded John every once in a while for information about Charlotte as he waited impatiently by the door. "Hey, come on, make yourself useful," said Diane. So he helped out, but still kept a watchful eye on the telephone. He didn't know why. His stomach was full of butterflies, but not the good kind. Charlotte was an hour late, and he had the vague sense that something was wrong.

"I'm going to step out a minute, get some air," he said. Michael gave him a brisk wave. John put on his coat and went out the door. Outside, the air was neither hot nor cold, but the perfect summer temperature to lie out in a field on a blanket and watch the nighttime stars. It was comfortable, welcoming, yet something about it was unsettling.

John glanced around at figures moving under street lamps, cars cruising by. After a minute, he found what he was looking for: she was seated on a bench under a tree, her head in her hands. She was crying. "Charlotte?" he said. He started jogging toward her. She looked up at him, her face wet with tears. "Aw, Hun, what's the matter? What happened?"

"I'm sorry," she managed.

"Don't be sorry, silly," John knelt down next to her and took her hand in his. It was shaking. "God, you're freezing. Tell me what happened."

"I can't go up there," she sniffled. "I can't meet your friends. I'm really sorry."

Now John was getting scared. The fluttering in his chest felt like burning, or like air trapped that couldn't get out. "Charlotte... what's going on?"

A Change of Faith

She shook her head. Her eyes were rimmed with red. She'd been crying a while. "I can't see you anymore, John. I want to more than anything, but I can't. There's something I need to do. But I can't do it and be with you at the same time. It's not possible."

He pulled back. "Whoa, wait a sec, what are you saying? What is it you need to do? We can do it together. I'll support you no matter what, Charlotte. You know that."

"No," she said, shaking her head again. "It's not possible. I'm so sorry!" Charlotte was bawling now, and John felt hot tears forming in his eyes. He tried to hold her but she stood up abruptly. "I can't make this any harder than it already is. Gosh, I can't bear it. I really can't. I'm sorry."

"Wait a minute," said John, but she was already walking away. He called after her. "Charlotte...Charlotte! What's going on? Please!"

She buried her face in her chest as she hurried away.

In John's apartment window, Michael was holding the curtain to the side and looking out at them. He turned from the window.

John stood on the sidewalk for what felt like an eternity, past the point when Charlotte rounded a corner and disappeared. Cars whirled past him and ruffled his clothes and hair. Passersby chuckled and told stories on their walks. He remained standing, too in shock to cry, too confused to move. Finally, he felt a hand on his shoulder. It was Michael.

John was dazed. "She's...gone."

"I know, buddy."

"I don't know what happened...I don't...my God."

"I know." Michael pulled John in and wrapped his arms around him.

Tears poured out of John's eyes, slowly at first. Then the floodgates opened and he began crying, burying his face in Michael's shoulder. "I love her," he said. "Fuck, Mike, what did I do? What did I do?"

"It wasn't you."

"How do you know?"

"Because I know, buddy. It wasn't you."

Michael let him cry softly in his shoulder for a while. Then they went up to John's apartment and Michael let the group know that John needed to be alone. They hugged and kissed him and said they were always there for him if he needed anything at all, then they left. Michael stayed with John. He poured two glasses of scotch and they sat listening to records until the wee hours of the morning. Michael tried to distract him, recounting stories of their travels, but John was mostly quiet and brooding, turning over every single moment he and Charlotte had spent together over the past three weeks, questioning every word, every move, anything he'd done in her presence that could have caused her to leave him. He could think of nothing.

The next morning, he tried to call her. No answer. He called her once a day for a week before deciding to give up. If she didn't want to talk to him, he wasn't going to push her. Although he was half-crazed by not knowing why the hell she'd left him, and he felt like his soul had been torn in two, he respected her wishes. He had no other choice.

Over the ensuing months, he fell into a deep depression the likes of which he'd never known. He refused to see friends and family. He didn't eat much and barely slept. The only thing in the world that gave him any solace was his work, so he worked obsessively, sometimes for 17 hours a day. He pushed Charlotte from his mind, telling himself that she never existed. She was just a mirage.

III

Throughout the next few months, John was so focused on painting that he lost sense of time, barely even stringing together any coherent thoughts. He was always vaguely conscious, though, of the fact that Charlotte was hanging onto the walls of his mind like drying paint. Days, weeks and months went by before John would poke his head out of his studio and catch a breath. His friends were concerned, and once a couple of them stopped by to check on him. But when they saw what he was creating, they understood.

In the eight months since Charlotte had left him, John produced 20 new pieces of work. Each was something special, with vibrant compositions that you could feel as you viewed them. Suddenly, John's talent and personality were oozing from everything he created. His paintings were oblique but wonderful in their inner-self, offering stories that were somehow unique to each observer. Everyone who looked at John's work felt separate vibrations as their imaginations were pulled in different directions. It never occurred to John to sell his new pieces. He was so absorbed in the act of painting, suddenly powerful and therapeutic, that despite the fact he was living on PB&Js, mac and cheese and soup, he was totally content.

Finally, Michael convinced John that it was time to approach some of the local galleries to exhibit his work and see how the public would react. Michael took six of John's pieces with a goal of visiting three different galleries, not anticipating anything exciting would happen. The Neumann Gallery, located in posh Birmingham, had exhibited John's earlier work without much success. The owner, James, who inherited the gallery from a business transaction gone south, had developed a reputation in the Midwest as running one of the most reputable galleries around, offering only legitimate pieces of original artwork. James did not sell limited-edition pieces, as he knew of too many knockoffs that were sold in the industry as originals. He wasn't particularly interested in meeting with Michael, but Michael, being a salesman, was persistent.

"Michael," James said gently, "I enjoyed meeting John. He's a wonderful guy and someone I could hang out and have a beer with, but his work lacks inspiration. I don't want to waste your time."

Michael asked James to look at just two of John's new pieces. He went quickly out to his truck, unpacked the pieces, both approximately 4' X 5', and carried them to the back of the gallery. There were a couple of customers roaming about, viewing other pieces on exhibit. The gallery was quite large, with eight separate exhibit areas, each capable of showing eight to ten pieces of work.

In the back of the gallery, Michael sat and waited for James. 30 minutes went by, and still no James. Then a customer came over and asked if he and his wife could look at the two pieces Michael was unwrapping. After some conversation, the gentleman, very finely dressed and quite confident, asked, "Who is the artist that painted these?"

"My friend John Adams," said Michael proudly, straightening in his chair. "He's a very up and coming artist. A true revolutionary." The gentleman wanted more information about John, and Michael gave him a brief biographical summary.

"And how much would he consider selling these two pieces for?" the man asked, scratching his chin.

Michael responded without hesitation, "$2,500 each."

When James finally found time to come over and look for himself, he was shocked to find that the paintings were sold. Michael wanted to say to him, "You snooze you lose, baby," but held his tongue, because James was now interested in seeing the other four pieces. With his past work, John had been unable to sell a single painting in two years. Now he'd made enough in one afternoon that his usual mac and cheese could be complimented with a $16 bottle of cabernet.

Michael went back to his truck and brought in the remaining four pieces. James reviewed the new work, in disbelief that it was painted by the same artist who had been such a flop not very long ago. He immediately asked for an exclusive management contract of all of John's work, but Michael was much too smart to agree to any contracts, especially without first talking to John. A normal gallery would ask for a 50% commission on all sales. Michael knew the interest developing with James, and seeing as he already had $5,000 in his pocket from the earlier sale, agreed to a 1/3 commission and immediately raised the price of the two pieces he agreed to leave to $4,000 each.

Once the proper paperwork was completed at the Neumann Gallery, Michael took the previous two paintings to the gentleman's house for delivery. The mansion, nestled into acres of sprawling yard-space, was located in Bloomfield Hills near the famous Cranbrook Institute, known for the architecture of Eliel Saarinen and Albert Kahn, both international architectural giants. Approaching the front door with the two paintings, Michael was greeted by the gentleman.

"Come in, Michael," he insisted. After some conversation, Michael learned that this was Frank McGann, an affluent businessman who made his living purchasing companies that were in financial disarray and turning them around. He was so good at what he did, he was asked to work on such projects as the U.S. Postal Service and Department of Defense. He was the son of immigrant Irish sheep-farmers who came to Detroit to find employment and were invited to work at a relative's meat market. Frank had spent many days in his youth processing whole sides of beef as they were delivered early each morning.

He'd attended school in Detroit with his brother and was not a good student by any means. When report cards would come around, Frank usually found himself in the basement receiving a few strokes on his fanny from his father's belt. To his parents' great frustration, that never seemed to help. The same was true in high school. Frank's buddies were all top students, and a number of them went on to become successful doctors and lawyers. Frank muddled through his time at the local junior college with his buddy Jim Zinners. While there, Frank started a graphic design business, providing murals to local companies. There was just one small problem: Frank had not an ounce of artistic skill. So he would quote out projects and subcontract them to students from the art department, keeping half the profits for himself. He never finished college, and if he had, he probably would have left many instructors alcoholics.

Frank was one of those people who didn't have time for academics, instead finding innovative ways to create business opportunities using other people's talents. He had a very simple business philosophy: Set your ego aside, find people much smarter then yourself, treat them well and always be honest with your customers. Though very successful, Frank never forgot his past and always treated everyone equally. At his golf club he could generally be found in the kitchen enjoying a cup of soup with the staff instead of in the members' bar.

Michael felt he was getting in way over his head, but he was excited to meet such a business icon. Michael explained that John had locked himself up over the past eight months and couldn't stop painting. John was in his own world, and it was wonderful and exciting. Frank gave Michael a check for the two pieces and asked if sometime in the future he could meet John, preferably at his loft. Michael assured him that could happen and left feeling he had known Frank a very long time. He couldn't wait to make the 30-minute drive back to John's loft and give him the news of all that had transpired. The afternoon had far exceeded their expectations. Could my high school best friend be a legitimate artist?

As Michael entered the loft, he carried in two other paintings and slipped behind the door a bottle of 18-year-old Oban Single Malt Scotch, John's favorite. John was hesitant to ask how it went, and of course, Michael wasn't going to let the good news out too quickly.

"Well old buddy, there's both good and bad news. Which would you like first?" John anxiously asked for the good news first, assuming he'd need it. Michael laughed. "I'm pulling your leg, John. It's all good news." Michael recounted the story of the afternoon; of his meeting with James Neumann and Frank

McGann. John was in disbelief, assuming Michael was messing with him.

"Don't joke like that," said John. "I'm not sure I can take a joke like that."

"John, I'm not joking. Look…" Michael pulled out a check for $5,000. Holding the check, John blinked once, twice, three times. "No," he muttered. "No way."

"Yep," said Michael, beaming.

John stared at him, and Michael saw in his eyes a sense of helpless wonderment. It was as if John were a child who'd been taken from his home at an early age, and finally as a grown man, granted a trip back to see the place where it all started. The air was replete with a sense of going home. Tears formed in John's eyes as he released all his pent-up anxieties. The two hugged and laughed, John sniffling and wiping his face, and the Oban was promptly opened. Over the next four hours, they enjoyed the entire bottle together.

John was still in disbelief, but the check certainly looked real, and Frank McGann certainly was a real businessman. As commission to Michael, Frank had even insisted that he pick out a piece from his vast fine art collection. "Please," he'd urged, "Pick any painting. I owe you much more than what they're worth."

John slept that night like never before.

IV

A week passed, and John was still in awe of what had taken place the previous Saturday with Michael. People really enjoy my work? The money was important, as John had to pay his bills and feed himself, but the best part was that people actually liked what he painted. The financial burden was temporarily taken care of, so now he could really focus on his painting.

It was Saturday, and like all Saturdays, John had his coffee and then visited his friends at the market below. But today everything felt different. Today he genuinely enjoyed saying hello, shaking hands and giving hugs. Everyone noticed the new smile on John's familiar face. "He's back!" they said.

Although John did in fact feel like he was "back," one thought still pulled at his mind: Charlotte. If it weren't for that one day almost nine months earlier when she visited his loft, John and his career would probably never have turned. He decided it was time to attend a church service at The Sweetest Heart of Mary, make an appropriate donation, and see if Charlotte would be there. He had to speak to her, but he didn't know what he would say.

John wasn't the most religious man, but he did believe in God and heaven. The Sunday services he attended were few and far between. Like many, he believed that living a good and honest life was more important than sitting in church.

The next morning, he dressed appropriately and

A Change of Faith

headed to nine a.m. mass at The Sweetest Heart of Mary, a stone's throw from the Eastern Market. The church was an absolutely stunning structure, built in 1893 with Polish cathedral architecture and soaring columns, amazing sculptures, high vaulted ceilings, gleaming marble altars, and beautiful stained-glass windows. If you didn't know you were in inner-city Detroit, you could have been anywhere in Europe.

John walked in a few minutes before mass and situated himself in a pew near the back of the church, which looked like it could seat approximately 600 people. It was only about 1/3 full. John wondered why it was so empty. He thought about his parents and grandparents and all they had given up for him and his brothers. They were amazing people, and as Tom Brokaw once said, "the greatest generation." His mind wandered as he looked around to see if Charlotte might be there somewhere. His heart felt fluttery in his chest. Would she even want to see him? What would he say to her? He hadn't seen her in the months since she left him, and now here he was, glancing over his shoulder towards the exit and wondering if he should leave.

As the organ began to play, everyone rose to greet the priest and altar-servers as they walked from the vestibule to the altar. John had his head down and didn't pay much attention to the procession. As the parishioners sat down, the altar-servers took their place on either side of the priest, and the priest slowly turned to face the congregation. John's heart jumped in his chest. He blinked hard and squinted, struggling to clear his vision. He must be seeing things. The person giving service appeared to be Charlotte. A female priest?

Charlotte had a glow about her, as if lights were pointed on her from the ceiling. Her eyes were full of love and completeness. As she spoke and welcomed everyone to the Sunday service, John could see that she was more than just a CPA. Her presence could be felt throughout the church.

As the service continued and Charlotte gave the sermon, John's mind was racing. He was mesmerized. The sermon was about developing an inner-happiness and appreciating the smallest of things given to each of us. She was in each heart that attended the mass. As John looked around, he could see smiles as parishioners connected to Charlotte's words. So often, sermons are just used to take up time and no one pays much attention to what's actually being said. But Charlotte had everyone's attention.

Later, the service was completing and the altar servers were beginning their walk back to the vestibule with Charlotte following in bright green, gold-trimmed priest's garb. As they walked by, John glanced at her, and as if she knew he'd be there, their eyes connected. She smiled at him.

What just happened? Who was she? Was she a female priest? He didn't even know the Catholic Church allowed women to become priests. John walked back to the vestibule and let the other parishioners shake Charlotte's hand as they left the church. Finally, it was just him and Charlotte in the church. Before John could say anything, she spoke. "I knew you'd come here someday."

John had to catch his breath for a second before he spoke. "Are you a priest?"

Charlotte laughed. "No. Not yet, anyway. But I hope to be one day. I've joined the seminary. I have a few years until I can apply as deacon. Then, God willing, I'll become a priest. Several years ago, the pope released a referendum in which Church members could vote on whether they thought women should be allowed to enter the priesthood. The results were not what was expected, very much in the affirmative. A vote was taken with the College of Cardinals, the recommendation passed, and it was decided three women would become priests as sort of an experiment. That's why I entered the seminary, John. That's…why I had to leave you."

"Hang on," said John, closing his eyes tight. "Sorry. Just a second."

She put her hand on his shoulder. "It's okay."

"It's a lot to take in, you know."

"I know. I'm sorry."

"That's why you left me? To become a priest?"

Charlotte was silent a moment. "Yes."

He looked up at her. "Why didn't you just tell me? Didn't I have a right to know?"

"Of course you did. I just didn't know how to tell you. How could I say it? 'John, you're the best man I've ever met, the man of my dreams. But I have to leave you because I'm going to become a priest.'"

"Yes! That. Something. Anything would have been better than what you did."

"I know…I feel awful about it," she said. "I guess… I was afraid you'd hate me for my decision, but mostly, I was afraid you would turn away from God. That you would blame Him for what I did. I couldn't have that. If my decision to leave you would turn you away from God, then I would have been a failure before ever entering the seminary."

"Well, when you put it like that…"

"I thought of telling you," she said. "For months I looked at the phone, willing myself to pick it up and call you. But there was a part of me that just knew it was God's plan, that I should leave it to Him to decide. I had a feeling you would come here and find out for yourself."

"I didn't know you were so religious. I guess that's another thing you didn't tell me," he muttered.

"I was afraid you'd think I was strange."

"Of course I wouldn't think that. And I wouldn't forsake God, either. Probably I'd have forsaken you more than I did."

Charlotte lowered her head. "I'm sorry."

John took a deep breath. "No, don't be. What am I saying? I don't want you to be sorry, I want you to be happy." He gestured around the church. "This makes you happy?"

"It does," said Charlotte seriously. "More than…more than almost anything I've known. But I miss you, John. I think of you all the time. I worry about you."

"There's no need to worry. I'm all right."

"Are you working?"

John nodded. "I sold my first painting the other day. Two of them, actually."

Charlotte's eyes widened. "You did?"

He couldn't help smiling. "I got five grand for them. I still can't believe it."

"Five grand! John, that's amazing!"

"Pretty unbelievable, right?"

Charlotte was beside herself. "No. Amazing, yes, but not unbelievable. You're an incredible artist. By now, your work must be amazing."

"I don't know about that…"

"Well, I do. In fact, I'd like to see it sometime…if it wouldn't be weird, you know."

John laughed awkwardly, looking down. "So, you're not a priest. Then why did you lead the service?"

"I'm friends with the priest," said Charlotte. "He was sick today and no one could take his place, so I was told to. I think I did okay."

"Charlotte," said John, astounded, "you were amazing. You were completely in your element."

"You're not just saying that?"

"No, I'm not."

They were silent a minute.

Charlotte gave him a weak smile. "Would you join me for a coffee, John? For old time's sake?"

John looked at this woman standing before him, at the freckles barely visible beneath the flush in her cheeks, and he felt the same about her as he had when he stood on the sidewalk and watched her walk away. "Yes," he said. "I'd like that very much."

Charlotte smiled. "Give me a few minutes to change."

She returned in a black turtleneck, jeans and a leather jacket. John followed Charlotte out the door. Once situated in the corner of their quaint coffee shop, John stared at Charlotte, his head swimming. He had a million questions he wanted to ask her. He'd spent so many bleak, frenzied months pacing around his loft reciting imaginary conversations, practicing all the things he wanted to say to her one day. She completed him. She shattered him. He loved her so much, yet hated her action so fiercely. But despite the chaos he felt inside, no words came to his tongue.

"John."

He forced himself to meet her waiting eyes, and his gut wrenched at the sight of them. For some reason, he'd expected them to look different. But they looked exactly the same as they used to. In fact, she looked completely unchanged, save for the glow of utter confidence emanating from beneath her skin.

"Female priest," he muttered in a trance, trying to remind himself not to lunge across the table and kiss her.

"The pope and cardinals in Rome realized that attendance for church services was dropping, with no end in sight,"

A Change of Faith

Charlotte explained. "They've been bucking the system for years, but this is a business, and the revenue generated years ago simply isn't there anymore. Most churches in the U.S. are running in the red and won't survive. There are a lot of problems with the system, including some unqualified priests. The old cardinals knew they had to do something dramatic, so...here I am."

"Here you are," John agreed quietly.

"I'm the only prospective female priest in the Detroit Archdiocese. They're planning to place me at The Sweetest Heart of Mary because many of them don't want to see a female priest succeed, and this church is bleeding losses. Attendance is so low..."

"Well, it'll go up once you're a priest, that's for sure. The crowd loved you."

Charlotte shrugged, looking down as she realized the insurmountable task in front of her. John had an impulse to reach out and comfort her. He fought it. "Maybe," she said. "It's going to be quite a challenge. The Church is the ultimate 'old boys' environment to break into, and I very well may never really break into it." She straightened up then, gathering encouragement. "But I'm a stubborn person, and I welcome the challenge. It'll take years to prove this experiment out, but I'm up for it. I'm no quitter."

John couldn't resist; he smiled. "Charlotte, this is amazing. I'm so proud just to know you."

Charlotte laughed. That laugh. "Thanks, John."

"No, I mean...watching you perform mass, I could see the people becoming...connected to you. You had each person's attention during your sermon. It reminded me of the way you captivated me with your words the first time you visited my studio; you changed my life that day. I know you're a humble person, but please feel very proud of who you are and what you're doing. You are an incredible woman."

Smiling, Charlotte glanced down at her coffee, and John detected an extra flush at her hairline and cheeks. "And so the question is," said Charlotte, looking back up with a sudden flash of sadness behind her eyes, "how do we remain friends, as you now understand I can never have an intimate relationship with you?"

John quickly averted his eyes, sensing he was now the one blushing. "I'm well aware of that. You want my answer? We can remain good friends and leave it at that. There's no sense in losing each other." He cleared his throat, finding courage. "But you'll always be more than a friend, in a way. You changed my entire life when you visited my studio. I was lost, totally misdirected in my art. When you came along, I felt a rebirth. And now I've finally sold some art. I now believe I can approach a gallery and request a one-man exhibit. My friend Michael has agreed to be my go-to-guy and is arranging such a show as we speak." John lifted both hands and crossed his fingers hopefully.

Charlotte broke into a wide smile, the mood lifting like a sheet to reveal real happiness, real friendship. "Are you enjoying yourself now?" she asked hopefully.

His eyes brightened. "When I sit at my easel now, I lose all sense of time. I don't know what day or even what month it may be. It's like someone is taking my hands and creating for me. It's so easy now. And it's all thanks to you."

A beat of silence passed between the two, during which a murmur of the coffeeshop's music filtered in. John cursed himself; he was being much too forward, much too clingy.

"Then, my friend," said Charlotte, lifting her chin high and looking straight at John, "let's toast to knowing that we both have someone we can talk to whenever times may be a bit sideways." They each lifted their coffees and brought them together with a soft clink. "With the barriers placed in my way, I could certainly use a listening ear now and again." Her demeanor darkened a bit. "As a matter of fact, Monsignor Karras of The Sweetest Heart of Mary is having a very difficult time accepting that a woman may become a priest here. Seems he doesn't think progressively and is doing whatever necessary to reduce my reputation before I even really have a chance."

"What is he doing?" John asked seriously, sensing Charlotte's unease.

She hesitated. "Well, it's not a very interesting topic to an outsider." John felt his heart wince in his chest. An outsider. That's what I am? "But as an older priest in the archdiocese, he has the ear of our archbishop. They have dinner together all the time, and I think he's spreading rumors about me."

John pursed his lips, determined to help. "Let me sharpen my pencil with my friends and see if we can't make some suggestions." Ha. She wouldn't be calling him an outsider for long.

A Change of Faith

"Wow. That would be amazing, John."

"Nothing will happen until we meet again. In the meantime, if you need anything, call me."

Charlotte seemed sad at the prospect of him leaving. "Yeah, it's…it's probably time for me to head back to the parish and continue my day, anyway." She glanced at her wrist and then realized there was no watch there. She giggled, rising and smoothing her hair with her hands. "I'd like to visit your studio soon to see what your new work looks like."

"You're always welcome to stop by," John said. "Always."

John rose, and Charlotte extended her hand. John took it, small and soft, but a firm handshake. Then, hands still clasped, Charlotte stretched up to touch her lips to John's cheek. He jumped, that familiar old tug coming alive in his chest. She smelled different than she used to, sort of smoky.

"Be safe," John managed, but she didn't seem to hear him.

V

Two years later, Charlotte's time at the seminary was coming to a close. As the first and only woman attending the seminary, Charlotte knew from the beginning that things would be challenging. As if the studying and testing wasn't grueling enough, having a woman at the seminary seemed to throw the entire system out of whack. Simple things like bathroom facilities and sleeping arrangements had to be specially adjusted for Charlotte, and although she sometimes felt like a burden, she reminded herself that she was doing something revolutionary. She often recalled John's words at the coffeeshop two years earlier: "I'm so proud just to know you."

Many of Charlotte's fellow students made sure to keep their distance, avoiding her as if her very presence would pollute their pure, godly minds. Others, mostly the boys who travelled in packs and laughed a little louder than the rest, frequently wanted to sit with her at dinner. Charlotte tried to hide her smile, pretending not to notice the way they leaned towards her, fighting for her attention. She was a rarity, after all.

The archdiocese wanted desperately to hide the fact that a woman was working to become a priest. It was as if they were ashamed, like they feared that if people saw a woman was capable of this male work, they would finally realize priesthood was a joke. Though Charlotte's presence was discussed in the hallways within the seminary, news about a female student was never mentioned on the outside. After all, she still had to do well in her remaining studies to be ordained. For many, there was still hope that she might not succeed.

The original idea of bringing women into the priesthood back in Rome was not easily accepted. The old guard of Cardinals fought very hard to oppose the concept. To say the group back at St. Peter's was a bit chauvinistic would be quite an understatement. It took a young, aggressive group to finally convince Pope Peter Paul that church attendance, especially in the U.S., was dropping incrementally each year, resulting in smaller and smaller income streams. Something had to be done. After years of deliberation, a final decision was made to let three women apply for the seminary in the States.

Charlotte had received word of the opportunity through the pastor at the Sacred Heart, where she and her parents frequently attended. Father Herbert Weir was a big brute of a man who used to be a professional boxer and gave the most colorful sermons. Father Weir knew Charlotte and her parents well. He was also a diocese monsignor and was exposed to inside information as it became available at the archbishop's dinners. He started the Sacred Heart from simple beginnings, performing mass in a public-school basketball court. Working relentless hours and recruiting as many parishioners as he could, he was one day able to place a down payment on 20 acres to start construction on a church. "The bankers never had a chance once I told them God was involved in the construction!" he boomed for years to come.

Eventually his parish consisted of a K-12 school, two churches (one converted to a gym), and a bingo hall. When Monsignor Weir was made privy to the idea of a female priest, his thoughts immediately went to Charlotte. He fancied her a very bright young business leader in the community, smart as a firecracker, and he knew her degree as a CPA would place her at the top among applicants. The vetting process would be small and private. Only four women in the area would be presented, and of these four, only two interviewed. Charlotte had spent months toiling over her decision to apply. Could she really give up life as she knew it and devote herself to the church?

She decided to throw her hat in the ring. After all, she

had to pass the intensive interview process and be selected, which seemed unlikely. The process itself was four days, and Charlotte met with various individuals and departments of the church. Her final interview was with the archbishop and lasted two hours.

A couple of days later, Charlotte received a call from Monsignor Weir; she'd been accepted. It was spring, and she still had to pass the test in philosophy by summer's end. There was much studying to do, and quickly. Charlotte knew this opportunity could open the door for a whole new generation of female priests; it could change the face of the Church everywhere. But was she really willing to give up her entire personal life for God? She was sacrificing falling in love and having a family. She talked the decision over with her mother and sister all summer.

She'd only ever had two serious relationships. Scott Miles back at MSU was the first. Like Charlotte, Scott was an accounting major, and they had a few classes together. 6'2" and handsome with dark brown hair, Scott was as polite as they come, the type of boyfriend you wouldn't be embarrassed to take home and introduce to the family. He was Charlotte's first true love. Weekends together were precious. They would study, cook, and attend tailgate parties at the tennis courts. Scott was from Petoskey, a beautiful little town located on Northern Lake Michigan a few miles South of the Mackinaw Bridge.

Scott's father Jim was an aspiring entrepreneur, having just started a local vodka company called Gypsy. After entering his blend and beating out 35 national applicants in a California competition, he pulled the trigger. Scott, along with his two sisters, worked at the distillery and tasting room during their summer breaks. Charlotte would visit when possible, but the four-hour drive from her Detroit home and her own summer job made it difficult to visit on any regular basis. Eventually, the distance took its toll, and Charlotte and Scott decided to see other people.

Then Charlotte met Aaron. An up-and-coming attorney at one of the state's largest firms, Aaron never stopped. Though the relationship wasn't a particularly long one, it was fast and furious. There was nowhere the two of them wouldn't go and nothing they wouldn't do. Together they went skydiving, sailed the Great Lakes, ziplined over gorges, and bungee-jumped off bridges. It was clear to Charlotte from the beginning that the pace of their relationship would eventually catch up to her. Aaron was relentlessly energetic and impulsive, and six months into the relationship, she waved the white flag and wished Aaron well.

It was obvious to Charlotte that relationships were not her forte, and she probably wouldn't be missing out on much by devoting herself to God. In fact, it would be a burden off her shoulders, in a way. The race to find a mate was exhausting and depressing. You know who doesn't work at a distillery across the state and who doesn't insist on an impromptu road trip when you have a test the next day? God.

But then there came John, who was different than all the rest. Quiet, contemplative, moody—beautiful in every way. From the moment she saw him at the market she felt her heart raging in her chest. She had purposely sidled up next to him at the asparagus stand, something she'd never told him before. She had deliberately made the first move. She just had to get a closer look at him, and when she did, she was so struck by him that she realized to get his number would prove disastrous if she had any thoughts about joining the seminary. Could she give up John for God?

Charlotte's time at the seminary was certainly an adjustment, but she quickly found herself adapting better than she thought she would. Her mornings started with six a.m. prayer services, followed by breakfast, and then a long day of classes. There was so much to learn and remember, Charlotte began to think maybe medical school would have been easier. As she was on an expedited curriculum, she was there all year long except for Christmas. There were still those who weren't buying into the idea of a female priest, but Charlotte's stubbornness and focus would carry her through. If she felt overwhelmed by a course or discouraged after a presentation, she didn't let it get to her. In fact, she was enjoying the challenge, amused by the men's reactions to her.

The days were long and tedious, but Charlotte knew it would all pay off when she became ordained. Near the end of her time in seminary school, she was requested to have dinner with Monsignor Weir and the archbishop. Not knowing what to expect, Charlotte entered the meeting a bit on edge. A few minutes into dinner, Monsignor Weir asked, "What do we call a woman in your position, Charlotte? A priest? A female…priest?"

Charlotte bristled, confused. "Oh, well, you call me a student, Monsignor. I'm only a student."

"Well for now, of course. But you won't be a student forever!"

Over baked salmon with toasted almonds and fresh vegetables provided by the fine folks at the Eastern Market, the three reviewed a long list of possible titles, eventually deciding upon "Vicar," as it wasn't directed at any particular sex.

"Vicar Charlotte," said the archbishop with a smile, "Welcome to the priesthood."

Sipping an Argentinian red Malbec, Charlotte started. "What? Really?"

The men laughed. "Of course! You've excelled in the seminary. The Sweetest Heart of Mary will be very lucky to have you, Vicar," said Monsignor Weir with a smile.

"You'll begin officially next month, of course, after studies conclude," added the archbishop.

Charlotte beamed. Vicar Charlotte. It had a nice ring to it.

VI

In the years since he'd seen Charlotte, John's paintings continued to improve. He created pieces that surprised even himself in composition and story. His two pieces that Michael left at the Neumann Gallery sold in the first four weeks. After spending years creating art even he didn't like, John now had a small following of people who genuinely liked his work.

In a just a couple of years since his first encounter with Charlotte, he had blossomed from a deeply unhappy painter into a real artist. It boggled his mind, and he frequently reminded himself that although he had sold some pieces and was certainly in a much better place now than he was a few years ago, he was no Picasso. He harbored a deep fear that his few successes would go to his head and all his friends would grow to hate him for his pretentiousness. The truth was, he was still eating hotdogs at Lafayette Coney Island and Ramen noodles most nights. He just didn't mind so much now.

James Neumann, who couldn't find time for John a couple of years ago, was now texting him regularly enquiring about more pieces. Michael stalled on returning phone calls to convince James that the work of John Adams was catching fire in other galleries. Michael told James he would try to convince John to allocate two more pieces for the Neumann Gallery, but he couldn't make any promises.

Then, the Webster Gallery in Chicago, one of the most respected in the nation, asked if John wanted to exhibit a few pieces there. When Michael turned his back to open a bottle of scotch, talking excitedly about the amazing impact this would have on John's exposure, John reached down and pinched the skin on the back of his hand. He still didn't wake up, so he pinched harder. He looked down at his feet, his left toes exposed through an unsightly hole in his sock. A rainbow of paint splatters, layers of yellow scrambled in layers of red, remained in place between his feet. Michael poured into a glass on the counter, ice crackling in the liquid. This was not a dream. This was distinctly real.

Michael flew to Chicago with a portfolio of John's work, and the folks at the gallery agreed to give John his own exhibit area of six pieces near the entrance. John couldn't believe what was happening, and again, he reminded himself sternly not to let this get to his head; he still had a very long way to go on the road to success. Michael was certainly no help in keeping John grounded; since the first paintings sold, Michael had been envisioning his name alongside John's paintings in textbooks for years to come. John needed someone who would remind him that he was just and always would be just John Adams.

Charlotte, John thought. She was always honest. John wondered suddenly if she was a priest yet, or what had become of the troubles she was facing, the rumors being spread about her. It had been four years and, despite their promise to each other, they hadn't spoken much; maybe it was time to invite her over for a glass of wine. Perhaps he had been too absorbed in his own work lately; what if she needed him? Then, there was that bit on the television this morning about a female priest crashing to her death. Something about the whole ordeal made John uncomfortable.

Suddenly concerned for her, John sent Charlotte a text with his new cell phone, and two agonizing days passed before he heard back. She apologized and asked if she could come over the next night. Her text was brief, and John sensed something was not right. He had the same uneasy feeling in his gut that he felt waiting for Charlotte to come upstairs and meet his friends so many years ago. The same feeling as when he heard of the female priest's untimely death.

The next evening Charlotte arrived at 7:00 p.m. They

shared a polite hug and kiss, from which John pulled away quickly. "How are you?" he asked, stepping back. "It's been a long time."

"I'm good!" she chirped tightly, standing in the entrance so that the backdrop of the door framed her like a piece of art. John frowned; even with years between them, he could see something was bothering her. Charlotte sat down at the counter while John prepared dinner. He poured her a glass of wine.

"So, it's been a while. Am I in the presence of a priest?"

"A vicar, technically. But yes."

John set the bottle of wine on the counter. "Wow. Congratulations, Charlotte. Vicar Charlotte!" He laughed. "That's amazing. Are you loving every second of it?"

"Oh, yeah," she said, spinning the glass on the counter idly.

John frowned. "Years ago you said it would be nice to have someone to talk to when something was bothering you." He raised his eyebrows. "Here I am."

Charlotte smiled, and John could see that her eyes were glassy and bright with tears. His heart twisted in his chest. Not yours to comfort, he reminded himself sternly, stuffing his hands into his pockets to keep from reaching out to her. He wondered who would comfort her, then. God? He frowned, doubting God could comfort her as well as he could. Did God know that she liked holding hands but hated cuddling? Did God know not to ask too many questions once she was crying?

"John...what I'm about to tell you has to remain strictly between the two of us."

"Completely confidential," he promised.

"Do you remember when I told you about the issues I was facing with Monsignor Karras?"

"You believed he was spreading rumors about you," John said, nodding.

Charlotte sighed. "Well, it's even worse than I imagined now that I'm officially a priest. He's been telling the archbishop that I've been having an ongoing affair with one of my parishioners. I know I'm going to be called in soon, and it'll be his word against mine. I don't know what to do. I don't know how..."

John served Charlotte some risotto. She didn't seem

to notice. He snapped into action. "Okay, let's think about the best way to handle this." John sat down and took a forkful of food, looking over Charlotte's shoulder as he considered how to help her. "We know he hasn't liked the idea of having a female in the Church and is very bitter and spiteful. If it's his word against yours, then we need proper proof that nothing is happening. Does he have an individual he's accusing you with?"

"He's planted someone who will testify that we had a relationship. I don't know what to do!" Charlotte threw her hands over her face, tears gleaming on her cheeks through the spaces between her fingers.

John put his fork down. "Do you mind if I bring my friend Michael into this conversation? He has contacts that may be able to help us. I meant to years before…"

"It's okay, John, things happen. If you trust him, then yes, let's bring him in."

John would normally never bother his friends on such short notice, but Charlotte needed help he couldn't provide. He texted Michael, who lived about 20 minutes away. Michael called immediately, and John explained Charlotte's situation.

"He's on his way over," John said as he hung up the phone. She nodded, her eyebrows knitted together.

"Thank you."

John stomped out the voice of reason that, thus far, had incessantly warned him not to get too close to Charlotte, not to look at her the wrong way. Now he reached across the table and grabbed her hand, looking right into her eyes.

"We're going to get this sorted out," he said. "I promise."

She squeezed his hand in return. "Thank you," she repeated.

On his way over, Michael had time to think about the situation and what could be done to handle it quietly. Ever since he sold John's first two pieces a couple years earlier, he had developed a strong friendship with one man who he knew could help: Frank McGann.

Michael entered John's studio without knocking and found John sitting across from a woman who wore her dark hair pulled back to display round eyes and a full mouth set into a broad,

A Change of Faith

fair face.

In rare form, Michael looked absolutely serious. He spoke quickly. "Charlotte, without your help, my friend and his work probably wouldn't be where they are today. If we can find a solution to your problem, we will. I have someone I'd like to talk to. I won't mention your name."

Charlotte looked to John. "What do you think about bringing someone else into this?"

"Michael knows his stuff," he assured her. Charlotte looked back to Michael and nodded.

Michael called Frank and shared Charlotte's problem without mentioning her name, and the next morning, Michael met Frank at the main entrance to John's studio. As they walked up the stairs, Michael could tell Frank McGann the businessman was excited to meet John and see his studio. As soon as they walked in, Frank smiled broadly and snatched John's hand.

"John Adams, in the flesh! I've been looking forward to meeting you since the day I purchased your pieces so long ago," said Frank hurriedly, still shaking John's hand. "Your buddy Michael here is quite the salesman." Still shaking. He glanced around the studio. "If you asked me to design an art studio for myself, I don't think I would change a thing from what you have here. Do you mind if I look at some of your new pieces?"

Shocked, John finally pulled his hand away as his biggest fan wandered off, examining the art that littered the floor and walls, leaning against cupboards to dry. This was really Frank McGann, standing here in John's dusty, poorly-organized studio. He made the whole place look nicer, more expensive.

"The pieces I purchased are very motivating and stimulating," Frank went on while John was silent. "Somehow when we view your paintings we just aren't looking at art, but feeling the emotion you incorporate with it. The pieces here have the same feel to them," he added, glancing around at John's work. "Yes, yes, very good."

John opened his mouth; he should really say something. Yeah, it was definitely his turn to say something. "Should I put some coffee on?" he managed.

"Sure thing, John. Coffee would be fine."

The three men took a seat at the counter, and John set

out a box of donuts he'd bought that morning; there were only a few left.

"Mr. McGann—" John started.

"Please, call me Frank."

"Frank," he corrected. "I have a friend who's a priest in the archdiocese."

"Ah, yes, your problem! Forgive me, gentlemen. I got caught up in all this wonderful art. Please, let's discuss the issue."

"Well, as I think Michael told you, our friend's been falsely accused of having a sexual relationship with a parishioner. The problem has been brought up to the archbishop by the monsignor, who doesn't happen to care for our friend and is doing what he can to disqualify them. We're trying to figure out the best way to handle it."

Frank dumped sugar into his coffee until John wondered how it didn't thicken into pudding. "I'm a member of St. Hugo's Church in Bloomfield Hills," Frank said commandingly, stirring his sugar. "I attend Sunday services regularly and have a good relationship with our pastor. With my position in town and my businesses, I'm also good friends with our archbishop. I believe everything you're telling me, and I know the uphill battle your friend faces as the only female priest in the archdiocese."

Michael and John exchanged glances. "How do you know we're talking about a woman?" asked Michael nervously, not wanting to reveal Charlotte's identity.

Frank laughed. "Gentlemen, I've been in business for many years and have been in meetings with every personality possible. I know things. I also know your commitment to your friend, and I will meet with the appropriate people in the archdiocese quite privately. Vicar Kotlinski will be just fine. Just like you know her and trust her, I trust both of you!"

There was a reason Frank McGann had the business reputation he did. After finishing their coffee, Frank agreed to meet with John and Michael again and give them an update under the pretense that they never met or spoke about this little issue. It was agreed.

VII

The next day, John called Charlotte and asked to see her as soon as she was available. She was busy with services all day; they would meet early the next morning at their favorite coffeeshop.

John seated himself in their usual quiet corner before Charlotte showed up. He sipped his coffee as he waited, eager to be the bearer of good news for her. The bell jingled over the door, and John turned to watch Charlotte stride in, her hair wild from the wind. She spotted him quickly and flashed a smile, reaching up to smooth her hair away from her face. John stood and they hugged and kissed, now their customary greeting. John was getting so used to it by now that the fire her closeness ignited in him almost didn't hurt anymore. All scar tissue now, perhaps.

"So what happened?" Charlotte asked quickly, taking a seat across from him. "What did your friend say?"

"Slow down!" John laughed. "Why don't you order your coffee?"

"John Adams, don't do this to me."

John smiled; he liked the sound of his name when she said it. "Michael and I met with an important local businessman yesterday, and in a very roundabout conversation, explained a friend's issue. This businessman has quite a say in the community, and he understood exactly what we were talking about. He's confident that he can resolve the issue without pulling you into the storm."

"That's it?"

John gestured with his hands. "That's it."

Charlotte blinked at John for a few seconds, her lips turning up into a slow grin. Then she stood up and reached across the table to hug him. "John Adams, I don't know what to say! Thank you. I don't know how I could ever repay you."

This reaction was worth the long meeting with Frank, worth waking up early for this morning, worth everything. "We're a team," he said. "You're the religious part of the team, and I'm the artsy one. Without you I wouldn't be where I am, and we wouldn't have met this particular businessman. It was a full circle of events."

Charlotte didn't seem to hear him. "I'm so excited. I can't wait for this problem to just go away, John, you have no idea. How is your friend going to do it? How will the archbishop be confronted without making this a political volcano? I just finally became a real priest, I don't want to lose my position already. I don't want it to be in jeopardy...I've worked so hard—"

"Hey, slow down, Vicar. Listen, this man just so happens to have key relationships with senior members of the archdiocese, including the archbishop. He quickly did his homework on the situation and found a few things that'll make the archbishop not only upset, but reactive. Seems this Father Karras [AF2] has had an affair himself, and his is a very real one. Besides that, he enjoys using some of his parish's donations for personal expenses. It's too bad his ego got in the way with your position; he could have gone on without anyone ever finding out. Now he'll probably be demoted and banished to some faraway parish."

"Oh my gosh," whispered Charlotte. "Are you serious?"

John shrugged. "As a heart attack. He put himself in this position and now he has to pay the pauper. You can probably expect to be requested to have a meeting with the archbishop himself after things settle down."

"So...what do I do now?"

"Just keep doing what you've been doing. Your reputation in the archdiocese seems to be very strong; in fact, I heard you've already turned the financial position at the Sweetest

Heart of Mary around and attendance has increased exponentially. I wouldn't be surprised if you're asked how you've been able to accomplish what you have so quickly! You're doing great. Everything will be taken care of."

"Wow." Charlotte sat back and laid her open palm on the side of her face, dazed. "Thank you, John. You're really saving me. Seems not too long ago we were buying some asparagus next to each other. Life is funny, isn't it?"

John smiled, trying to hide the fact that he couldn't quite breathe. Asparagus made him think of the beginning, and thinking of the beginning made him think of the end, which still brought him unimaginable pain.

"I'd better get to the parish," Charlotte said, standing. "I have service soon. Let's talk later."

"And I to painting!" stammered John, and watched her go. The Chicago Gallery was expecting some pieces, and those John thought he had on hand, Michael had already sold. Things were picking up.

VIII

John's father had worked in the bar business for the majority of his adult life, making many sacrifices along the way. When it came time to retire, it made the most sense for Brother Bob to take over. Bob had received his degree in hotel and restaurant management from Michigan State and ran a number of upscale restaurants in the Detroit area. Operating the bar came naturally to him, and unlike their dad, Bob figured out how to run it without working 70 hours a week, or 60, or even 50.

Bob was a jovial guy, an artful combination of Jackie Gleason, Archie Bunker and Rush Limbaugh. Ready to offer his opinion about anything political, when Bob was behind the bar, you could spend hours on end listening, debating, and possibly arguing. Bob wasn't known to be of the religious sort, but depending on what day it was, could still discuss theology with the best. Bob loved his wife and two boys and was always available if anyone ever needed help.

Today however, Bob was doing something he hadn't done in quite some time: visiting a church. Charlotte wanted to start a small soup kitchen in the basement of the Sacred Heart cathedral, and without Bob's knowledge, John had volunteered his services. John had sneakily invited Bob for lunch in the market. Once enjoying their food and conversation, John asked Bob to meet his friend Charlotte. Before Bob knew what hit him, he was in the basement of the church reviewing the small kitchen and things that would be required to mass-produce meals.

Much of the food and meals were being donated by the merchants at Eastern Market. Whatever they didn't sell would be picked up by a couple of parishioners and creatively used for meals. To his own surprise, Bob was actually quite enjoying his time at the kitchen, and he began attending frequently to help out. His conservative nature began to bend a bit more towards the middle of the road the more time he spent there with Charlotte.

During some of the kitchen's busiest hours, Monsignor Karras showed up, the man to whom Charlotte reported and who started the troubling rumors about her. Bob wasn't aware of the issues between Charlotte and the monsignor, but it was obvious the man wasn't happy. Bob lingered close by, keeping a careful eye on Charlotte, who he had quickly grown to feel rather protective of.

"Charlotte, may I have a word with you?" asked the monsignor. He was not always the happiest of men. He'd been passed over when a bishop's position became available. When a younger man with less experience was elevated above him, he'd found reason to make everyone his enemy. His general anger was obvious at his church services and sermons, and attendance shrunk as a result. The archbishop was aware of this, but hoped that the monsignor, now 60 years old, would soon retire. But after the accusations about Charlotte came to light, the archbishop had no choice but to react.

"Hello, Monsignor. Of course. How are you?"

"Vicar Charlotte," he snapped, ignoring her let's sit down gesture, "I had a recent conversation with the archbishop and it seems he was exposed to some issues that will certainly be affecting my future with the church. I'm not sure who he was contacted by, but it was someone significant outside the church. My position as Monsignor of our region will come to an end very soon, and I thought it would be best if I spoke to you directly."

"I'm sorry to hear that," Charlotte said, wringing her hands nervously. She glanced around, but no one seemed to be paying attention to the conversation, save for Bob, watching skeptically from the kitchen with a raised brow.

"News will be out soon about some internal issues

about…myself…that will be very condemning. Charlotte…I've made some severe mistakes over the past couple of years, some including you. I have to apologize for anything I did in regard to destroying your reputation. When I was told there was going to be a female priest in the church, my church, I was angry. I'm sorry for all I've done to harm you. Truth be told, you have been doing an amazing job at your parish, increasing attendance and revenues. We could all learn a lesson from your commitment to your parishioners. The folks truly love you, and this little soup kitchen is living proof," he said, gesturing to the air around him. "I'll be meeting the archbishop again soon, and I will be recommending that he consider you for my position."

Charlotte opened her mouth, unsure what to say. She had not expected this; neither the apology nor the potential promotion. "Monsignor, thank you for your candor, it's very appreciated. As a member of the Catholic Church and as a human being, I forgive no matter what the circumstances. And I do forgive you."

The monsignor nodded stiffly. "Well, then." All at once, Charlotte saw through the façade.

"But I wonder if you can forgive yourself," Charlotte went on. "I do hope your apologies aren't just because you're trying to appease yourself. I'm not sure if I feel sorry for someone in your position, or angry. Our church has experienced irreparable damages due to problems with our clergy. The way these problems were hidden by transferring the suspected clergy to outstate dioceses is very disturbing."

"Yes, well, Vicar, I certainly don't think I bear responsibility for all the problems—"

"I had many career options to choose between," said Charlotte, "and when Monsignor Weir approached me about this opportunity, I thought very hard about many things I would be giving up and decided this could be a chance to demonstrate that the Church is willing to change. So now here I am, and I'm committed to making a difference. There is much work to be done operationally, financially and spiritually. The truth is, monsignor, had you not set out to ruin my reputation, there are more people I could have helped by now. I have people waiting for me. Best of luck, Monsignor."

A Change of Faith

Charlotte walked away feeling upset. She brushed past Bob, who reached out to her with concern. She knew she should have felt some satisfaction after the conversation, but she found herself feeling restless and agitated. The Church had many pitfalls demanding her attention, and she felt the push now more than ever to work to straighten the system out. People like Father Karras were monkey wrenches. To fix the machine would require much focus and hard work, maybe more than she and her team were capable of.

By the time Charlotte pulled herself together and returned to the crowd, John had joined Bob and they were eating lunch together. John was instantly taken aback by the look in her eye, a fiery expression that was entirely new to him. This was a woman challenged and focused, someone who wasn't going to take no for an answer ever again.

"Vicar," John said with a sarcastic smile on his face, "what's new?" Bob didn't know what was going on, but he sensed from the look on Charlotte's face that she was viable to smack his brother.

"John, if I wasn't a vicar and surrounded by my parishioners right now, you'd be flattened!"

Bob and John started laughing, and Charlotte couldn't resist following suit. She was grateful they were there to take her mind off the monsignor. The more John and Charlotte looked at each other laughing, the more the laughter continued, growing from giggles to uproar. Watching them, Bob could see there was a special connection. He'd never seen his brother look at anyone the way he looked at Charlotte now, and if he wasn't mistaken, Charlotte had an interesting gleam about her eye, too. If only she weren't a priest.

"How about the three of us get out of here for a while?" John recommended.

"Yeah!" said Bob. "How about it?"

"I could use that," said Charlotte. I can meet you and Bob back at your place in an hour?"

"Sounds good. I'd like to get both of your opinions on my latest pieces before they head to Chicago."

Back at John's apartment, Bob grabbed a few things from the kitchen to make dinner for the three of them. A bottle of John's finest red wine was uncorked, now valued at $16. Once

Charlotte arrived, easy conversation bounced between the three, many laughs ensuing. It was just what the doctor ordered. John was grateful that Bob was handling things in the kitchen, because it gave Charlotte a chance to review his latest six paintings alone.

"If I didn't know you from a couple years ago," she said, "I'd never connect your face to these paintings. They are absolutely stunning. The composition is so deep, with each piece telling its own unique story. These are very impressive."

Pride swelled in John's chest, and he smiled. "So my face isn't absolutely stunning?"

"John!"

"Hey, you said it."

"I did not! Your face is perfectly handsome as it is."

"Well," John blushed, changing the subject. "I appreciate hearing that from you, because if I can trust anyone for a completely honest opinion, it's you." He studied the paintings with artistic precision. "Now I guess it's time to ship them to Chicago and see how the market reacts. Come what may."

A sheet of yellow composition paper, torn roughly at its edge, caught Charlotte's eye on a chair behind him. She peered closer; the words were stacked up into a tower. "John, are you writing poems?"

Poems? John didn't reckon he'd ever said that word, or even thought it. "I write to kill time…it's certainly not poetry," he said, embarrassed.

"May I?" Charlotte asked, reaching towards the paper. But of course he knew she wouldn't wait for his permission.

"If you insist, but be gentle with me," said John, his heart hammering against his ribs.

A Faraway Dream
As she wakes with a smile on her face,
Her dreams take her to a very different place.

In a world full of wondrous sites, Fields far away flying a million kites.

From there to a vast valley so green, So beautiful; this has to be my dream.

A Change of Faith

*I vanish now and awake in a room, It's a different language, one I
will learn very soon.*

*A door opens and to my surprise,
A beautiful Tuscan vineyard is dancing before my eyes.*

*"May I take you away?" this voice will say.
"It's time to go, it's the beginning of my day."*

*He says with a pleasant smile,
"Come with me, if only for a while."*

"John!"

"Remember, gentle!" John pleaded.

"You may have more than just painting in your future.
A short poem that so quickly takes your imagination away. Wow…"

John smiled sheepishly. This wasn't his real skill, he
was only having fun. Through the windows, the sun was beginning
to sink into the city, electric pink and orange spilling into the studio.

"Just don't tell Bob I'm writing poetry," he
whispered.

Charlotte laughed. "Whatever you say," she said,
folding the poem into a small square and slipping it into her pocket.
"But this one's mine.

IX

Over the next few months, Charlotte remained focused on her daily services and parishioners. As the only female priest in the area, she was quickly drawing attention from the public, media, and corporations. Charlotte was smart enough to use this personal publicity for the greater good of her church. Her young members attending grade school were being sponsored throughout the area by scholarships, home items and counseling. Many of these children were from broken homes with little direction or support.

It was clear now to the archbishop and his staff that Vicar Charlotte and the Sweetest Heart of Mary were exposing the Church in many positive ways throughout the greater Michigan area. A swell of support was developing, much of it due to her competence as an operator and the genuine care she offered her parishioners. She was asked for interviews from print-media and television stations, all hungry to hear from one of the first female priests in history. The vicar would begin her interviews by talking briefly about being a female priest, but always managed to quickly redirect the conversation to the church itself and the benefits it offered its members and the community.

Charlotte was turning into a public relations dream. The senior clergy members who had so fiercely protested the female priest idea finally had to accept that this wasn't going to go away. The archbishop requested a meeting with Charlotte. She was to present to him and four monsignors her overview of The Sweetest Heart of Mary cathedral, including operational changes, revenue gains, parishioner increase, school operations, and future goals and budgets for the next three years. Charlotte had much to do over the next week; there was a considerable amount of information to be accumulated. Her skills as an auditor and CPA would come in handy, but she was still a bit overwhelmed. One of her friends from the auditing firm, Robin Minano, with whom she had remained in contact, had once offered that she call him were she ever in a crunch. Well, it was time to call in the favor.

Robin arrived at Charlotte's rectory with empty arms, and by the end of the evening Charlotte had given him a box full of financial information to review. Robin was brought up on the Lower East Side of Detroit. His father left his mother when he was young, and his mother, his star from above, was a nurse at Detroit Receiving Hospital. She worked long hours to support the boys. As Robin was the oldest of three boys, he served as the role model for his brothers. An all-around sports type of guy, his skills on the football field yielded him a scholarship to the University of Michigan.

Though he wasn't the biggest or fastest guy on the field, because of his will to win for his mother, he started his final two years as a safety in the defensive backfield. His skills wouldn't provide a career in the NFL but would open many doors for him once he graduated and passed his CPA. Robin had a special place in his heart for Charlotte and what she was doing at her church. Together, their presentation next week to the diocese board would be significant. Their goal was to demonstrate that with proper skills and a business plan in place the church had the capabilities to operate in the black and grow throughout the region. This would be a huge hurdle to jump, but they enjoyed the challenge.

For the next five days, Charlotte was still running her day-to-day duties at The Sweetest Heart of Mary, but at night she and Robin worked late crunching numbers and designing an operations summary for not only her parish but the other inner-city parishes in her region. She and Robin understood that though the Catholic Church is a religion, it is also a non-profit business, which, with proper execution, can be very successful. This was why Charlotte wanted to become a priest in the first place.

John was painting on a daily basis. His six works displayed at the Webster Gallery had been there for four weeks, and two had already sold. The gallery director was thrilled with the reviews the pieces were receiving, and Michael was already negotiating adding a couple more pieces to the exhibit. He also tried to reduce the commission from 50% to 40%, but the gallery director wasn't having any of that. No matter; John's works were now priced from $7,000-$9,000, which was more than good enough for John.

The Neumann Gallery in Birmingham had agreed to a one-man exhibit in November. For John, this was a major accomplishment. One-man exhibits are significant to an artist's resume, and the fact that it would be close to the holiday season would be great for exposure. It was now the end of April and John had to provide 15 paintings, plus he still owed two to the Webster Gallery. His current inventory was four pieces. Michael was relentless, keeping John on his toes and brushes in his hands.

Vicar Charlotte, with Robin's help, was ready for her presentation. Upon entering the executive office, Charlotte was delighted to see Monsignor Weir there as one of the attendees. He pulled Charlotte aside before the meeting began.

"Charlotte, of the many decisions I've been required to make on behalf of the Catholic Church, you are my finest decision of all. You have stood up to so many barriers and handled them as maturely as could be expected. Now, here's the reality check: The other three monsignors here won't be giving you an ounce of room to prove yourself. None of them believe in female priests, and though you have done a remarkable job, you will be on the hot seat."

Charlotte nodded. "I'm ready."

"The archbishop, on the other hand, is quite open to this experiment and is very impressed by your accomplishments. Because I initially sponsored you, I will be attending the meeting, but I can't participate. I know you'll handle the situation with care. Just remember, they are only people. They put their pants on one leg at a time just like the rest of us."

A Change of Faith

Charlotte smiled. "Thank you, Monsignor."

"Break a leg, Vicar." He gave Charlotte a strong hug.

As Charlotte entered the meeting room, the archbishop sat in the center of a long, ornately-carved oak table. On either side of him were two monsignors. Charlotte immediately felt like she was in the "old boys' club," but thanks to her warning from Monsignor Weir, she knew she was well-prepared for the meeting. The room had high ceilings and dark trim, and a large fireplace of green marble was the center of attention. The area carpet looked like something from Rome, and light poured in through the large leaded windows to her left, leaving their faces lit in a chiaroscuro light. The archbishop smiled warmly, which was appreciated, as the three monsignors were as stoic as pieces of granite.

"Charlotte," began the archbishop, "this is a unique situation, but we are pleased to have you here." Still no smiles from the others. "Each of us has had an opportunity to read your overview, and if I may say so, it is concise and deliberate. Before we begin questioning...I know you were made aware of Monsignor Karras and the issues that took place. It's been a very unfortunate experience, but it's been put to rest. As you know he has been reassigned and requested early retirement, which we all agreed to. Speaking on behalf of the Church, please accept our apologies for the deeply inappropriate behavior and accusations."

"Your grace," said Charlotte, "thank you for your kind words. Let's consider the situation water under the bridge. There have been too many positive things taking place throughout the archdiocese over the past two years to worry about that. I'm here to give you my overview of the operations at The Sweetest Heart of Mary cathedral and offer suggestions about things that could increase parishioner attendance at surrounding inner-city parishes." She knew these comments would irritate the monsignors, but the archbishop seemed to be on her side.

"Then let us begin the questioning," he said.

One by one, each of the monsignors brought her financial facts and projections under fire, and one by one Charlotte provided concise and accurate answers. It seemed the group may have met their match as it became clear this vicar was much more than a pretty face. It finally became obvious to the archbishop that Charlotte was not only prepared, but fully ready to implement the programs being presented.

"Charlotte, if I may," said the archbishop, "before Monsignor Karras left his post, he and I had a meeting about the inner-city parishes in his district and their futures. Through his 11 years heading his churches, attendance fell, and revenues fell along with it. He made only one request, and it had nothing to do with himself. He suggested that we as the archdiocese executive committee review your resume and consider you for his position. He was quite adamant about you and your capabilities. If you don't mind, I'd like some time with my cohorts to discuss that. Please go and make yourself at home in my library."

Charlotte was in shock, remembering what she'd said to Monsignor Karras. She went to the library, but she certainly didn't feel at home. The more time that passed, the surer Charlotte felt that she wasn't going to be elevated to Monsignor. She remembered the cold looks on the faces of the three monsignors. Would she lose her position as Vicar entirely?

Two hours passed before a priest summoned her back to the room. As she walked in, not only did the three monsignors have firm faces, but so did Monsignor Weir and the archbishop. Charlotte's heart fell.

"It's obvious we had a long debate," said the archbishop tiredly. "There are many variables to this decision, as we have to think about not only the positives but also what negative events could possibly happen. This decision will not only open eyes in the local media, but will also be a shock to the country in all national archdioceses. Our holy Father in Rome has carefully reviewed my thoughts about this appointment, as he ultimately has to give his blessing to this elevation. I've had calls with him and a number of cardinals. We all understand the serious ramifications this will have."

Charlotte nodded solemnly. "I understand."

"All this being said, he has given me the go-ahead to elevate you to Monsignor. Congratulations, Monsignor Charlotte. We are pleased to have you."

"What?" Charlotte shook her head, taking it in. "Are you serious?" The archbishop nodded. She tried to fight her tears, determined not to cry in front of these men. She cleared her throat. "Thank you," she said. "So much. Thank you."

A Change of Faith

Did this really just happen? She looked up and saw all five faces at once, each with a wonderful smile. Monsignor Weir had tears in his eyes, as did the archbishop, and Charlotte felt her own begin to fall.

"Monsignor Kotlinski, would you kindly join us for a glass of wine in the dining room? We're all quite hungry."

During dinner, the archbishop and the three monsignors each opened up about their views on ordaining female priests. They all agreed that the Church was ready. Adding women would open up many opportunities for young ladies, eventually redirecting the Church in a positive direction. They wondered how Rome would look at this promotion. The fun would begin when the announcement was made on Sunday within the parishes. Charlotte wanted to get to Dearborn and tell her folks before word got out.

After dinner and one more glass of wine, the gentlemen excused themselves except for the archbishop and Monsignor Weir.

"Charlotte, Monsignor Weir and myself have been your staunchest supporters, though we've had to provide support as quietly as possible. What is about to happen will be a tsunami of interest that, quite frankly, we would prefer to deflect. But it will be coming, and in a very big way. We will require a good marketing strategy on how to handle all the upcoming questions. Many will never buy into female priests and will be bitter whenever your name is brought up. We must remain strong."

"I understand," said Charlotte. I don't care, she might have added. Bring it on.

"You've been almost magical in your performance at your church, but we have done everything in our power to keep you under the radar. That will change beginning Sunday. Your life is about to dramatically change. Go home and relax; you deserve a wonderful night's sleep, if that's possible."

X

On her ride home, Monsignor Kotlinski was in a daze. Did this just happen? Am I a monsignor? Any time I see Monsignor Weir, I think of him as someone so special, and now I'm his equal. Now who can I call and trust?

As she dialed the phone number, tears rolled down her cheeks. It was like all the pressure built up over the past few years was finally being released. "John, it's me. Do you have a minute?"

"What's going on? Your voice is shaking."

"You'll never believe what happened today. I'm in shock. I need to tell someone."

"Tell me."

"First you have to promise not to tell a soul. Promise?'

"Yes, I promise. You're scaring me."

Charlotte explained her long meeting and the angry-seeming monsignors. She said that b   y the looks on their faces, she just knew she was going to lose her position. "I'm no longer a vicar," she said.

There was a pause, and John said softly, "Charlotte, I am so sorry."

She laughed. "No, it's good!" She was hardly able to speak now. "I'm a monsignor. I've been elevated, and it had to be approved by the pope himself!" It was very quiet. "John, are you there? Say something!"

A Change of Faith

"Charlotte, holy shit! You're a monsignor? Is this a joke?"

"I'm shaking, I don't know what to do! Can we meet tomorrow? Can I see you?"

"Yes! Let's talk in the morning. Try and get some sleep. My friend is a monsignor…wow!"

The next night, Charlotte and John decided to have dinner at Armando's on the river and enjoy some Italian cuisine and exciting conversation. Charlotte was rarely seen in a dress, but tonight she wasn't Monsignor Kotlinski, she was Charlotte. They requested a quiet table in the corner of the restaurant, as her reputation was already becoming more public.

"John," said Charlotte in a low voice, "do you believe you're selling your paintings at almost $10,000 a piece, and I'm going to be a monsignor on Sunday? We both have each other to thank for our careers' progression! We've played off each other, listened to and motivated each other when we were down. Thank you. Without your positive attitude, I'm not sure I'd be here. I love you."

John started, almost choking on his wine. The moment those words escaped her lips, it felt like a warm knife was thrust into his heart. "I…love you too."

"Let's toast!"

They raised their glasses and lightly toasted. Though John was happy for both of them, he consistently thought about what it would have been like if Charlotte never went to the seminary in the first place. There was much more between them than simple friendship. Oftentimes, their customary peck on the cheek nearly grew into more. But as a priest of the church, living by the rules went a long way. John dispelled such thoughts.

An empty bottle of wine between them and another half-full, Charlotte asked, "John, where do you see yourself ten years from now? Would you like to meet someone, settle down and have a family?"

Even though it was coming from Charlotte, a woman he had come to love and admire, John found that the question felt totally natural. "I'll be turning 40 next year, you know," he said, "and only recently did that subject enter my mind in a serious way. I've been so focused on my career, and until recently, my lack of income. It would be nice to meet someone and even start a family. All of my little dinner group except for Michael and myself are now married. I wouldn't mind joining the club." John swirled the remainder of his wine around his glass, smiling a little. "As a matter of fact, I've been having casual conversation with a woman who goes to Brady's. I haven't asked her out, but I might."

"Do you feel that special spark when you're with her?"

"It's funny…initially no, I didn't. But now it's developing, and it's kind of nice. How about you, do you ever regret the direction you've taken and think about a family?"

Charlotte's face dropped, and she looked away.

"Oh, gosh, I'm sorry Charlotte. I didn't mean to…"

"No, it's okay. Really. At the beginning I did, but now with so many things happening and increased responsibilities, I find there isn't enough time in the day to look back and think what if. I made my decision. I'm not sure where life may take us, but I bet neither of us would have imagined we'd be sitting here tonight in the positions we're in. I guess we should be very proud."

"We'll both be very busy over the next few months, that's for sure. You have six parishes you'll be working with, and I have to complete works for the show by November. I'm so proud of you, Charlotte. I really am. I love you…as a very best friend. Forever."

Charlotte smiled. "Forever and beyond."

Friday came along, and Charlotte was excited to see her parents and sister for dinner. Because of her father's recent health issues, the dinner would be at her parents' house. John came by and picked her up for the 20-minute drive. On their way, Charlotte reminisced about her childhood and the ongoing support she received from her parents. Her father especially reinforced the fact that you can do anything you put your mind to. Her mother was always there for her. Tonight, she thought, they would get to see for themselves the results of their good parenting.

As they approached the front door, Charlotte was shaking with anxiety. She relaxed a bit when John was warmly welcomed by her sister Shawne, her parents, Robin, and Monsignor

A Change of Faith

Weir. Conversation was generic as everyone participated in the dinner's preparation in the kitchen. It was funny for Charlotte to see Monsignor Weir peeling potatoes with her dad, sharing Gypsy vodkas on the rocks. Once everyone was seated for dinner, Monsignor Weir began prayers, after which he turned to Charlotte.

"Earlier this week we had a little meeting at the archbishop's residence with a few monsignors," he began. "The topic was future development of the Church in the archdiocese, focusing on inner-city parishes. Our main presenter was Vicar Charlotte from The Sweetest Heart of Mary. The presentation went on for three hours with intensive questions and answers. Afterwards there was a review, and a decision was made. Charlotte?"

"Uhm." Charlotte glanced at the monsignor and smiled, a tear already running down her face. "Thank you, Monsignor. Yes, I was asked to develop a business plan for inner-city parishes. Fortunately, I had the help of Robin for the entire week prior. Robin, thank you; it would have never been completed without you. I guess the presentation went well, because when I was invited back into the meeting the archbishop had an announcement." There was silence around the room as everyone looked at her. "It seems...the Detroit archdiocese has a female monsignor."

There was a short moment of silence until Charlotte's parents and sister realized what she had just announced. Her father began to cry, and her mother blinked, mesmerized. Shawne jumped up and screamed. Everyone flinched, startled as Shawne ran around the table to give Charlotte a hug.

"My sister is the first female monsignor in the world. Oh my goodness, Charlotte!"

Her father took a deep, ragged breath, clasping hands with his wife on the table between them. "Dear, your mother and sister and I can't tell you how proud we are. Monsignor Weir, we are now in the presence of two monsignors at our table. To think our daughter will be following in your footsteps...there are no words. We are so very happy."

"Let me say this," said Monsignor Weir. "As a member of our clergy, I couldn't be happier to be sitting here enjoying this moment. Charlotte has proved to be an inspiration to not only members of our church, but to women and young people everywhere, and to many inner-city parishioners. This is truly a day of celebration. The holy Father himself had to approve this new position. Let's all enjoy this moment and be proud of our newest monsignor and her accomplishments. Charlotte, to a job well done. You have much hard work ahead of you, but tonight, enjoy this moment. You deserve it."

Everyone at the table raised their glasses and said in unison, "To Monsignor Charlotte."

The next day, the archbishop requested Charlotte come over. Her announcement would be made soon, and there was much to discuss. The archbishop had his public relations people attend, as this was expected to be significant. They'd already been contacted by all the local television stations, newspapers, and even CNN and FOX news for interviews. They were expecting every major national morning show to be requesting live interviews. Instead, it was decided that a press conference would be best, beginning with the archbishop and ending with a Q&A with the new monsignor herself. Some questions could be planted, like most politicians do, so some of the pressure would be taken off. The goal was to enjoy the moment for what it was and then get the new monsignor involved with her parishes. If all went right, in a couple of weeks Charlotte could be fully focused on her new position.

After a sleepless night, Charlotte rolled out of bed at 5:30 a.m. She was so excited for the day that coffee wasn't required, but she had her two cups anyway, thinking the routine might relax her. Church was at ten, and her family would be there at nine for congratulatory doughnuts. The archbishop arrived with the four monsignors from the meeting; they would all offer the mass together. It would be quite the ceremony. Little did Charlotte know that the pope wanted to watch the services from Rome. Cameras were quietly set up around the church. The archbishop thought it best if Charlotte wasn't made aware until after the service.

Finally, everyone was settled into the vestibule and ready for their walk to the altar. Charlotte had no idea about the television cameras in the choir loft. The church was packed. Family members and friends from Charlotte's childhood were all there to celebrate. At the stroke of ten, the organist began to play, and a procession of altar boys started their walk down the aisle, followed by Charlotte, the four monsignors, and finally the archbishop. The mass and ceremony were a blur as the archbishop gave a sermon about the unique abilities women would bring to the church. Monsignor Kotlinski was just the first of what would be a bright new direction of the church.

"Monsignor Kotlinski, over the past several years, has scaled walls many would consider insurmountable. She is a role model to many young women and minorities. Monsignor, job well done, but there is so much more to do."

Standing in the crowd was a stranger, a blonde-haired man in a dark suit with equally dark and penetrating eyes. He smiled with the rest of the crowd, but his eyes did not smile with his mouth. Charlotte glimpsed him clapping, and for some reason, she felt a wave of dread.

XI

One week earlier, Vicar Rita McPherson sat in formal silence in the semi-darkness of the confessional. It was 7:00 p.m. in Southie's Blessed Sacrament Church, a ray of hope in the otherwise grimy streets strewn with trash, sagging brick tenements and cars blaring hip-hop music parked on the corners of convenience stores, where tattooed men drank 40s and leered at passersby. The sun was setting over the neighborhood, its light piercing through the church's stained-glass windows and falling in colorful pools on the stone floor.

Vicar McPherson, a woman in her mid-50s with braided white hair and bright blue eyes, was eager to finish her duties and settle in for the night with a mug of hot chamomile tea. But just as she was about to exit the church, she heard the familiar echo of footsteps on stone. Then the door to the confessional creaked open and the wood groaned under the weight of a man. She listened as he got down on his hands and knees. Through the mesh, she could dimly make out his profile—light-skinned, blonde hair, dark suit. He spoke in a firm voice, "Forgive me Father, for I have sinned and will again. It has been six years since my last confession."

Vicar McPherson cringed at the word "Father." How long had she endured that word? But how was the young man supposed to know she was a woman and that the proper nomenclature was "Vicar?" She brushed it aside, ready to do her best to alleviate the fear and doubt from this man's mind. "God forgives all who seek penance in His name," she said solemnly. "Tell me, son, of the sins for which you seek penance today, and for those you say you'll do."

The man seemed surprised. He looked up. "You're a...woman?"

"Why, yes, I am," she said matter-of-factly. "I'm Vicar McPherson."

"The woman from the TV?" the coolness in his tone didn't change. "That is, the one who was accused of sleeping with her parishioners?" Vicar McPherson thought she heard contempt, but she brushed it too aside.

"No. You're thinking of Vicar Kotlinski, or perhaps Vicar Anderson, God rest her soul. Both have been exonerated from such rumors. Now as for..."

"Vicar Anderson," said the man. "How did she die?"

Vicar McPherson breathed a sigh. "She crashed through a guardrail alongside a mountain. Fell asleep at the wheel."

"Is that so?"

"It is. Now, what is the sin for which you would like your Lord and Savior to exonerate you, my son?"

"That's the thing," said the man. "I have no desire to be exonerated. I don't care either way. I receive instructions to kill, and I kill. It's that simple."

As sudden as the calm descending before a storm, Vicar McPherson felt surrounded by a palpable sense of dread. She realized for the first time that she was alone with this stranger in the vast church. And everything was much too quiet. "If you don't want to confess," said Vicar McPherson, trying to keep her voice from trembling, "I'm going to have to ask you to leave."

"Is that right?" The man's face was in front of the mesh now. He was staring in at her, his eyes unreadable. "You want to hear my confession?"

"No," she said, rising to her feet. "I want to call the police."

"My sin, Vicar McPherson, is that I killed Vicar Anderson. My next sin, however, I'm afraid you already know."

Before she could react, his hands plunged through the

77

mesh and wrapped a fiber wire around her throat, instantly cutting off her air. She clutched at the wire, trying to scream, but the man pulled harder and all that came out was a low gurgle. He violently yanked her into his booth. She could see his blond hair falling in his face, across his raging green eyes, his perfect teeth clamped down so hard she thought they might shatter into a million pieces. Vicar McPherson felt her temples pounding as her head grew hot, ready to explode. A black curtain descended over her eyes as she kicked and squirmed. The stranger pulled hard on the fiber wire until she stopped.

When he'd finished, the stranger left her lying face down in a puddle of blood. With tender care, he dipped two fingers into the puddle and brought them to the wall, writing. He didn't hurry; he took great care to make it right. Afterward he looked at his handiwork with pleasure. It was a quote from 1 Corinthians: "The women should keep silent in the churches. For they are not permitted to speak, but should be in submission, as the Law also says."

He straightened his suit and tie, slicked back his golden hair, and strode out of the church, soon disappearing down an alleyway overhung with laundry lines. From her cab's rearview, Sister Tamara glimpsed the man walking away before she got out and gathered her belongings from the trunk, fresh from a mission to Argentina. Three minutes later Sister Tamara was inside the church standing in front of the confessional, screaming.

XII

After a few months of hectic publicity, a calm finally began to settle in. Of course, the calm wasn't that calm, because Monsignor Kotlinski's new position was a demanding one. Many daily decisions were up to her alone. The six other parishes were all having serious problems staying afloat. Bills were piling up for them the way they were back when Charlotte began at the Sweetest Heart of Mary, when Sunday attendance was quickly dwindling. On top of that, after news began to spread of Vicar McPherson's murder, even regular attendees were growing uneasy.

Fortunately, Detroit was seeing a large uptick in millennials moving to the downtown area, so Charlotte knew there was hope for the struggling parishes. She just had to figure out ways to tap into that large group of successful young adults. If she could make attending mass cool again, it could start the rush she needed. Who were the coolest celebrities in town these people would love to hang with? She began accumulating a list of professional athletes, young business people and entertainers, including famous local rappers.

At one of the many dinner parties she was asked to attend, Charlotte met Kathy, the wife of Detroit Lions' quarterback Billy Cunningham, the highest-paid player in the NFL. The couple loved being involved in the community, and as Kathy and Charlotte formed a quick friendship, Charlotte realized Billy and Kathy could be very helpful in reaching her inner city goals.

"I would love for you and your husband to attend an event I'm putting together," said Charlotte. "We're trying to increase church attendance in Detroit. From young people, specifically."

"Well, I can certainly see why that's so important," said Kathy, nodding in agreement. There was just one problem: They weren't Catholic. Nonetheless, Kathy was onboard to help. Using her contacts, the friends coordinated 14 wives and girlfriends of professional athletes, along with six young female business executives and the wife of Detroit rocker Billy Rheins. On the day of the event, the women would embark on a pub crawl where people could come along, stopping at churches between the many Detroit bars. The parking lots of the churches would be littered with tents, each with its own band open for viewing. Billy Rheins agreed to sing a song at each church. The goal was to sell 2,000 tickets at $50 each and donate the proceeds to the churches.

Once word was out, almost 5,000 tickets were sold. Additional donations were coming from auctions, bar receipts, corporate sponsors, and tee shirt sales. The shirts were created by a local graphic designer. The front spelled out DETROIT in big letters, and the back read, "Cool to be Catholic."

The event was picked up by two Detroit radio stations, and by the end of the day, Charlotte and her team had raised $384,000, enough to operate one of the churches for an entire year. More events were being planned, but more importantly, people who didn't even know these churches existed had visited them during the crawl and discovered for themselves just how magnificent they were.

There were those in the archdiocese who were very impressed by the success of the event, but there were also those who thought the churches were being used for the wrong reasons. The archbishop enjoyed the exposure and the money raised, but he had to be careful not to display his feelings for fear of stepping on too many political feet. He was aware that stories were being made up in Rome about the rogue female priest in Detroit and the terrible things she was doing. Charlotte was always under the proverbial microscope.

A Change of Faith

John was so busy during this time that he didn't attend the pub crawl, and had barely talked to Charlotte in some months. He'd finished 12 of the 17 paintings he was required to complete by November. It was late September, and he had to paint five more pieces. Unlike Charlotte, who was in the public eye every day, John was cloistered in his studio, only coming out for the occasional burger downstairs at Brady's.

Brady's Pub originated in 1923, surviving the great depression and the Detroit riots of the 60s. Owned and operated by the O'Donell family from Southwest Ireland, the pub was more Irish in nature than most pubs in Ireland, the mahogany backbar imported straight from Limerick. Brady's didn't have tables, only booths and the bar, so a lot of "quiet business" was known to transpire there. Al Capone, John F. Kennedy, and Pope John Paul had all enjoyed a burger in those dark booths.

On this gray Wednesday afternoon, John emerged from his studio desperate to see some human faces. He ordered a corned beef sandwich at Brady's, noticing Maria, another regular who he secretly hoped would one day be more than just a friend.

"Hi, Maria," he said.

Seated at the bar, Maria looked up from her meal. "John! How are you?"

John sat down beside her. Her black hair was springing loose from its ponytail, clinging to the sides of her face. "Better than you," he said with a smile. "You look tired."

Maria worked for her family's company, Gardelli Wholesale Produce. It was one of the largest companies in the region, and her days began at 3:00 a.m. as produce began to arrive at their docks. The company had started with a handshake between Maria's great grandfather Tony and mobster Antonio Borcello, who operated the mafia's inner-city presence—prostitution, restaurants, unions, and wholesale markets. Borcello had a strong relationship with the Purple Gang, and if a business didn't do what the duo requested, it may mysteriously disappear. Over the years, as the mob was being disassembled by the government, Tony Gardelli was able to legitimize his business and it had thrived ever since.

John didn't know any of this. He only knew that Maria worked for the family produce business and that she was outrageously beautiful. Tall and slim with classic Italian curves, Maria had bright green eyes that glowed like a cat's. He knew she was 32 years old and lived not far from the market with two friends. He also knew that she had one sister and four brothers, three of whom also worked for the company. He hadn't met her father, Tony, but she talked about him frequently and the idea of ever meeting him made John nervous. Maria said that Tony, now in his early 60s, maintained a chiseled face and flowing gray hair. He was quiet and humble, but by his firm rough handshake, you knew you didn't want to get on his wrong side or interfere with the Gardelli family, whoever they were. He dressed in worn jeans every day but rumors had it that he could buy the entire Eastern Market if he so desired.

"You don't look so hot yourself," said Maria with a smirk. John glanced down at his paint-stained shirt and jeans. He hadn't thought twice before stepping out of the house; he was just eager for some social interaction. Now he felt himself blushing.

"Old clothes," he muttered.

Just as John knew little about Maria, she had no knowledge of his career as an artist. John was afraid that if he told her he made his living selling paintings she'd look at him sideways and politely say goodbye.

Maria poked her fork into a pile of fries. John chewed his corned beef sandwich, Irish football droning on in the TV overhead. A comfortable silence descended over them as they enjoyed their lunch. After a time, Maria broke it. "John Adams," she said, "are you ever going to ask me out?"

John stopped chewing and looked up at her, startled. She sat staring at him, waiting patiently. He broke into a smile and they both laughed.

"I was just about to, actually," John said. "You interrupted me."

"Ha! You liar."

He set down his sandwich. "No, really. I've been meaning to ask you out for a while. I'm a little embarrassed that I haven't, but absolutely, I'd love to see you outside of Brady's sometime. What do you say?"

Maria pursed her lips in mock-contemplation. "Well, I don't know. Let me think about this. After all, I'm an old-fashioned Italian woman whose parents will run their eyes up and down you like a polygraph instrument." She smiled. "Would Saturday night work?"

John was uncomfortable with Maria snatching the reigns, but there seemed to be no stopping her. "Saturday's great. Seeing as you've taken control of this date, where would you like to go?"

"How about up to Birmingham? I haven't been there in a while."

"I'll pick you up at seven," John said quickly, before she could choose the time herself.

"Seven it is," she smiled.

John's most recent painting was his largest ever, at 8' X 9'. It was also his most unique; he was incorporating newspapers, straw-hats, and even a broom handle. The colors ran the eyes left to right, from light and muddy to eclectic and zappy, a straw-hat dangling from the broom handle on the right. According to John, the piece told an interesting story about the 1920s. He was having so much fun creating that he was unable to stop even when his eyes grew sore.

On Saturday, John made reservations at the 440 Bates Steakhouse in downtown Birmingham, an upscale city where the more affluent people in Detroit frequently hung out, dined, and shopped at the many unique stores and art galleries. As John drove to Maria's apartment, he wondered what awaited him. He'd hardly had a serious relationship since Charlotte, which was practically five years ago. He smoothed his hair back nervously with his hands, trying to ease his rapid breathing. Was this just a fling, or something more?

As Maria answered the door, John realized with a jolt that this was the woman he had been thinking about for a long time. She wore a short, silky black dress that was cut low in the front, and heels that made her legs look long and muscular. John couldn't help himself—he stared.

"Hello?" she said with a laugh, waving her hand in front of his face. Her hair was curled like nothing John had seen at Brady's…everything about her right then was completely new to him. Her green eyes sparkled. "Earth to John?"

He swallowed, thinking for a moment of Tony Gardelli, the protective Italian father who happened to be even more dangerous than he knew in that moment. "Maria, you look beautiful," he managed. "Stunning."

They jumped in John's Subaru and headed up I-75 to Woodward and then to Birmingham. During the drive, they talked about their families and how hard their previous generations worked to get ahead. Maria spoke passionately and proudly about her ancestors, and John reached over and placed his hand on hers. She entwined her fingers through his, never breaking the pace of her story.

At the restaurant, they were seated in a round corner booth overlooking all the tables. John ordered a bottle of Cornelius Cabernet, their fingers never separating. They talked about their childhoods and their careers. John still didn't fully expose his primary means of income or the acceptance he was receiving in the art community, and Maria refrained from delving into her family's business connections.

The waiter slid John's and Maria's plates onto the table, and they lifted their glasses to toast. After the clink, John looked to Maria, and their smiles slowly fell away. They both leaned in, and suddenly they were kissing.

When they finally broke away, Maria said quietly, "Since the first time we met at Brady's, I was hoping this evening would come. I felt your charm and warmth, and I admire the love you have for your family and friends. There's something different about you, John Adams. I don't know what it is, but I'm dying to find out."

The lighting was growing dimmer and dimmer, and the two could hardly make out their facial expressions anymore. "The feelings are mutual," said John. They were practically whispering; suddenly the atmosphere felt very intimate. It was as if the restaurant were empty, save for John and Maria. "I'm glad there's a Brady's Bar and that you walked in that door one day."

After dinner, they decided to go for a walk up Old Woodward. They popped in and out of quirky stores, admiring useless trinkets. Wandering down the streets hand-in-hand, laughing under the streetlights, they eventually found themselves staring into an art gallery.

A Change of Faith

"Oh, let's go look at the art!" Maria said eagerly, tugging John's arm.

John looked up at the sign: The Neumann Gallery.

"Eh, really?" he said, trying hard to sound disinterested.

"Yes! Come on."

They made their way in. They inspected the artwork on the right side of the gallery, John knowing his three pieces were hanging just on the other side. He was hoping Maria would lose interest and want to leave.

As they circled the back and started towards the exit, Maria stopped at a particular painting and cocked her head. From the corner of his eye, John watched her nervously. She was squinting, her arms crossed over her chest, looking at the piece as though she had seen it before.

"John, this artist has your same exact name! Isn't that funny?"

A man who John recognized as one of the gallery managers approached with a smile. "Hey, John! We haven't seen you here in a while. Are you ready for your one-man exhibition?"

Maria turned to John, perplexed. "These are your pieces? You're John Adams?"

The gallery manager shifted uncomfortably. "Oh boy! We'll be in touch, John," and he scurried off.

"I guess I am," John said softly.

Maria stared at him, her eyes glinting in the overhead lights. This is it, he thought. It's only the beginning, and it's already ending.

"You big stinker!" Maria exclaimed, her face opening up into a bright smile. Her laughter came like music. "Why didn't you say something?"

John felt himself relax. "Well, I wanted to make sure we appreciated each other for who we are as people," he said. "Instead of participating in a popularity contest. It's about John and Maria. You know?"

Maria was flabbergasted. The thought of standing with the artist of these three works was very…cool. She leaned down to examine the title and price, and her mouth fell open. "John, this says $12,000!"

John grinned. "It does, but my career certainly didn't begin this way."

Maria looked back up at him and laughed. $12,000!

The conversation on the ride home was very different from the one they'd shared on the ride there. Maria's potential boyfriend was a well-respected fine artist...how about that?

"I was a miserable excuse for a painter," John explained as they drove down the dark highway, "until my friend Charlotte gave me some of the best advice I've ever received."

Maria listened intently. She was familiar with Charlotte and her position at the church. "Are you very close with the monsignor?" she asked.

"Yep." He glanced over at his date. "We bounce ideas off each other. In fact, I think she'll be very excited to meet you."

"That would be nice. I admire her. I can't imagine how difficult it is, what she's doing. She must be quite a woman."

"She is," John said, quickly adding, "as are you."

Maria was dropped off at her front door with a warm kiss. Without any words, the two shared a clear understanding that what happened tonight was the beginning of something very special. "Goodnight John Adams," she said, "you stinker."

Though the college of cardinals had ultimately voted to approve women in the priesthood, the vote was very close with much animosity. Of the 218 cardinals involved, only 117 voted to approve the change. Many were so angry that they were investigating ways to implement the church's canon law 1024 and change the rules back to males only.

Three cardinals were spearheading the vote's retraction. To ensure their efforts would be successful, they hired a highly-regarded private investigative company in Washington D.C., Gottfried and Co. Gottfried was the company many high-profile politicians used in their campaigns. In the last presidential election they were responsible for digging up even the minutest dirt on opponents. They were being retained under a strict non-disclosure from cardinals Stefinnes, Gonremy, and Montross, all over 60 years old.

These pompous cardinals were involved in the

coverup of pedophile priests in the U.S. They thought by moving the problematic priests to other locations they could keep the issues swept under the carpet. This problem was eventually exposed and cost the Church a reputational beating along with tens of millions of dollars in legal fees and settlements. Still, the attitude in Rome was that the problems would subside with time. After all, this was the Church. No one could take the power away from the Church. Right?

Gottfried was to begin the process of digging up as much dirt on the rising number of U.S. female priests as possible, focusing on Monsignor Kotlinski. The goal was to start a smear campaign that would eventually lead to a retraction vote in Rome. The cardinals had their PR departments prepped, and a strategy was put in place. They were not fans of the pope, who was kept in the dark about the entire operation.

Digging up dirt on these women was proving more difficult than the politicians in Washington. Each of the vicars led quiet and dignified lives. Gottfried could try to put a spin on Charlotte and her past relationship with Aaron, suggesting they had a resurging romance while she was in the seminary, but that would be a stretch. So, after speaking to Cardinal Gonremy, it was decided that stories would have to be prefabricated. Illicit relationships, monetary misappropriations, lying; with the help of Gottfried, the cardinals would spread whatever rumors they could about Monsignor Kotlinski.

The first leak was initiated as a tweet about Charlotte. It was a small rumor about her and a personal situation with a parishioner, but it didn't take long before others followed that were more specific and more condemning. The archbishop's PR team picked up on the tweets quickly and immediately notified him of the situation. The rumors were also exposed to a local newspaper. From there things snowballed quickly, but Charlotte had been so absorbed in her work that she still had no idea. Then Monsignor Weir called.

"Charlotte, we have to meet soon," he said urgently.

Charlotte was working in her office. Things were looking positive for her parish; her hard work was finally paying off. "Is everything okay?" she asked. She'd detected a hint of something in his voice—was it pity?

"There are things developing…they aren't good."

Charlotte drove to the monsignor's parish in

Dearborn, her stomach in knots. She'd never heard him speak that way on the phone before.

"Come in, come in," he urged when she arrived. "Let's go to the den."

Charlotte followed her old friend towards the back of the church. "What's going on?" she asked as they sat down, unable to bear the anticipation any longer.

Monsignor Weir leaned forward, placing his elbows on his knees and folding his hands. "More rumors," he said gravely.

Charlotte felt fear sweep in like a wave, quickly mingling with despair. She could prove to those who knew her the type of woman she was, but how could she change the tide of public opinion? "Why are they doing this?" she asked, looking up to Monsignor Weir as if truly awaiting an answer. The monsignor informed Charlotte about the details of the quickly developing rumors. Charlotte shook her head, defeated.

"I don't understand," she said quietly. "I know it can be difficult to accept change, but this change has brought only positive results. I'm a good monsignor. I'm a good person, aren't I?" It was becoming anger now. "When will they let me do my job in peace? Who is doing this?"

"Whoever it is, they've created this smear campaign very meticulously," Monsignor Weir said sadly. "Someone wants to ruin you and any other female priests that are currently in the seminaries. They're facing similar issues. The archbishop and I have a suspicion of where this is coming from, but it will take some work to verify. The archbishop is speaking to the other bishops where your various cohorts may be assigned. They hope to come up with a reliable strategy that can clear all of you. But in the meantime, we can expect more negative news. Have you heard about Vicar McPherson?"

"From Boston?" asked Charlotte. "No. What about her?"

Monsignor Weir sighed deeply. "I thought you knew..." He shook his head, plainly disturbed. "She was found strangled in her confessional a few hours ago," he managed. "There was a quote from scripture about women's subservience written in her own blood."

Charlotte went pale. "No... no, no, no."

"I'm afraid so."

She rose to her feet, pacing, biting her nails. "She was targeted?"

"We're not sure, but it seems that way."

Charlotte's eyes grew wide. "And Vicar Anderson, who crashed on the mountain. Monsignor! Do you think…"

Monsignor Weir raised his hands. "It's no use jumping to conclusions. We've found no evidence of a conspiracy. But you must be careful, Charlotte. Okay? Be careful." Charlotte looked defeated. "This won't stop until they completely destroy you, but we're doing everything we can to fix this. For now, go to your church and keep doing your work. The diocese will put a counter-campaign in place."

Charlotte shook her head, looking at this man who had encouraged her to enter the Church in the first place. He had only kindness in his eyes. Had he misled her? "No offense, Monsignor," she said, "but how am I supposed to stay focused on my work with all this developing? I feel like something terrible is about to happen."

"Well, it will be quite difficult, I imagine," he said. Charlotte had never seen Monsignor Weir maintain such an air of seriousness. It was extremely unsettling. "We have a good idea of what's going on. We've been suspicious for a while. You just focus on your parishes."

In her car, Charlotte threw her head on the steering wheel and began to cry with frustration. These were supposed to be men of God. They had attacked her once before, and now they had come back with a vengeance. It seemed that the harder Charlotte worked and the more fruitfully her life and parish grew, the harder the Church tried to tear her up from the roots. Her parents lived nearby, and she thought it might be nice to have some company, but she couldn't bring herself to go there. Instead, with shaking hands, she dialed John and left a message on his voicemail.

"John, it's me, I need to talk to you. It's something kind of terrible, can you call me?"

When she got back to her rectory, she sat down in the den, never turning on the light, and certainly not the radio. She knew it was irrational, but she was afraid she'd see a headline about the scandal, hear a radio broadcaster announcing her newest disgrace. She thought of Vicar McPherson, that poor old woman, strangled to death in the church she loved. She listened to any sound outside the door, clutching a large candlestick, then placing it beside her. An hour in the dark and the quiet passed before her phone rang. She picked it up without checking the ID.

"John?" she said.

"Charlotte, what's wrong?"

It was him.

"I need to see you as soon as possible," she said, her voice breaking over the words. She was beginning to cry again. "Please."

"Are you home?"

"Yes."

"I'll be there in 20 minutes."

The next 18 minutes were even longer than the previous hour. When John walked in the front door, Charlotte stood, ran, threw her arms over his shoulders and began to weep in a way that she hadn't wept in years, probably not since she walked away from John outside his apartment that very first autumn.

"Charlotte, my God, what's wrong?" he asked anxiously, trying to pry her away from him. He wanted to look her in the eye and see what was wrong, understand what was happening. But she clung to him fervently, unable to speak.

Walking carefully with Charlotte latched onto him, her feet dragging limply across the tiled floors, John sat down on the couch in the den and waited. Finally, Charlotte unhinged from him and sank into the cushions, her cheeks red and swollen. Her eyes, bright with crying, glazed over as she stared ahead and took a few trembling breaths. She felt nauseous. John reached up to turn the lights on.

"John, it's happening again."

"What is?" he asked.

"Someone is defaming me, accusing me of having an affair."

John frowned. How much must she endure? "Not again. Do you have any idea who it is?"

"No, but Monsignor Weir indicated they might know, and it's someone significant. But that's not all."

"Charlotte, just tell me," he said. "You're making me

nervous."

"A woman priest from Boston was found strangled to death just a few hours ago. Written in her own blood was a quote from first Corinthians."

John didn't speak for a minute. "What was the quote?"

"The women should keep silent in the churches. For they are not permitted to speak, but should be in submission, as the Law also says."

"Fucking hell," John muttered. "A sexist psychopath. Do they know who it was?""No," said Charlotte, staring blankly in front of her. "No leads."

John took a deep breath. He grabbed Charlotte's hands. "What did the monsignor tell you to do?"

"They want me to perform my daily work, but how am I supposed to do that when there's a female-priest-hating monster on the loose?"

John thought a moment. "Frank McGann and I have grown to become good friends. If anyone can help, it's him; let me call him tomorrow."

"You think he can help?" Charlotte asked desperately.

"He's Frank McGann. Of course he can. It's so late, you should get some sleep. Is Mary here tonight?"

"Yes, she's asleep."

"Do you want me to stay here with you?"

"Yes, but with these rumors going around…"

John punched his knee. "Dammit. All right, you got a pen, notebook and camera?"

She looked confused. "Yeah, why?"

"Let me borrow them."

Charlotte went to her room and gathered the items and brought them to him, frowning. He took them and stood up. "All right, now I'm a reporter, and I'm going to camp out in my car all night long for the chance to catch a glimpse of the infamous Charlotte Kotlinski."

"You don't have to do that."

"Too late," he smiled. "I'm doing it. And if I see anyone, and I mean anyone, meander up these steps, they're gonna be sorry."

Charlotte gave him a weak smile. "Thank you."

"Don't sweat it. Now get some sleep, okay? We'll talk tomorrow." John gave Charlotte the best hug he could, wrapping his arms around her and holding on tight. He kissed her forehead. "It will be okay," he said. As he left Charlotte on the couch and headed towards the exit, he heard her begin to cry again.

I promise, he vowed.

The next morning John called Frank. As he explained the situation, Frank made it clear that he would make the proper calls and set up a meeting, and this time everyone would be included. Frank had befriended Charlotte after he first met her with John. He found her to be sincere and honest, and he understood the barriers she consistently faced as a female monsignor. He was already well aware of the newest accusations against her, and he was eager to be of help. Frank enjoyed a good battle, and this was sizing up to be just that.

Over the next couple of days, Charlotte attempted to continue her normal work, but she was highly unproductive. Her thoughts were in shambles. Where would she live after she was kicked out of the church? With her parents? Had they already heard the rumors? What if they believed them? Was someone going to kill her? Finally, the archbishop's office called and invited her to a meeting the next day at his house. Everyone would be there.

The attendees included Charlotte, John, Michael, Frank, the archbishop, and Monsignors Weir, Stanton and Trbovich. Also present were two people from the archbishop's PR office. Charlotte looked around at all the kind, intelligent men surrounding her, hopeful that together they could help her out of this mess. Suddenly, the lack of women present struck her. She trusted these men, but perhaps the best person to help a woman was another woman. But the meeting had already begun.

Then James Neumann walked in the door. Everyone except Frank looked up at him in surprise.

John straightened up. "James, what are you doing here?"

Frank smiled. "Let's begin the meeting and you'll understand."

A Change of Faith

"First I welcome everyone to this quickly coordinated meeting," said the archbishop. "The issues and external stories that have taken place about Monsignor Kotlinski are completely unwarranted and must be stopped immediately. We are here to review what is taking place, put in place our own PR campaign, and find the individuals fabricating these stories. We have been able to get some good internal information over the past two days with the help of Mr. McGann and Mr. Neumann." John and Michael glanced at each other, confused. "Frank, I will now let you chair the meeting."

"Thank you," said Frank, standing. "You were stunned to see James walk in here. Well, he's here for good reason. Michael, when you and I first met at the gallery, I was there visiting James, as he and I are old business associates from when I was doing work for the Department of Defense. James at the time was Deputy Director of the National Security Agency, where he and I had many interactions with internal government issues. Thanks to our experience, James and I, through some existing Washington contacts, were able to get a good idea of what's taking place. This situation is being directed out of Rome at the highest levels. There's a company in Washington by the name of Gottfried and Company. They market themselves as a public relations company—if you visit their website, you'll see everything looks very legitimate. What they are behind the scenes is an investigative house that digs up dirt on companies and individuals to defame and incriminate them. With that said: James, go ahead."

James Neumann stood up while Frank sat down. "Thanks, Frank. John, once we clean this up I'd like to know how your paintings for your exhibition are coming along."

John nodded, in shock that the gallery owner also happened to have a significant past career in the NSA.

"When Frank contacted me two days ago and explained what was taking place, my first calls were to some old contacts in Washington who are well-connected throughout the cybersphere. After just 24 hours of investigation, they were able to identify where the tweets had originated. Gottfried is very good at what they do and would never tweet any information themselves, but by investigating the origin of the tweets and working backwards, we were led to them. Once we knew it was Gottfried, we were able to contact someone who was able to identify the individual that retained the company. The original source is from Rome, and though not the pope himself, they are individuals with significant power."

James turned to Charlotte. "Why are they doing this to you? It's quite simple: There is still a faction of cardinals that greatly resents female priests and would like to reintroduce a procedural vote eliminating them. The way they would build support would be to defame you and the rest of the female vicars, more of them joining the ranks all the time. And with the recent and highly disturbing homicide of Vicar McPherson and probably Ford, we will take these matters very seriously. It will be up to us to put a plan in place that exposes these individuals."   "Now," Frank cut in, "this will not be an easy process. The men behind this will hide behind the veil of the Church and deflect any accusations. They're senior members of the clergy. Our goal is to get a couple of the fine folks at Gottfried to talk, which shouldn't be difficult. Once we verify the individuals behind this, the archbishop has agreed to speak to His Holiness. We'll fly to Rome and meet directly with the pope. We are all fully committed to seeing this through. Charlotte, the men behind this think you are just a pawn in their game , but they will be exposed and treated accordingly."

The archbishop now spoke: "In the meantime, our PR department has been working on a counterpoint strategy which should help deflect some of the stories that are spreading. I'm sure you'll still receive calls, Charlotte, but politely pass on answering questions for now. We'll work as expeditiously as possible to put this issue to bed. Personally, I'm extremely upset by all this, as are the bishops at the other dioceses. Keep your head focused, Monsignor Kotlinski; we're making progress."

She nodded solemnly. "Thank you, Archbishop."

"I'd like to thank Mr. McGann and Mr. Neumann for all their help so far," said the archbishop. "Without it, we would be lost. We will keep everyone notified on progress as it happens. That's all for now."

"Well," James said to John and Michael as everyone stood and dispersed, "I guess this is kind of a surprise, isn't it?" Dazed by the overload of information, John and Michael said nothing. "Sometimes you can't tell a book by its cover, can you?

A Change of Faith

Don't worry, I'm still James Neumann from the Neumann Gallery." He extended his arm, preventing John and Michael from moving into the hallway. He lowered his voice. "I'd appreciate if you don't mention what you learned about me in there. I'd rather be a gallery owner, if you don't mind."

Both nodded rapidly.

"So, John!" James said, very loudly now. He slapped a hand on his back. "How's the painting coming along?"

John, flabbergasted, finally spoke. "James—uhm, Mr. Neumann..."

James laughed. "John, it's James now."

"James. I have 13 paintings completed, wrapping up the final two next week."

"Good! The exhibit is in three weeks, after all. We've already started our marketing campaign. This should be fun."

"James," asked Michael as the three men walked towards the exit, "who are you, anyway?"

James laughed. "Consider me your friendly neighborhood vigilante." He gave John a friendly wink. "That's all I can say on the matter."

XIV

Maria was falling in love, but John was so busy helping Charlotte and trying to get his paintings completed that she hadn't seen him since their first date. As more and more women began entering the priesthood in Charlotte's shadow, public unrest grew, and Maria knew John was nervous for his friend. People were constantly talking about Vicar McPherson's murder; as her death now hung like a heavy fog over the nation. A rising threat.

Maria missed him. They agreed to meet Saturday night for dinner at Maria's parents' house. John was normally pretty laidback, but frankly, he was terrified to meet her parents. They were hardworking old-fashioned Italians, which meant they'd want to know who John was, what he did and what were his personal goals. He was concerned that if he answered anything incorrectly, he could be exiled from Maria's life indefinitely. Already he couldn't bear the thought of losing those bright green eyes or the peacefulness he felt when he was with her.

Maria was doing John a huge favor. The old Italian way would have been to invite everyone to the dinner, including brothers and sisters and aunts and uncles. But that would have been an Italian overload for poor John, and Maria knew it. He was nervous enough to meet her parents, especially her father, who he was beginning to hear strange rumors about which centered on the mob.

A Change of Faith

John could imagine the scene as if it were already a memory: "An artist?!" Maria's father would bellow as her mother wept into a satin handkerchief. "An ARTIST?" Maybe he'd throw a chair.

"Daddy, I love him!" Maria would scream.

"MY daughter, with an ARTIST?"

There was an article in the Detroit News about John Adams' upcoming exhibit at the Neumann Gallery. It included a brief biopic of the artist's "rise to success." It even mentioned how much his paintings were now selling for due to their high demand. John asked Maria to place the article on her desk at work. Eventually, as per John's plan, Maria's father stopped by her desk.

"Looking forward to dinner tomorrow, sweetheart," he said with a smile, leaning against the open door frame.

"Me too," said Maria, looking up from her paperwork. "John's a wonderful man. He comes from a very hardworking family."

"What does he do?" Tony asked. Unsurprisingly to Maria, he'd gotten straight to the point.

She took a deep breath; this was what she'd been preparing for. "Here," she said, pointing quickly down at the article. "This was in yesterday's Detroit News."

Slowly, her father picked up the paper and read the article. "It says he sells his paintings for $10,000," he said after some time, his brow furrowed.

Maria nodded eagerly. "Sometimes more."

Tony paused, his jaw set firmly. "Does anyone buy them?"

"As a matter of fact, he sells whatever he paints. He's very good, very well-respected."

Again, Tony paused, looking down at the article on his daughter's desk. "Baby girl, if he can support you and a family, your mother and I look forward to meeting him."

Maria was amazed. "Really?"

Tony smiled. "I'm sure he knows better than to mess with a Gardelli."

John was struggling to complete his final two

paintings; he'd been distracted by worries. Since the murder, he hadn't been able to stop thinking about Charlotte alone in her parish at night. Someone should really be there with her, he kept saying. One evening he even went himself again and sat in her den with her while she finished up paperwork late into the night. The Detroit police department had a surveillance team on call 24 hours a day as the archbishop pulled all the political strings he had. Frankly, painting seemed unimportant at the moment. But the exhibition was a week away and he was running out of time. Michael would be over in the morning to begin packaging some of the pieces.

Meanwhile, Frank and James made a trip to Washington D.C. to visit some old government friends. Some were retired now, but they'd all held significant positions of power at some point and still had consulting positions with companies that provided intelligence and IT services. Frank and James wanted to make sure to gather all the necessary information before they scheduled their trip to Rome. Their first meeting would be with the director of the NSA, William Beauchamp. William had reported to James many years earlier as a new hire. He'd received his degree in electrical engineering from MIT and his business degree from Stanford. He was a MENSA member and was not only academically inclined, but was also blessed with an acute degree of common sense, quite an effective combination for a man in his position.

Even though William would easily be able to provide all the information required, Frank and James also had meetings scheduled with two senators in charge of the Senate Intelligence Committee and a friend who worked for Samuel Services, a highly regarded investigative company specializing in IT intelligence. They knew that because of the severity of the church's issues and the character of cardinals who were suspected to be involved, they'd need to have a strong case prepared for Rome. All their information must be fully factual. The archbishop of the Detroit diocese was committing his reputation to this meeting. If things weren't completely investigated, he would meet the wrath of the senior cardinals in Rome.

Frank and James sat side-by-side at an outdoor table, both looking down at their watches.

"He's late," said James.

A Change of Faith

Frank laughed. "Late for being early, perhaps." He was practically a decade James's senior, and wore well the extra patience that had earned him. Frank picked up his coffee and drank calmly. James frowned.

They were at a small diner across the Potomac in Virginia, waiting for William to join them for breakfast, although neither intended to order any food. The door to the restaurant opened with a ding and William walked in. "Bill!" Frank said, rising from his seat. He extended his hand, palm open to the sky. "Pay up."

There were always bets placed between the three of them between the Detroit Lions and Chicago Bears, where William was originally from. William laughed and shook Frank's hand, clapping James on the shoulder before sitting down across from them. "Bill," James began, "it's always nice to see you and catch up, but Frank and I have this little situation that has developed, as per our previous conversation, so we'll skip the small talk. We have a good friend who's one of the few female priests in the U.S. She was ordained some years ago and has since been elevated to Monsignor in the Detroit archdiocese. Her name is Charlotte Kotlinski, an intelligent and sincere woman. Her reputation has been attacked and unjustifiably slandered recently with Twitter releases and now newspaper articles."

"Waiter," William called, raising one finger into the air. "An omelet with everything in it, please. Whole wheat toast, bacon, orange juice."

The waiter, young and skinny, looked nervous. "Everything in it?"

"Everything ya' got," said William.

"We're quite certain this is being done by a group of cardinals in Rome who want to destroy her reputation and that of the other female priests before a meeting of the college of cardinals next month," James continued as the waiter hurried off. "I'm sure you've heard about the murders of Vicars McPherson and probably Anderson. We're growing quite concerned. The cardinals' goal is to request a review of female priests in the Church and retract the vote from years earlier that approved female priests. They'll stop at nothing to get rid of these women. Evidently even by murdering them."

"Now," Frank interjected, "we can't be certain of that just yet. But our initial homework has led us to our old friends at Gottfried."

William rolled his eyes. "Those assholes."

"They were retained by what we believe are some significant cardinals in Rome spearheading this campaign," said Frank. "With your help, we'd like to scare the hell out of a couple of employees at Gottfried, no pun intended. Get them to understand the significant problems they're facing. With their help, we can accumulate the required information, including Gottfried's involvement, who the people are back in Rome that retained them, and why."

William's food was placed in front of him. He picked the omelet up with his fork and knife and placed it on his toast, then topped it with the bacon, then the other piece of toast, creating a tall, lopsided sandwich. He took a bite and chewed slowly. "Frank and James, I'll make my office and staff available to you for these services. Being a Catholic and attending parochial schools in Chicago, it makes me sick to think after all the issues the Church just got over, now this comes up. I can understand why you have to make sure everything is carefully orchestrated; these cardinals, if that's who it ends up being, will be able to politically protect themselves and probably throw others under the bus in their place. Let me see who would be the best people in my office to work on this. I have a couple of folks I know would enjoy digging into such a project. Give me a day."

"Absolutely, Bill," said James. "We appreciate your help, and that of the NSA. I'd like to say I miss the excitement, but it's kind of nice living under the shroud of an art gallery owner back in Detroit."

"I don't doubt it," said William. "Now, let's see if we can't get Frank to buy us this breakfast."

When the archbishop was made aware of the meetings Frank and James had coordinated, he was amazed by the significant people with whom these men held connections. He would feel much more comfortable making his initial call to Rome and the pope knowing the weapons he had in his arsenal.

A Change of Faith

Heading into the capital building, Frank and James quietly reviewed with each other the questions they would ask, as the senators were giving them just 10 minutes of their time.

"No, I'm asking that," whispered James as the elevator doors dinged closed.

"Fine, but you have to make it brief," whispered Frank.

"Don't you think I know that?" James frowned.

The doors opened and they strode down the hall. The men had been working closely with one another for almost a week now, staying in adjoining hotel rooms and sharing every meal together. Frank was accustomed to being the most powerful man in the room, and so was James. The stress of the situation was beginning to show in their furrowed brows and clipped words.

It was always difficult making time for meetings, especially with two senior senators at the same time. The senators were Tim Mosher from Illinois and Donald Mills from Utah. They'd both served as elected officials for many years; Frank and James knew they would be capable of pulling all the right strings. Plus, the senators were both in a pleasant mood, since unlike most meetings they attended, no one was asking for any government funding today.

"Senators," Frank began, "James and I very much appreciate your time. We know how squeezed you are on a daily basis. We will keep this as focused as possible."

"Frank," said Senator Mills with a smile, "we've known you for a long time. We respect you and your reputation as a businessman. The work you and your company did with the DOD saved our country billions of dollars in project cost overruns. And James, your work at the NSA is unparalleled. The least Senator Mosher and I can do is give you a few minutes. We know neither of you would request a meeting if it wasn't important." He nodded. "Go ahead."

James gave the senators an overview of the situation with Charlotte and the other vicars. Though this wasn't a direct government matter, both senators understood the grave consequences this could have in the Catholic Church. Senator Mills was Mormon, but Senator Mosher was a devout Catholic.

Senator Mosher looked at Senator Mills, who nodded. Senator Mosher spoke. "Gentlemen, Don and I understand that bringing us into the loop will legitimize your meeting with the pope. We'll make ourselves available in any way possible to help rectify this problem. If you require internal investigations into Gottfried, please let us know and we'll be happy to video conference in while you have your meetings in Rome. The Church doesn't need another problem like this, and I'm sure they won't want this publicized. Call us anytime."

Frank and James were feeling confident as they headed to their final meeting, heads held high. Everyone they needed was getting on board with them in support of Charlotte and the other victims. Their case in Rome would be strong.

They met their friend Adam Conrad from Samuel Services. Both men were in communication with Adam on a regular basis. Adam was famous for internet IT investigation and they were hoping he would be able to verify the information that would be provided by William and the NSA. He would be the final person they spoke to before they wrote their report. Frank and James were hyperaware that lives may be depending on them. Their meeting with Adam was brief, but Samuel's reputation as a company was topnotch, and their name on a report was worth its weight in gold. They got the go-ahead.

With their meetings behind them and their nerves raw, Frank and James headed to Old Beggars Pub in Georgetown for a bite to eat and a nightcap. "Productive day," Frank said brightly, relieved to be sitting in a comfortable chair in a dimly lit room with an old scotch in front of him. He just might close his eyes.

James nodded. "It was."

After that, the men seemed to sign some sort of an invisible agreement in the air between them not to bother trying to create any further conversation in the restaurant. They were tired, looking forward to their flight home that night in Frank's Citation X jet. In the mutual silence, they drank.

Finally back in the comfort of his own home, Frank reclined in his armchair and looked out at the first painting he'd ever bought from John Adams, framed on the wall in front of him. He smiled. He loved that painting, and Frank knew when he loved something, that meant it was worth something.

A Change of Faith

He called Charlotte, proud to be able to deliver her some positive news.

"I can't tell you about everything that's going on behind the scenes," he said, "but I can tell you James and I were in Washington yesterday and had some important meetings. We feel confident that in the next week, we'll have enough information for the archbishop to make his call to Rome. We're quite certain that when the smoke clears from this you'll be vilified."

Charlotte spun her hair on her finger. She had been anticipating a call, and she was grateful that it seemed to be positive. She'd been trying hard to remain optimistic but it had been a challenge. She was being attacked from multiple directions. "Thank you, Mr. McGann. I really needed to hear you say that. It's been terrible having my reputation pulled over coals, especially as a monsignor. When will things begin to happen?"

Frank could hear rustling on the line, like Charlotte was fiddling with something. "We're quietly but quickly putting all the required information into presentation form for the pope. We won't want anyone back in Rome to know what we're doing. If word gets out, they'll begin deflecting the story. The goal is to provide our findings at the next College of Cardinals meeting; a total surprise, not giving any of the cardinals a chance to run. If we do this correctly and the pope will go along with us, none of this will come to public knowledge. A strategy will be put in place that clears your name. Don't tell anyone about our discussions. This has to remain between us."

Charlotte nodded. "I promise. But I have to be honest, it's been difficult. Parishioners who have always gone out of their way to see me are avoiding me. Thanksgiving and Christmas will be especially hard. Very sad." Charlotte paused, remembering that this was not her friend John, but businessman Frank McGann. "Thank you for all your help. James too. You really are quite businessmen."

Staring ahead at his painting, Frank smiled. "Quite the friends," he corrected.

XV

John's final painting for his one-man exhibit had proven itself his most challenging yet. For days on end he had wrestled with the beast into the night, standing and staring at it until six in the morning. He had fallen asleep with brushes in his hands. Why wasn't it good enough? Or maybe it was a masterpiece? He wasn't sure. There's an old rule when looking at an artist's work: don't give him a critique until the work is complete, and try not to use the word "interesting." John tried to follow that rule for his own work.

Strange as it sounds, he was grateful when Saturday finally rolled around, when he could focus all his nervous energy away from the painting and on dinner with Maria's parents. He threw a sheet over the painting so he wouldn't have to think about it, showered and shaved. Then he headed to the wine store to buy two bottles of Brunello. John knew little (nothing) about Italian wine, so he was hoping the store owner wasn't misleading him. Then he stopped at the market and purchased a bouquet of wildflowers, deep green and gold and purple. When he got home, he showered again.

Dressed in slacks, a button down, and a wool sport coat, he was ready to pick Maria up at her apartment at seven. In accordance with Italian tradition, dinner wouldn't be served until nine, with a few appetizers prior. John was feeling pretty confident in his best clothes, but when Maria opened the door, he suddenly felt like a slob. Once again, she looked outrageously beautiful. In a navy sundress, her dark hair curled away from her face, she resembled Sophia Loren. Heads always turned when the two were out together, and John knew it wasn't him they were admiring.

Maria's parents lived in Grosse Pointe, an affluent city just east of downtown. In the car manufacturing heydays, many automobile tycoons lived there, including the Fords and Dodges. There were still affluent families that lived in the "Pointes," wearing their appropriate khakis, blue sport coats, and pink shirts. The Gardellis lived on Little Italy Street, where rumor has it many mafia families had lived; some still did. Safety on this particular street has never been an issue.

"You nervous?" Maria asked on the way. John glanced over at her; her knee was bouncing. He reached out and stopped it.

"Not as nervous as you," he said.

"Don't be afraid to talk about politics and religion and all that," she said. "My dad likes those kinds of conversations."

John's eyes widened. "Well I don't."

"When I bring spineless guys home, he eats them up and spits them out," said Maria. "He's tired of people being so afraid of him that they just agree with everything he says."

"What if I do agree with him? Why are you telling me all this right now?" John asked, growing agitated. He'd been trying to remain composed, but Maria's nerves were bringing out his own.

"It's this one," she pointed to a large sandstone with a U-shaved driveway and a fountain in the middle of the yard.

"You don't say." John pulled in. Maria leaned over the center console and gave him a warm kiss.

"Let's just go have some fun. They're good people. Don't worry."

As soon as Maria opened the front door, she was yanked inside. Tony held his daughter firmly by the shoulders and gave her a kiss on each cheek. Then he reached out and pulled John inside, shaking his hand hard. "John, come on in and make yourself comfortable. Can I get you something to drink? How you two doing, anyway? Hope you're hungry." John stood in the entryway with his mouth hanging open as he thought for what to say. "Let me help you: Maria said you like single malt scotches. So do I. Shall we?"

Tony turned away, and Maria grabbed John's hand and led him to the kitchen. "Momma, this is John."

A slender woman with olive skin and beautiful green eyes like her daughter smiled warmly, and John instantly felt comforted. She didn't look like a classic Italian mother cooking in the kitchen; she didn't even look old enough to be a mother.

"Maria has told me so much about you. She tells us you're a successful artist."

"Mildly successful," John said.

"Oh stop it," Maria pinched him. "He's just being humble."

"Well, I look forward to hearing more about your paintings." She stretched up on her toes to give John a kiss on each cheek.

They congregated in the den around an enormous fireplace with crackling flames. The room was trimmed out in beautiful walnut paneling. A few candles were lit on the coffee table, and spicy Italian pork meatballs, hot antipasti dip, and prosciutto with arugula were all waiting to be tasted. John tried to pace himself, reaching out for another bite only when he saw Maria do so.

"John, please," Mrs. Gardelli said sweetly, "Eat all you can stomach. Nothing warms a mother's heart more."

John felt himself blush. Maria laughed. Tony asked about John's family and career, listening carefully, a crease between his eyebrows. John explained how his parents had worked so hard to support him and his brothers, and nothing was taken for granted in the family. Tony nodded. "And where do see yourself ten years from now?"

"Dad, this isn't an interview!" said Maria.

John smiled. "It's okay." He tried to answer the question, explaining that he hoped to be relaxing with someone he loved and still doing something he loved. To his surprise, no chairs flew across the room. Soon 30 minutes had flown by and John found himself feeling relaxed. He might even be having fun, he mused. Maria's parents were kind and interesting, and they were beginning to realize that John's family was very much like their own.

Then Tony asked a question John didn't see coming.

"It's obvious your parents sacrificed a lot for you their children. No one appreciates that more than I can." He leaned in. "So tell me, what's the one moment you remember most about them?"

John panicked for a moment, unsure of how to respond. What kind of answer was Tony looking for? Then he realized it was about digging into the heart. Okay, he thought. He could do that.

"Sir, that's something I haven't really thought about, to tell you the truth. But if there's one thing, I guess it was when I played football in eighth grade. My father worked long hours: 12 per day, six days a week. The other fathers would always show up for the games and even coach, but my dad was always working. I knew he'd love to be there, but his business kept him away.

"The last game of the year, I was on the field when in the corner of the in-zone I saw a figure standing there with his long overcoat and hat; it was cold, just getting dark. No one else was near, just him with his hands in his pockets. It was my dad. Somehow, he found a way to get out of his bar to come watch me play that last game. I'll never forget that figure all alone. He didn't show up until the beginning of the fourth quarter but when the game was done and I walked over, he put his hand on the back of my head and gave me a hug. He didn't say anything. He really didn't have to."

Looking up, John saw that his three listeners were quiet. Maria's mother's eyes were glistening with tears. Encouraged, John continued, "Mr. Gardelli, I suspect this would be true with your family as well. My parents and grandparents are my heroes. They all sacrificed so much to make things work in this country and took nothing for granted."

Mrs. Gardelli was dabbing at her eyes. Maria watched John from the other end of the room, touched to see him bonding with her family.

"John, you're so right," said Tony. "We've all worked hard for what we have. It doesn't matter how many zeros are in your bank account; it's about the family and the love."

Dinner was served, John's wine uncorked and

decanted. There appeared to be enough food for 12 people. An antipasto salad was followed by hearty ribollita soup, which Mrs. Gardelli explained was from the Tuscan region and was traditionally made of leftover bread and vegetables.

Fortunately, the courses were served intermittently, giving the stomach a breather between courses. For the main entree, Mrs. Gardelli served manicotti casserole with fresh vegetables and a side of chicken piccata. Although he'd been stuffed after just the appetizers, John was a member of the clean plate club by the end of dinner at 10:30. After everyone helped cleaning up, cannoli were served with cappuccino back in the den. It was a fun evening, but everyone was beat. The Gardellis generally rose quite early, and John was tired from painting.

As John helped Maria into her coat, he said as nonchalantly as possible, "You're both more than welcome to attend the exhibit in Birmingham. My folks will be there. It should be quite a party."

"We'd be honored," said Tony with a smile.

"We're honored just by the invitation!" interrupted Mrs. Gardelli. "How exciting!"

The drive home was dark and quiet, hands held on the center console. At a red light, John looked over at Maria in his passenger seat. She was staring ahead at the road, smiling to herself. She turned to look at him, and he laughed.

"What are you so happy about?" he asked.

"I—"

"Wait." He looked at her, her face glowing red in the traffic light. "Maria Gardelli, I love you."

Maria laughed. "John Adams, that is exactly what I was going to say to you."

"I thought this time I'd better be first."

They kissed until someone behind them honked their horn. John stepped on the gas, the car bubbling over with laughter.

Maria didn't find her way home that night. She wanted to see John's paintings, but mostly she didn't want to say goodbye to him. It felt too good being cuddled against him, knowing they were in love. They enjoyed their night, and as the sun rose on Sunday morning, they shared their first morning coffee together and watched the market open below.

A Change of Faith

Charlotte blinked herself awake and sighed, burying her face in the pillow. Just like all the other mornings over the past few weeks, she was tired of facing her parishioners, knowing they were unsure if she was the same priest they'd loved and trusted the prior year. She believed in what Frank had told her, at least she wanted to, but he wasn't the one living her life.

She kept telling herself that she just had to survive the next seven weeks, get through the holidays, and hope that once the college of cardinals met, things would go back to normal.

She trusted John; she had to.

XVI

John's pieces had all been shipped, and the gallery was hanging them. Everything was now in the hands of James and his staff. Fortunately, the Neumann Gallery was known for their precise preparation and significant marketing skills. Members of the press would be invited not only from the Detroit area, but because of the Neumann's reputation for discovering new talent, several national publications would be present as well.

Patricia Menstom, chief art columnist from The International Arts Magazine, had agreed to attend the open house. Highly-regarded among other industry critics, she was responsible for having found a number of artists who went on to lead significant careers. John knew if Patricia didn't find an artist's work to be moving, she wouldn't write anything at all on them.

John invited a number of friends and family to attend the exhibit, eager to introduce them to the local celebrities and business executives who would be there. A typical open house was 50% collectors and 50% industry professionals, celebrities, friends and family.

Maria came to John's the night before for dinner and found him surprisingly relaxed and comfortable. "Wow," she said as they cooked together, "I expected you to be a little stressed tonight."

John laughed. "I've worked a long time to get to tomorrow night. It's out of my hands now, so there's no sense in worrying." He truly felt less pressure than he had in a long time. He'd already done all the hard work; tomorrow night was the payoff. In fact, he was really just excited. His father hadn't been well the past year, so seeing him at the show would be nice, and he was excited for his and Maria's families to meet.

"Well, no matter how tomorrow goes, you know how I feel about you. Let's just go and have a great time." She kissed his cheek. "I'm so proud of you."

John put down the pan he was cooking with to wrap his arms around her.

"That's going to burn!" she laughed.

He bent down to kiss the crown of her head, her temples, between her eyes. The pan sizzled. "Don't care," he said.

"John!"

"Fine." He turned and lifted it off the stove. "Hope you don't mind that I invited Charlotte," he said. "She needs some fun. Getting away from her parish for a couple of hours will be good for her."

"Not at all," said Maria, smoothing her hair down. "I look forward to meeting her. You'll be quite busy. Want me to keep her company?"

"Sure, baby. I'm sure you'll get along well."

Their night together was quiet. Spending nights at John's was becoming more regular, and going home alone was becoming increasingly difficult. Maria normally had to work on Saturday mornings, but her father gave her a special pass for the day. She enjoyed a slow morning with John, having coffee and reading the paper together. She made John breakfast, then the two went down to the market. Winter was moving in quickly. They buttoned their coats up to their necks to look through fresh breads and local coffee. From the squash stand Maria blew John a kiss, and he watched her white breath travel through the cold air, dissolving in front of him.

Back at the studio, the two shared some pastries they'd bought and watched the Michigan-Ohio State football game before preparing for the trip to the gallery. As John got ready in front of the mirror, he tried to pump himself up. This was his night, after all. This was all he had worked for, all he had struggled so many long and lonely years for. Behind him in the mirror, he caught a glimpse of Maria reaching back to pull on her shoe, and all his self-empowering thoughts fizzled out. In a black pantsuit, Maria looked straight from a business magazine.

She was going to pick up her folks for an early dinner before heading to the gallery, so John drove himself. He was asked to be there two hours before the show began. As he pulled in, he finally began to feel a bit nervous. Inside, he was quickly greeted by James and his staff.

"Welcome to your exhibition! I want to show you something." James walked John to six of his pieces. "Notice something about these?" John looked, and to his surprise, the information tags identifying the paintings each had a red dot on them.

"What?" John breathed. "No..."

"Yes, John," James said, "you've already sold six paintings. Well done, my friend. That's quite a start to the night."

"How?" John asked, dumbfounded.

"It takes three days to prepare the exhibit, and we don't close the gallery to our customers, so a few of them enjoyed your artwork enough to purchase pieces before we even opened."

The paintings that sold were priced between eight and 12 thousand dollars. John might splurge and purchase a bottle of $18 wine for his next dinner with Maria, or maybe even buy a new pair of jeans.

James introduced him to his staff and a few media members before the show began. Patricia Menstom arrived quite early and meandered around, looking distinctly uninterested in any of John's pieces. James knew Patricia's MO: arrive early and avoid speaking to anyone, including the artist, until she's had an opportunity to review the work. She didn't like speaking to the artist until her review was complete, as she didn't want to attach the artist's personality to the work. She wanted the art to speak for itself. She was meticulous in her review, each piece given ample time for inspection. Once James saw her finally sit down on a bench, he tentatively approached.

"Enjoying the pieces, Patricia?"

She looked up from her clipboard and smiled politely. "It's quite an exhibit."

Without breaking eye contact, James waved John over

to join the conversation. John hurried to his side. "John, I'd like to introduce you to Patricia Menstom from The International Arts Magazine. Patricia flew in from New York just for your exhibit."

John smiled as if this was news to him. "Great to meet you, Patricia."

"It's quite a pleasure to meet you," Patricia replied. "James insisted I come review your work. I have a difficult time saying no to him; he has a good eye for the arts." She winked at James. "I find your work unique. The pieces have wonderful composition. It's unusual to attend an exhibit like this and see each piece capable of having its own life."

John scrambled for something to say, but fortunately James spoke first. "Patricia reviews many exhibits each year and has an excellent eye for new art. I'm not going to ask her what, if anything, she may write about your work. We'll have to wait a couple days to find out." This time, James winked at Patricia.

"Ms. Menstom," said John, "thanks for taking the time to see my show. No matter what your thoughts are, I greatly appreciate you being here. I paint what I feel, and though I care about my work, the priority is to create what I enjoy. It's made painting fun and fulfilling. Really, it's changed everything for me."

Patricia tilted her head as she listened. "Rest assured, those feelings resonate in each piece. It is noticeable." She nodded two times in rapid succession, indicating the end of the conversation. "Well, it was a pleasure coming to see them. I look forward to seeing you again, maybe next time in New York." She glanced at James. "See you later for a nightcap?"

"Wouldn't miss it," James smiled.

The exhibit opened to the invited guests. People strolled in as James set out light appetizers with craft beer and local wine. He introduced John to a number of his patrons, names John was quite familiar with and surprised to be meeting in person. He felt like a minor celebrity. Around 6:30, John's parents showed up with Brother Bob and Diane. They were beaming with pride.

"Mom, Dad," said John. His parents looked out of their element. John Sr. had made an obvious attempt at dressing up, looking dapper in a tucked-in checkered shirt with his graying hair pomaded back. Mrs. Adams was in a floral-patterned dress looking and feeling so proud. "By the looks of you guys you were expecting

Kennedy's inauguration, not a little exhibit for an unknown artist."

Mrs. Adams pinched him.

"Son," said John Sr., gazing at the paintings around the room like they were holy relics, "I couldn't be any prouder than I am right now. Sincerely. This is…really something."

"Well hey," John clapped him on the shoulder, "I couldn't have done it without that chat we had a few years ago. So thanks for that. Come on, I'll show you around."

His family was surprised by the quality of the gallery and all the people there. His parents were modest people, not used to such style and class. They strode around the room in a half-daze, oohing and aahing at the pieces and the special guests. As John walked them through the exhibit, his dad glanced at the identification cards next to the pieces. "Are these prices what you're really selling these paintings for?"

John grinned. "Yes they are."

His father frowned. "$12,000?"

John shrugged. "Guess people are beginning to like my work. And look, there are nine red dots, meaning those are all sold!"

John Sr.'s mouth dropped and he gaped at his wife.

The pieces were selling better than even James expected. James saw so much artwork come through the gallery, but when he saw Patricia's face and listened to her comments, however brief, he knew something good was happening for John Adams. He purchased a piece for himself. Just in case.

Around seven, Charlotte entered the gallery. Dressed in wide-pleated black slacks, black boots and a dark brown oversized turtleneck, she looked like a Peruvian gaucho. No one there would have guessed she was a monsignor, her hair and makeup done up in a way that was almost provocative. James spotted her first and made a beeline for her. "Wow, you look fantastic!"

Charlotte blushed. "Thanks, James."

"Let me ask you something," he said. "I'd like to introduce you to some of my friends, but do you want to be Monsignor or Charlotte tonight?"

She gave him a warm hug. "Monsignor. That's who I am, and it would be good to let people see the human side of a priest. But I'm here to relax and have fun."

"Monsignor it is." He made a showman gesture. "Let's begin."

John glimpsed Charlotte, stunned. He still couldn't quite believe she was a priest. That night, she could easily have passed for a famous Hollywood actress. He excused himself from the people he was talking to and went to see her. "Monsignor, I'm glad you could make it."

Charlotte shook her head, glancing around the exhibition in awe. "John, this is amazing. All these people are here to see you. Can you believe it?"

John glanced around, smiling broadly and shaking his head. "It's more than I could have ever dreamed of," he said. "I know you're tired of hearing this, but it wouldn't have happened without you. This is your show as much as mine." He gave her a hug, whispering, "Next we're going to take care of the other issues. Frank and James are singularly focused, and so am I. You'll be safe. It'll all be over soon."

A flood of emotions swept across her face. "You really think so?"

John gave her arm a reassuring squeeze. "I know so."

She let out a sigh of relief. "Thank you. For everything."

"Don't mention it."

She gulped, nodded. "Let's enjoy the evening then. Lord knows I haven't had a good night for a while. Go on, show me your paintings."

Together they walked around the show, John slipping pleasantries to people viewing his work and answering questions whenever asked. Michael was there too. He was excited to see Charlotte attending the show. "Can you get a load of this?" he said excitedly. "It's unreal. I think our friend Mr. Adams might just be the next Picasso!"

Around eight, Maria and her parents showed up. The gallery was shoulder to shoulder. No one seemed to want to leave and people kept showing up. Before John could get to Maria, James told him 12 pieces had been sold. In total, the sales were well over a hundred thousand dollars. John simply shook his head and laughed. Finally reaching Maria and the Gardellis, he apologized for the packed gallery. He studied her parents' faces; it was obvious they were astonished.

Maria was beside herself. "My goodness, John, this is so exciting! I had no idea what to expect, but it certainly wasn't this. Let's show my parents your work."

As they took their first tour—John's eighth—he squeezed her side and whispered into her ear, "Babe. We've already sold 12 pieces."

"12 pieces?" she repeated. "How much per piece?"

John couldn't help it. He was grinning. "Over ten grand."

Maria couldn't help herself. She grabbed his face and kissed him. "John Adams," she said, "I'm so proud of you. I love you."

After a half hour, a few of the attendees began leaving and the gallery became more breathable. John was able to round up his family, Charlotte, Maria and her folks. The gallery had a small sitting area which one of the managers was able to reserve for John because his dad needed to have a seat. Finally, John introduced his family to Charlotte, Maria and the Gardellis. Everyone got along, and soon there was a chorus of comfortable laughter echoing throughout the gallery.

John pulled Maria and Charlotte aside. "Ladies," he pointed to his mom, "along with that woman sitting right there, you two are the most important women in my life. I can't thank you enough. For everything."

"Monsignor—or can I say Charlotte?" asked Maria. "I can't tell you what a pleasure it is to meet you. For not only helping John, but for your own accomplishments. You're a hero around these parts. Can we do dinner soon? All together?"

Charlotte nodded. "I'd like that very much. But I'm not the only one who deserves a thank you. For as long as I've known John, I've never seen him so happy. There's so much love in each of your eyes, it lights up the whole room. I'm so happy for you both."

Normally, two women with a shared history with a man might be artificial or judgmental with each other, but Charlotte genuinely meant what she was saying, as did Maria. There was a great deal of respect between them. John breathed a quiet sigh of relief.

As his parents left, John put his arm around his father while walking him to the car. "Dad, remember that day you and Mom told me to go find myself and I'd be fine? Well, without those words I wouldn't be here now. You guys did this. I owe it all to you. I love you, Poppy."

John Sr. didn't have to say a thing. He put his hand on the back of John's neck and gave him a hug. "Love you, son." A few tears moistened John's eyes. He knew his dad wasn't feeling well. Also, he never used the "love" word with the kids. He felt something was amiss, but he didn't want to push it. He'd let the old man rest and save that conversation for another day.

They stood outside, John watching his father amble slowly to the car after standing around for far too long. He wasn't in the driver's seat, which was unusual.

"John!" He whipped around. James was rushing down the steps. "I did a final count on the paintings." Charlotte and the Gardellis looked up. "My friend, I'm happy to say: you are officially sold out."

John's friends cheered, congratulating him, patting him on the back and shaking his hand. Maria kissed him. He stood in a daze, blinking. "All 15 paintings?"

James was smiling ear to ear. "That's right, son. 15. Sold."

John didn't hesitate. With tears in his eyes, he gathered his friends and went next door to order a few bottles of champagne to celebrate. He sat smiling to himself as he sipped his champagne, watching the people he loved chatting together under one roof like family. All of them there to celebrate his success. He took a sip, contentment filling his bones. After all these years, he'd done it.

John Adams was an artist.

XVII

Frank McGann purposely stayed away from the exhibition, as did the archbishop, though both were invited. They were making sure there wouldn't be any slip-ups and no one would notice anything peculiar. Every effort was being made to keep things quiet. Much work had been taking place behind the scenes both in Detroit and in Washington.

William Beauchamp regularly provided updates to Frank. Once the folks at Gottfried found out the NSA was involved with an investigation, they were quite motivated to talk. Nothing in their job description included prison time.

Now it was a matter of putting all the pieces together in a proper presentation that would make the archbishop comfortable enough to contact the pope's office. Frank was visiting the Archbishop the next day to update him on the progress of the investigation, and William Beauchamp would be sending one of his staff to help with the specifics. If the archbishop was comfortable with the information provided, he would go ahead and contact the pope's office.

The next day, Frank went by the gallery to pick up James for their drive to the archbishop's residence. During the drive, instead of talking about the upcoming meeting, James gave Frank an update on the previous night's exhibition, knowing Frank wished he could be there.

"I think those paintings you purchased from John may be worth a bit more today," he said. "The show was completely sold out."

Frank looked astonished. "Completely?"

James nodded.

"Well," said Frank, sitting back in his seat. "Can't say I'm totally surprised. That boy's got the gift."

"The review from Patricia Menstom should be quite positive. I met with her after the show for a nightcap. Unlike some of the other exhibits she attended, she immediately went into a Q and A. She's good at keeping her feelings in check, but a direct invitation to New York was beginning to make things pretty obvious. I wouldn't be surprised to see an invitation in John's mailbox from one of the more significant galleries out there." James chuckled. "Hope he remembers the 'ole Neumann Gallery for future exhibits. I could use the exposure."

"Man like John Adams? No. He'd never forget his roots."

They pulled into the archbishop's driveway, parked, and entered the foyer, where they were met by NSA member Rick Prescott, sent by William Beauchamp. Instead of reviewing information while waiting, they enjoyed some coffee and went over Washington politics. After ten minutes, the archbishop came out and greeted them. "Sorry for the delay, gentlemen. I perform 8:00 services on Sunday mornings; it keeps me on my toes. Come. Let's go to my den."

The den was a sunny room with floor-to-ceiling bookshelves lining the walls. There were plush chairs and a coffee table with a platter of croissants, coffee, tea, and milk. Once seated and given refreshments, the four men dug into the purpose of their meeting. Rick Prescott spoke about his background and responsibilities at the NSA. Then he gave his review. Each attendee was given a booklet with all the pertinent information.

"Your Grace," said Prescott, "we believe what you'll find in this booklet, along with what I'm about to go over now, should give you enough evidence to bring the matter to Rome." He gave his overview, going through the information page by page. By the end, he'd revealed a concrete paper trail leading back to three cardinals in Italy who had orchestrated the entire smear campaign.

They now had incontrovertible proof.

The archbishop nodded solemnly. "Gentlemen," he said, "first of all, I know how much time, effort and expense you've committed to this, so on behalf of myself and the Church, thank you. Mr. Prescott, this information is more than adequate to request a meeting in Rome with the pope. But if this gets out to the media, it will create a PR nightmare that would rock the Church from its foundation. The pope will try to take care of this issue even before the college meets in January. If this were exposed there with all those cardinals and staff, it would surely get out. Let me complete my review, make my call and suggest a meeting in Rome. We may want a representative from the NSA to attend, as it will legitimize the information. Let's put this to bed as soon as possible. Any questions?" There were none. "Very well." The archbishop stood up, preparing to leave.

Wanting to get some more insight, especially about Gottfried, the three men requested a little time alone in the den. "Take all the time you need, gentlemen," said the archbishop. "We'll meet again soon. God bless you."

Rick gave Frank and James a more in-depth review explaining specifics about the Gottfried employees. They'd signed non-disclosure agreements when their project began, but certainly weren't thinking something this big would develop.

"There's no feeling sorry for them," said Prescott. "They were aware of what they were doing the whole time. They've worked on countless projects that have ruined reputations. It would be nice to see them get their due."

Frank and James thanked him for making the trip north, deciding it would be him or William Beauchamp joining them in Rome to meet the pope or his immediate staff.

Frank and James went out to lunch at the Bayview Yacht Club, a local sailing club known for its expertise in developing highly-skilled sailors. They had more than once snuggled up to the bar at the club on the Detroit River, watching Great Lake freighters drift slowly by, hauling iron ore.

Frank spoke first. "If you'd told me ten years ago I'd be flying to Rome to meet with the pope, I would've put you away in the old folks' home. It's a hell of a thing, God forgive me."

"He doesn't," James quipped.

A Change of Faith

Frank took a sip of water. "It's possible to keep this quiet, I think. But hey, what am I saying? Tell me more about our artist. I need some good news. What's next for John Adams?"

"Well, unfortunately for the Neumann Gallery, we might find John's next exhibit in New York. Once written up in some of the media, especially by Patricia, he'll be a hot topic. Guess we should have purchased a few more pieces. But it's great to see it happening to a local artist, especially John. He's a good guy. He's involved with Maria Gardelli; she was at the show with her parents. Wouldn't it be interesting to hear what Tony Gardelli thinks about his daughter being involved with an artist?"

Frank nearly choked on his food. "Tony Gardelli's daughter?"

"That's right."

"Good lord. Betcha John's not aware of the family background. I remember some of the news out on Tony, what was it, 20 years ago? It had to do with the teamsters. Him and a couple of others in the family controlled the electricians', plumbers' and truckers' unions in the Midwest. The family business, though legitimate, is just part of the spider web of outside influences. Then again, their daughter being involved with an artist with a name like John Adams helps legitimize things and will certainly keep her at an arm's reach from the overall operations. John better behave himself. That's all I'm saying."

But James was still thinking about the art. "I wouldn't be surprised if we don't see John's work selling for $30,000 soon. He might find himself loaning money to Tony and the family."

Frank laughed. "And with John painting an average of 30 paintings a year, he'll be making a pretty fine income. He might be leaving his Eastern Market studio soon enough."

The two wrapped up their lunch and finished it off with a hummer, a national drink invented at the Bayview bar by then-bartender Jerome, made of Rum, Kahlua and ice cream. Frank raised his glass. "To helping friends."

The archbishop didn't waste any time reviewing the information provided by Rick Prescott and the NSA. He sat with his Chief of Staff, Father Billings, a bright young priest with a law degree from Emory University. The archbishop wouldn't be surprised to see him assigned to Rome sometime in the near future working directly with the Vatican's legal staff. He had just finished reading the report and was leaning back in his chair with a thoughtful expression.

The archbishop spoke. "What are your thoughts, Father?"

"Your Grace, there's enough information in this report to convict the three cardinals in Rome of felonies, let alone get them expunged. This is very serious. The Holy Father will have little choice but to bring them to justice. It'll be interesting to see what he decides to do with them, but I suppose the bigger question will be how the Church will keep this quiet. There are just too many staff members involved with these three cardinals."

"You're comfortable with me making the call?" asked the archbishop.

Father Billings stared at him. "These female priests are being blackmailed and their reputations destroyed because of this awful campaign. Monsignor Kotlinski is one of the most qualified priests we've had in the diocese in years. We can't let this happen to her. For them and the two priests who were murdered, make the call."

The archbishop nodded, his brows furrowed. "Very well. Contact the appropriate office in Rome tomorrow. Let's see if we can't schedule a call with his Holiness this week. We're moving into the Christmas season, so this has to be handled very soon. Don't be surprised if we don't find ourselves in Rome next week."

The next morning, Father Billings called and was directed to the pope's Chief of Staff, Bishop Sanchez. Their conversation lasted 80 minutes, the bishop asking dozens of questions to understand the magnitude of what he was being told. He asked Father Billings to overnight the report directly to his office and only to his attention—he didn't want it sent in email form, where it could be picked up and shared. "Eyes are everywhere in the Vatican," he said. "Please, keep this quiet."

The bishop agreed to read the report and then present the issue to the pope, recommending a face to face with the archbishop and his team the following week. Bishop Sanchez understood the problem had to be resolved prior to the College of

A Change of Faith

Cardinals' meeting in the beginning of January. He suspected the three cardinals had already planted their intentions with various other cardinals.

Father Billings received a call from Bishop Sanchez the following day at four p.m., quite late in Rome. "I've read through the report," he said quickly. "It's even more pressing than I thought possible. I've already sat with the Holy Father this afternoon and reviewed the information with him. He's asked a meeting with all involved next Tuesday. Can you make proper arrangements and arrive Monday?"

Father Billings agreed.

"We don't want people here to know about this," said the bishop. "We'll meet at the summer retreat in Castel Gandolfo, 16 miles outside Rome on Lake Albano. I recommend you spend Monday night somewhere in Rome. Tell the archbishop we apologize, but due to the privacy required, it's best if he spend the night with your other guests and dress appropriately."

"Understood, Bishop Sanchez. Who'll be attending on your side?"

"The Holy Father and myself. You must understand, all the walls in Rome have ears. We must exercise the utmost discretion."

"Of course. I'll send you a list of attendees with brief biographies," said Father Billings.

"Thank you, Father. I look forward to meeting. See you Tuesday."

Father Billings notified the archbishop, who asked him to contact Frank, James, and William Beauchamp.

They were going to Rome.

Sunday evening, both the archbishop and Father Billings met Frank, James and William at the Detroit Metropolitan Airport wearing layman's clothes. It was different seeing the archbishop in slacks and a sweater, looking more like a retiree off to some tropical island than an emissary of God. If the archbishop of Detroit were noticed going to Rome this time of year, antennas would go up immediately and questions would be asked.

Once in Rome, they had dinner at the Ambasciatori

Palace Hotel, located a 40-minute walk away from St. Peter's Basilica. William shared with them more incriminating information supplied by the two Gottfried employees, who were now open books, exposing everything from paying members of the media to writing defamatory articles about the female priests to full-blown harassment. They didn't disclose any information on the recent murder of Vicar McPherson, however, nor did William think they would, doubting a couple of lawyers wanted anything to do with a homicide. William left that bit out of the conversation. There just wasn't any proof.

The archbishop looked forward to making good on saving the priests' reputations. There was much to be done to turn things around, especially if his Holiness wanted to keep things quiet. The five of them had a pleasant dinner and then retired for the night, eager to get started the next day.

The next morning, two cabs picked them up for the drive to Castel Gandolfo, located in the hills overlooking Lake Albano, its inviting azure waters shaped in a perfect circle. Their meeting with his Holiness was set for 10:00 a.m. with no end-time scheduled.

They pulled up to the Apostolic Palace of Castel Gandolfo, a massive 17th century castle with 135 acres overlooking the lake. The men stared in awe at its sweeping tan façade. Father Billings' mouth hung open. "Sweet mother of…"

"Gentlemen!"

Approaching was Bishop Sanchez, arms outstretched. He was a short bald man with kind eyes and a warm smile. "Welcome to Palazzo Apostolico di Castel Gandolfo! I trust you had a comfortable trip?"

"Can't complain," said Frank. "Remarkable place the pope can get away to."

Bishop Sanchez admired the palace proudly. "The oldest parts date back to the 13th century. A sight to behold, no?"

The men nodded in agreement.

"Come. His Holiness awaits your presence in the library."

They were directed up the stone steps, where they entered a huge door and passed through several massive rooms whose sculpted ceilings were so high any number of homes could have fit within the walls with room to spare. Hung on the walls were priceless works of art from the masters of the Renaissance: sketches from da Vinci and Michelangelo; dark, austere paintings by Boticelli and Caravaggio, as well as sculptures the perfect precision and beauty of which the men had never seen. "James," Frank muttered, his eyes glazed over like a child's during its first time at the fair. "Imagine having a collection like this?"

"Wouldn't be living in Detroit if I did. I think I'd take up residence next door." He glanced at their host leading the way. "Bishop, any vacancies?"

The bishop laughed.

They made their way into an expansive library whose painted ceiling resembled that of the Sistine Chapel. A hundred thousand books sat on three levels of mahogany bookcases surrounding them. The air was cool as a cave and smelled of old vellum and cellar dust. They waited with their hands thrust in their pockets, too intimidated to touch anything.

Within a few minutes, his Holiness Pope Peter Paul entered the library dressed casually in a summer polo and slacks. The men were quietly taken aback. They stood to greet him, but they were confused on the etiquette. They'd never greeted a pope before.

The pope waved his hands. "Gentlemen, please be seated," he said in perfect English. "It is I who owes you recognition this morning. Good morning, Archbishop Morley." He bowed slightly. "It's wonderful to see you, though unfortunate it has to be under these circumstances."

The pope was from Columbia. He had visited the U.S. frequently as a priest, hence his fluent English. "I thank each of you for the hard work you have put into exposing this issue, as sad as it is. It is a very difficult time for the church, but when something like this takes place, we must take aggressive actions. I'd like to take our time and hear from each of you. Please be frank about giving me your thoughts. Difficult decisions must be made, and I want nothing other than the truth."

That said, the group agreed it would be best if William spoke first. He had most of the internal information and could fill in the blanks if there were any. "Your Holiness," he said, "It's a great honor to meet you, sir. As you're already aware, these issues are significant not only for the Church, but for parties back home, since they hold legal problems for those involved. I understand the Church will want to keep this as quiet as possible, but we also have to see how to prevent these cardinals from being charged in the U.S. with felonies. We have enough information and witnesses to accuse them of blackmail, character defamation, bribery and possibly murder. Any of which, if prosecuted, would mean prison time."

The pope brought his hand to his chin as William continued. "So, how we move forward with this will be a bit tricky, to say the least. We may even have to inform the president, which I hope to avoid because if that happens more players come into the fold and then the news will surely find a way out."

The Pope nodded solemnly. "How do you suggest I proceed?"

"By making it quick and simple. I suggest you summon them here tomorrow for a personal meeting. We sit with them and expose the information we have. They'll probably deny everything, but ultimately with the information and the potential legal issues they face in the States, they'll come to understand these problems are significant. From there, it will be up to you how you want to move forward with them. But if the repercussions are right, we can agree here and now to waive any sort of legal ramifications back in the States, protecting any outcry against the Church."

"I agree," said the pope. He turned quickly, all business. "Bishop Sanchez, please contact their offices and request a meeting here first thing tomorrow morning. These gentlemen will be present in that meeting as well as yourself. But no one else. And no one is to speak of it."

"Of course, your Holiness."

Then the pope turned to the men. "Gentlemen, I can't tell you how much I personally appreciate what you've done for the Catholic Church. This event would have been destructive and embarrassing to our reputation, to say the least. Because we'll be spending the evening here, let us reconvene at six for dinner. Archbishop Morley, please come with me to discuss this further. The rest of you, treat this palace as your own home. We have a lovely garden you might enjoy."

James, Frank and William gave their thanks and left

the library to spend the afternoon visiting the local town and landscape. As soon as they were gone, a dark look came over the pope's face. He seemed suddenly drained of energy and will. "Archbishop Morley and Father Billings, we have a grave problem here. Once the cardinals hear the information provided by the NSA and understand the legal issues they face, it is obvious what we'll have to do with them. I'll have each forced into retirement and sent to different locations, none of which are near Rome. I never want to see any of them again. They will be banned from the Vatican and any communications with staff or other cardinals. If they don't abide by this, then they will be prosecuted.

"More importantly, let's discuss the female priests. The loss of Vicar Anderson and now McPherson is very upsetting. The new vicars, along with Monsignor Kotlinski, are now the ones we have to save. I'm sure she's been deeply affected by all this. What can we do?"

"Your Holiness," Archbishop Morley said, "we've been working with the largest public relations firm in Detroit to help keep our own monsignor in a positive light with her parishioners and the public. It's been difficult. We weren't able to expose to the firm helping us what's really happening. Because of this, we haven't been able to effectively restore her reputation. Then, there's the matter of the recent...homicides."

Again, shadows crept over the pope's face. "Has anything been discovered to establish a connection between the two vicars' murders and the cardinals?"

The archbishop shook his head. "No, your Holiness."

The pope breathed a sigh of relief. "Very well. Because if that were the case, God help them."

"We need your help, your Holiness. Across the nation there's talk about Vicar McPherson's death. Some say this madman, whoever he is, had a hand in Vicar Anderson's accident on the hillside some time ago. I'm not one to subscribe to conspiracy, but there's a very real worry that this...demon, is actively targeting female priests. Women in the seminary are nervous about their futures. Can you imagine that? The opportunity of their dreams has become somewhat of a nightmare. They're fearful. They need hope."

The pope grew quiet for a moment, thinking. "Here's

what we're going to do. Plan on me coming into Detroit mid-January, prior to the college meetings. Make sure a number of the new female priests are in town. We will perform mass at Monsignor Kotlinski's parish. At that time, during my sermon, I will discuss the issues and offer some solutions. Can you put together a larger service somewhere? I'd like to have the monsignor perform mass with me. Would this help?"

The archbishop stammered, humbled. "Your Holiness, a visit from you would certainly help more than any PR firm ever could! Of course. We'll make sure we have everything in place for your visit. Thank you so much."

Later, the archbishop and others congregated, each of them in disbelief of having met the pope and impressed by how quickly he acted on the information provided. The cardinals in question were senior members of the Church with whom the pope had had personal relationships for many years. Now he had to expel them from the Church and Rome. It was like a father kicking his sons out of the house. It was not going to be an easy discussion.

The archbishop informed the men of the pope's decision to travel to Detroit in January. He had to find a significant location for a large mass. Frank suggested Ford Field, home of the Detroit Lions. He knew Mrs. Ford and would be happy to make the call, he said. It was settled.

They had dinner that evening in a stately dining room with centuries-old portraits of previous popes lining the walls. Dangling from the high ceilings were three ornate crystal chandeliers, twinkling like so many diamonds, with tall white candles flickering among them. The room was cool, fragrant with the buttery scent of fried fish, garlic and herbs, which came out individually in small cast iron pans set in front of each guest by the humble wait staff. A fine chianti was decanted and poured into glasses set on the long table.

Conversation came easily, like coffee with an old friend, and before long another chianti was being decanted and laughter filled the cavernous room. When everyone had settled down and dessert was arriving, James eyed the pope at the head of the table, dressed casually in a white button-down shirt.

"Your Holiness," he said. "This might seem like an odd question, but would you tell us about yourself?"

A Change of Faith

"Not odd at all." The pope's eyebrows furrowed as he tilted his head to one side, remembering. "I was born the fourth child out of six in Santa Marta on the Colombian coastline in a city with approximately 450,000 people. My father had a fish processing factory, so my brothers and sisters were raised in the factory cleaning and processing fish. I wasn't the best fisherman, but now I represent Peter and all fishermen; funny how that worked out."

Chuckles around the room.

"I was a bit of a teenage troublemaker," he continued, "so naturally, my parents decided to send me to a private parochial school where rules weren't broken. Probably the best thing to have happened to me. While there, one of the priests befriended me, I think because my father would send fresh fish to the school once a week. Though I wasn't a very good student, I enjoyed theology, so it seemed like a normal evolution to enter the priesthood.

"At 20 I was the youngest seminarian out of 43 students. By 24 I was ordained. My first church assignment was in Bogota at what would be considered an inner-city church. At that time, cocaine was a very serious problem, with many young people getting involved in the drug trade. We saw happy families splinter and break apart, murders and kidnappings in broad daylight. The cartels were in total control of the country.

"As a priest, it was difficult supporting our parishioners without breaking the rules of the street. If such rules were broken, the cartels had no issue eliminating a priest or anyone else who challenged them, be it God Himself. I was assigned to a number of churches in the inner-cities before being granted my own parish in a small rural town 20 kilometers outside of Bogota. I was just 29, and the little town was a headquarters for the traffickers. There wasn't much there we weren't exposed to, including prostitution and cocaine houses. It was a very bad business. I remained the pastor of our church for three years until the Archbishop in Bogota required someone with experience to become the pastor of The Cathedral of Columbia. An astonishingly beautiful cathedral. Honestly, I could have remained there for my entire career and been very happy. The place was protected, untouched. Not even the cocaine barons dared step in its halls. Those were glorious times."

The pope took a deep breath, gently swirling the ruby

wine around the rim of his glass as if lost in a distant dream. He looked down, breathing slowly. "My oldest brother and youngest sister were driving home one night from a friend's house when a gang and the cartel got into a fight. They opened fire on each other, and my family was caught in a crossfire. They were both killed. Since that time and since I was elected to this office, I have worked hard to do whatever it takes to break up the cartels. I am fully committed. I'm no stranger to evil plots hatched by misguided men. However, witnessing such a plot in my very own church is nothing less than harrowing. It feels as if I've been betrayed by my own children. Now I know what God must think of Judas. How saddened, disappointed."

Looking up from his wine glass, his eyes glittered wet in the candlelight. "Not in God's Church. I will not allow it. Now, let us toast to the defiance of evil, and to the rise of a better world."

The men at the table raised their glasses. The pope nodded and drank. They followed suit, watching him with quiet respect. "Please, let's move on to other subjects. Something good."

Frank brought up the World Cup, which, except for in the U.S., was the biggest worldwide sporting event. There were smiles and laughs around the room, though everyone could see the sadness written on the pope's old face as he contemplated the next day's meetings. Watching him, they realized the enormity of his position. One lone man commanded all the responsibility of an entire religion.

The next morning, the men were up early in the dining room. Due to morning prayer services, the pope was not in attendance. William Beauchamp had a number of printed files in hardback ready for the meeting with the cardinals. Tension hung thick in the air like a storm growing.

At 9:45 a car pulled up and the three cardinals entered the villa. They immediately noticed how quiet it was. Staff was nowhere to be seen, when ordinarily they would be rushing every which way.

The cardinals were guided into the meeting room, where a long, ornate oak table with 12 chairs stretched across the center of the room. At 10:00 sharp, the pope, with Bishop Sanchez by his side, entered the room. The air went still. The cardinals were used to people kissing their proverbial asses, and now they were the ones who would have to do the kissing.

"Your Holiness, if you don't mind," said Cardinal Stefinne stiffly, determined to have the first word, "each of us has schedules we had to cancel to come here. We hope this meeting is important." Cardinal Stefinne, known for his arrogance, probably thought he should have been elected pope. He had little patience and treated others with little respect. The other two cardinals, Gonremy and Montross, also had pompous characteristics, but not nearly to such an extreme as Stefinne. None would be missed walking the executive hallways of the Vatican.

"Gentlemen," the pope said calmly, "I asked each of you to attend a meeting this morning for good reason, and requested we have it here for discretion. I'd like to introduce you to a few men who have flown in from America to help me identify an issue that seems to have developed over quite some time." He nodded to Bishop Sanchez, who ushered the men in. "From Detroit, Michigan, I'm sure you're familiar with Archbishop Morley and his executive assistant Father Billings."

"Why are these men here?" barked Cardinal Montross, his face reddening.

"Please, let me finish," said the pope, trying to keep his voice level. If the cardinals continued to display such arrogance, he would have no trouble seeing them out of their jobs. "I also have three other gentlemen here."

"What is going on?" demanded Cardinal Stefinne. "This is smelling pretty ugly; we demand answers!"

"My dear Cardinal Stefinne, you are absolutely right. You deserve to know why you have been requested to this meeting, and you will be fully informed shortly." The pope leveled his eyes on the man, who looked away angrily, quiet at last. "This is Mr. Frank McGann and Mr. James Neumann, two significant businessmen from Detroit with resumes that include much internal work within the U.S. government. Mr. McGann is a self-made success story, doing business with many private companies, but also with the U.S. Department of Defense. He has a significant resume. Mr. James Neumann was the assistant director at the government's National Security Agency for ten years before retiring and beginning his own business career."

When the NSA background was mentioned, the arrogant attitudes flashed to panic. "We demand to know what is going on here! You are wasting our time!" snapped Cardinal Gonrenny, fear buried beneath the anger in his tremulous voice. "Do you have any idea what the three of us are capable of doing with the college of cardinals?"

The pope nearly smiled; he would enjoy this more than he thought. "Finally, I would like to introduce William Beauchamp, the director of the National Security Agency."

Cardinal Stefinne jumped to his feet, his chair toppling to the marble floor with a clatter. "That's enough, I'm leaving!" he announced, turning to go.

"Sit down, Cardinal Stefinne," said the pope in a chilling voice that quieted the room, making half the men look down for fear of meeting his eye. The cardinal froze. "These men have flown here on their own dollars for this meeting," said the pope in a measured tone, "and you will sit and listen." Cardinal Stefinne replaced his chair and sat between the other two cardinals, silent.

"With these introductions out of the way, I'd like to move forward," said the pope. "It is no secret that a while back when a vote was taken with our college of cardinals to allow females to become priests, there were those who vehemently disapproved. Since that time, three female priests were ordained in the U.S. to see how this experiment would work out. As you are aware, two of the priests have lost their lives very suspiciously. Recently I was made aware of issues developing with our lone remaining Monsignor Kotlinski. Seems she stands accused of having illicit relationships, committing theft, and other parishioner grievances. Mr. Beauchamp, please pass out the information and let's review your findings."

You could hear a pin drop as Father Billings passed a hardbound copy of the NSA report to each person. "Your eminences," began William, "my office was contacted about an issue a couple of months ago. It seems a company by the name of Gottfried was retained by some individuals in Rome to put in place a plan to accuse three female priests in the States and seriously defame their reputations." The cardinals' faces paled in unison as they looked blankly down at the report. "Our investigation was supported by two United States senators who both sit in on the intelligence committee. We had their full support to investigate the issue. We contacted two Gottfried employees who informed us about the contract and who it came from. Gentlemen, you can read through the information and see exactly what was provided to us."

The pope was ready to complete the task. "My fellow cardinals, it is obvious that defaming the female priests would have made it much easier to request a retraction of the previous vote of female priests at the upcoming college next month. What has happened is criminal, and so disturbing that personally, I'm having a problem sitting here with each of you. Two of these poor women have lost their lives and the last has been living in daily hell because of you. Your actions and your pompous, arrogant attitudes are enough. You can try and fight the action I recommend, but if you do, it will expose this issue externally, your reputations will be destroyed, and the Church will have another international PR problem."

There was no more uproarious clattering of chairs on marble, no more shouts of objection. The room was silent as the pope paused to survey those within, good men on one side and bad on the other.

"Here is what I suggest each of you do. Over the next 60 days, so this doesn't look obvious, you will retire. You will be banned from entering any locations at the Vatican. You will give up your staffs and any responsibilities with the Church. I will assign each of you to a location somewhere outside of Rome. You will retain your positions as cardinals only because too many questions will be asked if I fire you. Now, please leave my home, where you are no longer welcome, and figure out who retires first."

The three looked at each other for a moment, like guilty boys after a good reprimand. Then they quietly stood, heads lowered, and walked out.

The pope sat down, placed his hands over his face for a moment, then raised his head. "That may have been one of the most difficult yet pleasing things I've ever had to do. Those three are terribly dismal characters. Without your help, we would have encountered an issue with the entire college, which would have been so unfair to our female priests and any future ones. They have performed well above our expectations and the loss of our two vicars leaves me with grave pain."

His features softened. "At any rate, Monsignor Kotlinski could teach any of us how to market and increase revenues at our churches. I look forward to my trip to the States to see what we can do to reestablish her reputation and honor the memories of the others." He looked up and gave them all a warm smile. "Until then. Very safe travels, my friends."

With that, each man shook the pope's hand, and he retired to another room with Archbishop Morley and Father Billings to coordinate the upcoming trip. There was a gift left for each of the visitors: a beautiful bible personally signed by the pope. Frank, William and James loaded up their bags and headed to the airport.

"Well guys," said Frank in the car, "that was the most amazing day of my life. Don't tell my wife, but more significant than marriage or childbirth. William, thanks for all your help. I think the pope was greatly relieved and vindicated by the end of the meeting."

William and James agreed. It was one of the most important days in the Church's history, and they were a part of it. They fell asleep on the flight home, wandering into the same dream.

XVIII

When Archbishop Morley returned from Rome, he had his office contact Monsignor Kotlinski for a meeting. He was excited to break the news to her about the pope's decision to visit Detroit, but wanted to do it with both Frank and James in attendance.

It was the second week of December, and Charlotte was busy coordinating Christmas services with the pastors and their churches. But when she received the call from the archbishop, she dropped everything. She was asked to be at the diocese offices the next morning at 10:00, which allowed her a chance to complete morning services at The Sweetest Heart of Mary beforehand. She quickly agreed.

James couldn't make it, but when Charlotte arrived the next morning, the archbishop and Frank McGann were both already there waiting for her.

"Come in, Charlotte," said the archbishop. "Frank and I have a few things to talk about." Charlotte's heart sank as she sat down. The men were not smiling. "Thank you for coming in. I know how busy you are this time of year. Frank and I, along with James and two other attendees, just returned from Rome, meeting with someone most significant. Over the past few weeks there has been much work done, mostly by Frank and James meeting with important contacts in Washington about your issues."

Charlotte nodded, wringing her hands beneath the table. Her eyes went from one to the other nervously. "Please," she said. "Just give it to me straight."

The archbishop continued. Frank was fighting to keep back a smile. "Upon some in-depth investigation, and you could say a little arm-twisting, things were exposed that were very incriminating to some senior members of the church. Once we were able to review the information, a meeting was coordinated in Rome. We just returned yesterday from where we spent significant time with his holiness. Upon review of the information, some important decisions were made by the pontiff that will have an immediate effect on you and the memories of the other two vicars. We can't provide you with the specifics of the meeting, but what I can tell you is the negative publicity being given to the media will end immediately."

Charlotte let out a deep sigh.

Frank smiled warmly at her. "After the meeting, the pope spoke with Archbishop Morley about you and about the damages done to your reputation. The holy father is impressed with your marketing skills. Because of that, he thought it would only be appropriate if you would meet with him."

Charlotte's mouth fell open. "The holy father wants to meet me?" she echoed, dumbfounded.

"Yes, he does," said the archbishop with a smile. "Not only that, but because of what's happened to harm your reputation, he thought it would be best if he came here to hold services with you at The Sweetest Heart of Mary."

Charlotte stared out at the men before her. "Okay, I get it," she said with a smile, pointing a finger at them. "You two are pulling my leg, aren't you?"

The archbishop shook his head. "The pope will be here the second week of January. He intends to hold mass services at your parish and somewhere a bit more significant, possibly Ford Field, where he wants you and three other female seminarians to join him for mass. The holy father understands what you've been through and how your parishioners aren't sure what to believe. He commented that the only way this can be resolved is if a strong PR campaign is put in place. So it begins with him."

"How…"

A Change of Faith

"Charlotte, it's no secret there were men trying to reverse the laws passed about female priests. You have lived in a hellish nightmare, and now it's ended. We have much to do to prepare for the papal visit."

Charlotte sat in a daze, taking deep breaths. "Maybe I'll be redeemed and trusted again by my parishioners," she said, choking on the words as tears welled in her eyes. "Thank you, gentlemen. I...I can't believe what I've just heard."

"I'll have my staff begin working on the pope's visit. We'll have to coordinate with the Detroit police department and other national security offices. Frank will be meeting with the Ford family about the use of Ford Field, and we'd better make sure your parish is prepared, as there will be a long list of attendees who'll want to be there. We're announcing the event tomorrow; it won't remain a secret for long. Now we have to focus on Christmas services and a papal visit..." he said, shaking his head. "My, my."

Charlotte laughed. "We can do it, Archbishop Morley!"

"With God's help," he agreed with a weak smile.

There was a lot to do over the next 30 days. Leaving the office, Charlotte sat in her car for a few minutes thinking about the conversation that had just taken place. The pope, the pope, was coming to Detroit, was coming to Charlotte's own parish. She wanted to call her parents, but before that, she wanted to call John. Not unusually, his voicemail picked up.

"John, it's Charlotte. Can you and Maria give me a call? It's something big." She paused. "But not bad at all!" she added quickly. Then she dialed her parents' number, which also went to voicemail. "Mom and Dad, I have some amazing news. Can you call me whenever you get this message? Love you!" Finally, she tried Monsignor Weir. Thankfully, he actually answered; she needed to tell someone. She was brimming with excitement.

"Hello Monsignor, I have amazing news," she blurted out. "The pope is coming to Detroit in January and performing mass at my parish!"

There was a brief pause. "What? Charlotte, what in heavens are you talking about? Have you been sipping the Eucharistic wine?"

"No, Monsignor! I just left the archbishop's office

meeting with him and Frank McGann. They just came back from talking with the pope in Rome, and he said he wanted to come here and perform mass at my church with me."

"Holy...Charlotte, you're not kidding me, are you? The pope is going to be here next month? That's unbelievable!"

"Monsignor, can we meet with my folks soon? I need to get this off my chest."

"Of course, dear, let's plan on something soon!"

Back at her parish, Charlotte was trying to do her work, but she found herself unable to concentrate for even a minute. She had to get out for a while. She tried John's number, but it went to voicemail again, so she decided to try Maria instead, who answered quickly.

"Hello?"

"Hello Maria, it's Charlotte."

"Charlotte? Oh my gosh, is everything okay?"

"Yes, absolutely! Are you and John available?"

"John's at the Neumann Gallery reviewing the results of the show. Is everything good?"

"Very good. I'd like to tell you and John face to face."

"Okay, let me call him and give you a call back."

Charlotte went to the coffeeshop at the Eastern Market and waited for a call. The one time she really wanted to share an amazing story, and no one was around. Finally, John called. His voice was frantic.

"Maria said you called. Is everything okay?"

"John, this is way better than okay, way better than amazing. Can I please see you guys soon? I'm about to burst!"

"I can be there in 30 minutes. Coffee shop?"

"Yes, thank you!"

The next half hour chugged by, and two refills later John and Maria walked in and met Charlotte at their normal corner table. They shared hugs and sat down.

"I'm assuming you won the Mega Millions," John said.

"Nope, better!"

"Hmm, what could be better?" John laughed. "Your smile is wrapped around your ears!"

"Well..." began Charlotte, folding her hands on the

table and leaning forward. This was her news to tell, and she was going to tell it right. "As a priest, what could be the coolest thing that could ever happen to you?"

Maria, eager to play along, chimed, "You're going to Rome to meet the pope!"

Charlotte laughed. "Very close. But this is even better."

John and Maria looked confused. What could possibly be better than meeting the pope? "I just met with the archbishop, and he informed me that the pope is coming to Detroit next month to perform mass with me at my parish. So yes, I am meeting him. But he's coming here."

John swallowed his coffee hurriedly, his eyes bulging. "No shit."

"He'll be at my parish and maybe Ford Field for a larger mass. I'll be performing with him at both."

"Charlotte, you're dead serious!" John said.

"It's incomprehensible, isn't it? I'm not even sure what to do, what to say, I'm, like, totally dumbfounded and lost, and just so grateful…"

Maria jumped up and gave Charlotte a huge hug. "After all that's been dumped on you, I'm sure the pope is coming to correct the hateful rumors," she said, squeezing Charlotte. "His appearance with you at mass will be proof of his belief in you."

"They're releasing the news tomorrow, and I'm sure once word gets out the media will be all over us," mused Charlotte.

"Maybe we should sell tee shirts," suggested Maria with a mischievous grin.

"The Pope Does Detroit," laughed John. "I'll buy the first one."

Charlotte drove to her parents' house in Dearborn and met Monsignor Weir there. There were a few bottles of nice chianti opened and many smiles shared as Charlotte shared the good news. For the first time in a long time, she let go. In fact, she let go so completely she had to spend the night. She giggled with her mom and sister in the kitchen as Monsignor Weir and her father sat in the library and told old war stories. It couldn't have been a better night.

Meanwhile at the Neumann Gallery, James was meeting with John about the exhibit's results.

"We had pretty big expectations. The work you provided was exceptional, but we certainly didn't expect a sellout. First sellout we've ever had. The articles were very positive. Now let's look at what the famous Patricia Menstom had to say." James picked up the paper and began to read:

"This past Saturday, I was invited to an exhibition opening at the Neumann Gallery in Birmingham, Michigan by an old friend, James Neumann. I went there with simple expectations because, like many of us, I tend to believe the art world revolves around New York and my core group of artists. Upon entering the exhibition, I was shown 15 paintings by the artist, John Adams, a Detroit native who works out of his small, no-bedroom studio overlooking the outdoor Eastern Farmer's Market located near the downtown area. Though I didn't have an opportunity to visit his studio, I was told it is compact and quite eclectic. Of course…what else would you expect?

"As I viewed his first painting, like some other exhibitions, I was impressed with the piece but figured the best is always the first that you're presented. The painting 'Morning Storms' was approximately 4' X 5' and, unlike its title, was whimsical but presented serious composition and story. As I reviewed Adams's pieces, I felt like each piece was an exhibition on its own and each required its own description. John Adams, if he can maintain this quality of work, is an artist to be reckoned with. He was able to move me into his world and keep my attention tuned into each piece. His skill at creating compositions that make you think far beyond the canvas they are created on was something special. I hope we find him at one of our New York galleries soon, though my friend James Neumann might put up a good fight."

James finished reading and took his time folding the paper. He smoothed the crease against his knee and finally set the paper down, looking nonchalantly up at John. "Well Adams, any comments?"

John hesitated. "I'm not sure what to say. I've been told she rarely gives positive reviews. Did you buy her dinner or something?" He suddenly looked shocked. "Oh, God, James, you didn't sle—"

"Of course not!" James blurted. Then, with a proud smile, "Though I can't say I never have before..." He shrugged, thinking fondly of the encounter.

"James?"

"Right." He snapped out of his reverie. "Patricia's one of the most highly-regarded art critics in the world. She's seen most every type of art humanly possible. What you showed her was something so different and so good she had no choice but to write what she really felt. Where we go from here is your choice. You'll surely be approached by international galleries after her column, and though I know this isn't super relevant to you, your works will be appreciating in value."

John looked down at his shoes, the same shoes he'd worn for years. Not long ago, painting made him sick. Not long ago, he was wandering around his studio, brokenhearted, directionless, completely broke.

"James, let me say, and I'm sure Michael will agree, the Neumann Gallery will always have a piece of my art available. Without you and your team, where would I be? I have a core group of people responsible for my success, and none of you will ever be forgotten. That's my word, and I will not break it. It's wonderful having this recognition, but none of it matters if you don't have friends to enjoy it with."

James nodded warmly. "If you'll allow me and my team to work with you, we can make this journey so much fun. I haven't had the opportunity to work with someone of your skillset...ever. This will be like winning the Kentucky Derby, Super Bowl and World Series wrapped into one!"

John outstretched his hand, and James took it.

"James Neumann, you have yourself an artist to work with."

XIX

After Christmas, it was time to regroup and prepare for the papal visit. Everyone was on pins and needles, including the archbishop. A pope hadn't visited Detroit since Pope John Paul many years ago, and back then there wasn't as much of a problem with political hate and terrorism. The mood was different now... heavier. The security divisions of all local and national departments were coordinating. Thousands of police and national guard would be working during the three-day visit.

Though word was released the pope would be staying at the archbishop's residence, he would quietly be spending his two nights in Bloomfield Hills at Frank's house. The McGann house was very large with two separate wings where the pope and two members of his staff would be staying. Though the McGann house already had significant security in place, the entire grounds were installed with additional cameras, motion detectors, heat sensing, and a 24-hour security team.

The pope would be arriving on Friday. He'd spend a couple of hours with the media, then meet with some church benefactors and local politicians. That evening, he requested a quiet dinner at Frank's with the archbishop, a couple members of his team, and Charlotte. The next day would be services at The Sweetest Heart of Mary, with only invited guests allowed. The mass would be televised and national networks invited, as the whole idea of the pope's visit was to talk about women priests in the Church and the honest job they were doing. The sermon was specifically constructed for that purpose. That evening the pope would meet with children at the local boys' club, and the next day would be the mass at Ford Field with 70,000 attendees. At both masses, Monsignor Kotlinski and the three female seminarians would be the main participants directing the services behind the pope. Once Sunday mass was over, the holy father would be escorted to his plane and head home. It would be a relatively quick trip, but one that should be effective in kickstarting the PR campaign to protect female priests.

Pope Peter Paul landed at the Detroit Metro Airport at noon on Friday. Security was heavy, with numbers of politicians and press members waiting to greet him. The pope's motorcade took him to the Fox Theatre on Woodward Avenue in Detroit, a majestic old theatre with large gold leaf columns, marble floors, and chandeliers hanging everywhere. The pope sat on the stage by himself to take questions from the press, no cameras allowed. He wanted this to be an intimate one-on-one, with approximately 100 journalists from around the globe. Questions were not planted; he wanted it to be as open as possible. After all, he had nothing to hide about the vicars. The first question was why the Church ever voted in favor of female priests in the first place.

"Thank you for asking that question. The Church for the longest time believed the priesthood should only be open to men. There were many reasons for that, some quite legitimate, but the more we reviewed the matter, the more it became obvious the Catholic Church was designed for equal representation for all. But centuries ago, some senior members decided to initiate rules that would ignore opportunities to anyone other than men. We had a choice when this vote was introduced to the college of cardinals on whether we wanted to live by rules that were artificially installed centuries ago, or be more proactive. It was a bitter meeting, and there were those who adamantly, even to this day, want to live by past laws. The vote was very close, but passed.

"I personally am in favor of female priests, or as we call them, vicars. The three women who were ordained have each done remarkable jobs performing their duties in their parishes and with outside parishioners. The loss of Vicars McPherson and

Anderson has left me with great personal pain. Though on a happy note, Vicar Kotlinski had done such a wonderful job reestablishing her parish that we elevated her to Monsignor. She has taken her first parish, then five others, and increased attendance by 63%. Before she came along, each church was bleeding red numbers. Now all six parishes are in the black, and these are churches all located in your inner-city.

"We've become so impressed with the success of these women that four years ago we opened 12 seminaries around the world where 173 more women are being trained for the priesthood. 40 of them complete their classes this spring and will be ordained. Our goal is to ordain 12,000 female priests in the next 15 years. That may sound significant, but the church has 415,000 priests worldwide serving 1.4 billion Catholics."

When the pope closed his mouth, someone new spoke quickly. "Your Holiness, it's no secret a smear campaign's been launched against these priests. Can we assume that's why you came here, to help rebuild reputations?"

"Yes, that is one of the reasons I am here. These women had been living a nightmare, bearing daily negative reports. There has been conversation about what we have to do to retract these allegations. Having you here and giving us an opportunity to talk about this issue is a good start."

The question and answer went on to cover a variety of subjects, and the pope answered each question meticulously and with extreme patience. After 90 minutes onstage, he excused himself and went on to his next meeting. Considering he was 71 years old, he displayed a strong level of energy. He went on to a private room at the Fox to meet donors and politicians, after which he was escorted to his limousine.

A decoy motorcade led the press to the archbishop's house, while the pope's real motorcade, along with a small group of police cars, took the holy father to the McGann residence. Once there, he was able to change into more comfortable clothing and take a nap, during which time the dinner guests were arriving and meeting in the den: Monsignor Kotlinski, Archbishop Morley, and two of the pope's direct reports. Frank and his wife excused themselves to attend a friend's birthday party at Orchard Lake Country Club down the street.

A Change of Faith

In the den with Charlotte, the archbishop diverted her attention to some discussion about Christmas and how her churches' attendance measured up. He could see her nerves building, her eyes darting to the door and back. "Charlotte, please be calm," he said kindly, trying his best to sound comforting. "I know that may be difficult, but you will find his Holiness is very down to earth and just as excited to meet you as you are to meet him."

As the archbishop completed that sentence, Pope Peter Paul walked in the room. His presence immediately silenced everyone and settled all attendees into their seats, starstruck.

"Charlotte, it is my complete pleasure to finally be meeting you," the pope said warmly. Charlotte gaped up at him, wordless. "This is the true highlight of my trip. Over the past couple of months we've been made aware of how your reputation was being manipulated and abused. Before we sit, please accept my personal apologies for this. We are working hard to alleviate this problem and bring the perpetrators to justice. I am only so very sorry that Vicars Anderson and McPherson aren't here enjoying this moment with us. If we may, let's go enjoy dinner and talk."

As they were seated, Peter Paul made extra efforts to put Charlotte at ease. He understood the significance of the meeting and could plainly see by the look on her face that she was overwhelmed, but the goal was to have open and casual conversation. He'd become good at initiating that.

"Folks, if you enjoy good pizza, next time you come to Rome I'm going to arrange for us to go to my favorite little restaurant, hidden down a small side street near Fontana de Trevi. But first, let's enjoy our wonderful meal. And I must apologize in advance—I may last only a little while. It's quite late for me, being on Vatican time."

"Of course," came a hurried murmur from the archbishop, finally finding his voice.

Though the pope was interested in listening to each guest, his real interest was biased towards Charlotte, as he was impressed that she was able to take chapter 11 churches in the inner-city and turn them around. He could use her skillset in Rome to implement some of her programs internationally, but he knew they needed her in Detroit.

I'm sitting here in the presence of one of the most

powerful and important men in the world, thought Charlotte. Is this really happening? Throughout dinner she and the pope talked nonstop, and to her surprise, her unease quickly evaporated into a warm sense of calmness. Like she was drifting in the ocean on a sunny summer day, the waves lapping over her. She marveled at the man, so intelligent and kind, his eyes the more enigmatic feature of his face: this was a man who couldn't lie. If he did, his eyes would betray him like neon signs. But she saw he was incapable of lying. He was genuine and true down to the very marrow of his bones.

The dinner lasted almost an hour before the pope began to stifle yawns and force his eyes open. Finally he set down his napkin and gave each participant a beautiful rosary and a book about Saint Peter's Basilica, signing each copy.

As he left, he turned around and shook Charlotte's hand. "It's been a pleasure, dear."

His eyes smiled.

Before the sun began rising, dozens of media trucks had already parked in front of the archbishop's house watching for any sign of the pope, who was enjoying a hearty breakfast with Frank and his wife Carol. Frank received a call from John.

"Morning, John. Hope this is important. I just excused myself from the pope."

"It pertains directly to the pope," said John in an unsettled voice. "I was with Maria last night when she received a call from her father. He heard a rumor about something going on in Rome. It's about the three cardinals. All he could say was something about a direct threat to his health..."

"The pope's health?" whispered Frank. "Are you indicating what I think you are?"

"I have no idea, Frank, but I don't think we should take any chances. I'd like to have the pope take a few minutes and meet with Tony. Can you make that request?"

"Gardelli?"

"Yeah."

Frank was silent a moment. "No one can know."

"I'm sure that can be arranged, Frank."

The pope agreed to meet with Tony after mass. The

A Change of Faith

Gardellis were large contributors to their own parish in Grosse Pointe and were respected parishioners. Besides, the pope was used to dealing with multiple serious issues at once. He wouldn't let this affect his mass with Charlotte and the other seminarians; this was their day, and nothing would change the excitement that was building.

After breakfast, the holy father went to change and say his morning prayers, after which his two staff members accompanied him in his black Suburban with other security patrol to the cathedral. At 11:30, the choir and orchestra from the Detroit Symphony began to perform, television cameras and news anchors giving their overview about the mass outside. When noon came, the music went to processional songs and the mass procession began, ten priests each carrying tall candles, followed by Monsignor Kotlinski and a handful of female seminarians, then the archbishop, and finally the holy father. It was a tremendous moment as Pope Peter Paul made his walk to the altar and took his seat. The music continued for an additional five minutes, and then the pope rose, followed by Charlotte, then the entire congregation. It was a sight no one would ever forget.

When it was time for the sermon, the pope was eager for the opportunity to praise the vicars. It was, after all, the purpose of this trip. "Good day, and a blessed Saturday to each of you."

"And to you," the crowd chanted in unison.

"I decided to come visit you at this beautiful cathedral here in Detroit with a specific purpose in mind. Some years ago, the college of cardinals met and made one of the most significant votes in the history of the church: a vote to allow women to become priests. Many continue to disagree with the decision. Today, I am here to introduce you to Monsignor Kotlinski and to remember the lives of Vicars Anderson and McPherson. Each of these heroic women put their personal lives aside to join the sacred sacrament of the priesthood.

"For the past 12 years, these women have lived under the microscopic scrutiny of the church in Rome and the international media. Each has handled herself very professionally and should be proud of her accomplishments. Over the past few years, a media program was put in place to not only embarrass them, but to destroy their reputations, and now we have the very unfortunate deaths of two of them. I am here to remember them not only with my own support, but that of the Church. We cannot allow these women and their memories to be abused by illegitimate information designed to destroy them. These vicars have been as good as any priests we have had in the Church."

The pope stepped over and took his time shaking the hands of Charlotte and the three seminarians, the congregation staring on in silence. "I will with all the power in my position make sure that these women are protected. If anyone attacks them, they do so with the knowledge that they challenge the might of the Church itself." He then slowly lit two large candles in memory of the dead priests.

The mass went on for 90 minutes, after which the pope was led to Charlotte's rectory to meet with Tony Gardelli, Frank and James.

"Your holy father," said Frank, "I'd like to introduce you to Anthony Gardelli, a friend of the church. His daughter Maria is good friends with Monsignor Charlotte. He has something important he'd like to say."

"Mr. Gardelli, it's a pleasure to meet with you," Pope Peter Paul said with a smile. He knew a bit about Tony's background, so he was certainly interested in what he might have to say.

"Your holiness," began Tony with a respectful bow of his head, his accent strong, "my daughter Maria is very good friends with Monsignor Charlotte, and my family happens to own a produce business here in Detroit that has operated for the past 80 years. Because of some of the men we have as business partners, conversations sometimes develop beyond the topic of produce."

The pope nodded intently. "Certainly."

"Well, some of our partners live in Italy and are involved in a broad variety of industries. During your visit here in Detroit, things were being set in motion in Rome…serious things. Your holiness, we're aware of the meeting with the three cardinals demanding early retirements and reassignments outside of Rome. Though two have left, there is one who has made his own decision. This week when you get home from this visit, the college of cardinals will be meeting. At that time, they are going to try and reverse the decision about female priests."

A Change of Faith

There was a heavy pause as Tony, James and Frank watched the pope anxiously. He seemed unfazed, his hands folded comfortably between his knees. He was thinking, a crease forged between his eyebrows. "Excuse me, Mr. Gardelli, but how do you know this?"

"Your holiness, my friends have ears everywhere. They found out about this almost immediately after your meeting at the villa took place." Frank and James exchanged glances. Tony was part of something larger than they knew. "An associate in Rome received a request from someone having to do with your health and safety. To be frank sir..." Tony looked down and cleared his throat. "To be quite frank, they requested you be poisoned here in Detroit. Because I happen to live and do business here, I received calls just prior to your trip. If you're eliminated, the three cardinals could reestablish themselves, go to meetings with the other cardinals, and because of their historic power, probably pick their own new pontiff who would be in their pocket. The vote to eliminate female priests in the next college would most certainly receive the 66% requirement, and the church would revert to the old laws."

"How and when was this poisoning supposed to happen?" asked James, the word poisoning coming out bitterly, almost sarcastically.

"The pope meets with many people during his visits. A person was in place who would meet him, and with a simple shake of the hand, poison his holiness, with no antidote available. We were able to find the individual and take care of the issue. The problem going forward is that unless the initiators aren't dealt with properly, another attempt will take place back in Rome."

"Anthony, what are you suggesting we do?" asked Frank.

"I'm asking that you give us permission to take care of this issue, as something will certainly be in place by the time the pontiff gets home. We can take care of the problem without any unusual media news, making it look like a normal event. Your holiness, there are some very angry people who want you eliminated. If they are successful, it will be terrible for the Church. For all of us."

The pope remained sitting calmly, a look of quiet

thoughtfulness in his aged features. "Mr. Gardelli, may I have a word with Frank and James for a moment?"

"Of course, your holiness. Take your time." Tony stepped out of the room, pulling the door closed with a click. A beat of silence followed.

"Gentlemen, I'm sure we all understand what he's saying," said the pope. "What are your opinions?"

Frank quickly said, "This is an unthinkable plot that without Tony's assistance may have already taken place. The cardinals are stepping beyond any boundaries imaginable. It doesn't appear they'll stop until you're eliminated. I suggest we never had this meeting and let things in Rome be dealt with as Anthony sees fit."

"Your holiness," said James, "being an ex-NSA director, I know that sometimes things are best handled without official procedures. In this case, and because of the timeframe we're looking at, I agree with Frank. Give Mr. Gardelli the opportunity to make his calls and let his business associates handle the problem."

More silence as the pope looked down at his hands. He seemed to emanate a sense of sadness. No fear, no anger, no sense of urgency—just sadness.

"Gentlemen," he said quietly, "I am the pope. I'm seen as a source of supreme good." He sighed softly. "I…I can't believe I'm having this conversation. Yes, I understand everything being said, and I know that without help this could all have a very negative outcome. The police in Rome aren't capable of handling it without some form of corruption taking place. We seem to only have one option." He looked to Frank knowingly, who nodded. "Please speak with Mr. Gardelli. I'll give him my best now as I leave." With some effort, the pope rose and passed through the doors.

Frank and James continued their meeting with Tony, who informed them that appropriate care would be used to eliminate the threat. This was all a bit uncomfortable for Tony, as things were usually never discussed outside the family, but this was a very unusual circumstance. The men had to trust one another.

That evening, the pope went to the boys' club and met with approximately 100 inner-city children. It was a warm and emotional hour hearing some of their stories and the tribulations they'd encountered. Monsignor Kotlinski was invited along with a few other church members, including Monsignor Weir. The pope tried his hardest to stay focused on the children, but he couldn't get his mind off the meeting with Tony. He found himself glancing nervously at everyone who wanted to shake his hand, and that broke his heart. These were his people. This was his job, it was his whole life, and now he was being forced to betray his own beliefs, his own sense of moral goodness.

The pope had requested his staff not be informed about the assassination attempt; he wanted as few people as possible to know what was at stake. On the ride to Ford Field for the international papal mass, he contemplated the events that would take place in Rome. Tony said the problem would be "handled." The pope watched the world whir by his window, buildings going and then gone in the same instant.

Security at Ford Field was significant, with local, national and international law enforcement at hand. With all this security, how could someone possibly enter the papal inner-circle? For the first hour, the pope politely met with invited guests. His mind racing with echoes of Tony's words, instead of shaking strangers' hands he kept his hands pressed together as if in prayer, bowing his head in greeting. Though mass wasn't beginning for an hour, the stadium was filled to capacity, music provided by a compilation of local choirs totaling 150 singers. He put on his alb, the plain white dress considered the undergarment. The silk chasuble went on top. Pope Peter Paul was ordinarily a casual person, but due to the significance of the mass, this piece was very elaborate, trimmed in gold. The pallium was the final piece and resembled a collar, and finally a skullcap was placed on the head and capped by a larger, pointed headpiece called a mitre.

He would be assisted in the mass by 20 priests, six monsignors, and three bishops. Just before him in the procession would be Charlotte and the other female seminarians. A huge stage was prepared, an elegant altar surrounded by four 20-foot columns draped in long silk valances. Four of the "priests" in the procession were actually secret service agents, along with two more who would walk directly behind the pope, though no one in security was aware of the present threat.

Finally, the mass began with an orchestration of Handel's Messiah. The pope welcomed the audience and took his place at the altar, cameras from all over the world documenting the service. When it was time for the sermon, he decided to break the plans and bring Charlotte and the seminarians with him as a way to send a message to Rome. He wanted to make it very clear where he stood with the female priesthood. Those assisting with the mass glanced around nervously as the careful plans went askew. The sermon revolved around the family and raising children, then shifted focus to the value of the female priesthood.

Once mass was completed, the pope closed his eyes and tried to relax on the way to the airport. The last three days had been some of the most exciting, saddening, rewarding and scary days of his career. He had accomplished his objective of supporting the female priests, but there would be so much more than that to think about in the coming days.

XX

It was raining as Frank drove towards the Eastern Market and Gardelli Produce. When he first met Michael a while back at the Neumann Gallery, he'd never have guessed he'd become involved in such an international development. Fortunately his career, though still very active, moved according to his own schedule these days.

Gardelli Produce was located on the west end of the market. An enormous warehouse with 20 loading docks, the business was an anthill of activity from 3-9:00 a.m. Produce was known to fly in and out at record speeds to the company's almost 900 customers every day. The offices were anything but fancy, scenes frozen from a 1920s business. Things were very simple; if you wanted to see someone, you walked in and asked. There was no front desk, just people rushing about, doing their jobs. Frank walked in and immediately saw Maria.

"Mr. McGann, great to see you!" she said brightly. She knew exactly why he was there but played naïve. She was used to it.

Frank smiled. "Heard John's receiving remarkable accolades from the papers. How are you both handling the recognition?"

"We're still in the clouds," Maria said, stepping away from a busy worker on his way to somewhere that must have been important. Frank took Maria's elbow and led her to a corner where there was little activity. "John never thought this would happen to him," she went on, "but it's great having Mr. Neumann and Michael look out for him. He's got a good sense for business, but everything's happening so fast his head is spinning!"

"James'll take good care of him. He loves working with him. And Michael, he's a hoot."

Tony entered, surprised to see Frank in his offices. "Well, look at you two. Let me guess, we're talking about some guy named John who happens to be an artist." Maria smiled bashfully. "Would you ever have thought I'd agree to my daughter falling in love with an artist? Wonders happen all the time. Sweetheart, mind if I speak with Mr. McGann for a while? We have something to discuss."

Maria bowed out as they headed into Tony's office, and Frank immediately smiled. The office was everything he'd expect from Tony. Desks were littered with family photos, small trinkets and collectibles. The walls were lined in framed photos of celebrities of the entertainment and political world. It's not often one sees a signed photo of the entire Rat Pack acknowledging Tony during his stay at the Sands. There were photos from each president from the past 30 years. Finally, Frank studied two photos of popes, both taken while Tony was visiting the Vatican. Was there anyone this man didn't know?

"Mr. Gardelli—"

"Please Frank, for the sake of this discussion and others going forward, let's go by first names."

Frank smiled politely. "Anthony. You seem to be aware of almost everything that's taken place over the past few months. Hell, you could probably tell me more about what's happening than I'm supposed to know. So, my question is: how much time do we have to help the pope?"

Tony sat down behind his large desk and gestured for Frank to take a seat across from him. Frank sat, struggling now to maintain eye contact with Tony over the heap of treasures decorating the surface of the desk. "In my family's profession we don't have a choice but to know everything, including things that take place in other countries. As a small, family-owned business, we've developed relationships with partners from around the world.

A Change of Faith

These partners are sometimes part of situations that require each other's help. What's happened here over the past two days could have been catastrophic. We couldn't let that happen to such a good man. The family made an internal decision to take care of the issue, but now it turns even more significant. There are those, as you are aware, who want Peter Paul eliminated, and it goes beyond the three cardinals. We're capable of taking care of some of the immediate issues, however, we'll require some external help. The murder of Vicar McPherson was not committed by a lone person and the tragic death of Vicar Anderson was not an accident."

Frank straightened his glasses as the mood turned dark. He leaned forward in his chair. "You know this?"

Tony nodded.

"What kind of help?"

"Your friend James and his buddy William Beauchamp. The NSA has resources that may be required as the threat increases. The pope has the female priest issue going against him, but on top of that, he's also supported the recent Israeli/Saudi pact, which has created many enemies in the Muslim world. His assassination will be attributed to the female priest ruling, but in reality, the people involved with the cardinals are from a small but very powerful faction in the Middle East. They want Pope Peter Paul gone more than anyone else. And they are powerful enemies."

Frank didn't know what to say. The issue seemed to endlessly unfold into something larger and more dangerous. It was now a worldwide political matter that could totally change the entire climate in the Christian world. "Tony, what the hell are we supposed to do to prevent harm coming to the pope?"

Tony used his finger to push an antique-looking tobacco pipe back and forth across his desk. "We have our own ideas for how to take care of the issues over the next week. But once that problem is eliminated, they won't stop there. The 'resolution' to the problem in the Vatican will be exposed through the media as if there's a war with the pope and cardinals. This is where we'll require external help. This will get very dirty, and big resources from the government will have to be given. The good thing is, we know the people involved all the way to the top. If they see all their lieutenants and captains being eliminated, they'll soon disappear."

Frank followed the pipe with his eyes as it scooted across the mahogany. "How do you suggest we move forward?" he asked.

"It's best if we never meet with William Beauchamp in Washington. I'll leave it to you to coordinate a meeting over the next couple days, but we have to move quickly. Let's talk tomorrow and try and get Beauchamp into town. I'll have a couple of my friends attend."

Frank nodded.

"Now, back to work, Frank. I have tomatoes to ship." Tony grinned. Just another day in the life. Frank didn't envy him. He stood, dazed. Walking through the misty parking lot, he had a sour feeling in the pit of his stomach that he couldn't quite place. Then he found it: no matter what happened from here on out, people would die.

Monsignor Kotlinski, on the other hand, was on cloud nine. She was a superstar in the local papers and within her church, and she was embarrassed to admit that after all the rumors and negative press for so long, she was quite enjoying her newfound adoration. The pope's trip had accomplished its goal; Charlotte and the female seminarians were on proper ground with her parishioners and the press. Despite wanting to bask in the joy of finally receiving recognition for all her hard work over the years, Charlotte knew she had to get back to work. She had bills to pay and services requiring her attention. She had churches to run.

The archbishop was only peripherally exposed to the issues that had taken place during the pope's trip to Michigan, so he was still extremely pleased with how everything fell into place and the responses he received from his peers. He was beginning to think about retirement, as he was now 68. He would have a say in who would become his predecessor, though ultimately a bishop's approval would have to come from the pontiff himself. Thoughts about recommending Charlotte certainly crossed his mind; she'd been performing wonders in her district. The Detroit area diocese included over 290 parishes and chapels covering an expansive geographic area. The archbishop had a significant support staff, some of whom would be up for his position once he did retire.

A Change of Faith

Charlotte was only 42 but very well-qualified. He put the thought on the shelf.

While Frank was busy trying to coordinate meetings with James and William, the three cardinals in Italy were receiving unwanted visitors at exactly the same time so calls couldn't be made to warn one another. The message for each was simple but direct: "For the sake of your own health and that of your family, it's highly recommended you leave Rome and enjoy your retirement. Anything happens to the pope, and you won't be far behind him, though it might be a bit more painful an experience. You have 24 hours to find your way to your newly appointed location."

The visits seemed to work, as all three, if not already at their new homes, would be there soon. Tony and his business associates in Rome were quite effective in helping people make decisions they may not agree with. They always seemed to make the right choice in the end.

Frank's call to William initiated a flurry of calls at the NSA, and a meeting was scheduled for the next day in Detroit, where a government jet would arrive at the Oakland County Executive Airport around noon with the guests. Frank asked his wife to leave the house for a couple of hours so the attendees could meet there in private. In attendance were Frank, James, William, Tony, William's assistant director Peggy Percy, and a gentleman by the name of Brett Patterson. They were all familiar with one another and their professions with the exception of Brett, who explained he was there to represent some of the other government agencies and would help coordinate whatever additional services may be required.

"Folks," James began, "we're all aware of the assassination attempt on the pope. As of yesterday, the three cardinals were handled thanks to Mr. Gardelli and his associates. Now we have a much more severe problem at hand. Tony has informed us there are Middle Eastern mercenaries still involved."

Despite all the power and influence the NSA and other national agencies had, it was the produce man from Detroit who took over the meeting. "A few months ago, my associates in Italy were informed that an assassination attempt would take place on the pope," said Tony. "The cardinals would be the scapegoats, and ultimately, they would be eliminated, taking care of any street gossip. The goal was to put in place a pope who'd be more user-friendly to the Middle Eastern cause. The people involved included some leaders of powerful organizations and countries. My friends were able, with some help from internal Middle Eastern contacts, to put together a list of the people involved. We came up with about 30 people who must be handled in order to eliminate the threat and increase the pope's chances of a continued healthy life, and we are ready to pass this obligation on to you. My friends and myself, being Catholics, feel an obligation to the Church and his holiness. We respect him and the job he's performed. I'm leaving the list here with you and will excuse myself—I have tomatoes to ship."

Tony strode out of the room and was gone before any reply could be made. Silence hung between the remaining men in the wake of Tony's speech, his absence oddly stark.

"Well," said William, gathering the group to attention. "We have the list sitting in front of us. If I didn't know Tony and the services he's provided, I'd tear this up and leave. But we have to believe him. We'll do a bit of homework to complete our own verification process, but we don't have much time. That said, and now I'm asking for extreme secrecy, I'd like to provide a solution. Brett Patterson does not represent other government agencies, but is the director of his own. I'll let him explain."

"Thanks, Bill," said Brett, folding his hands together on the table. "When the second Iraq war broke out under President Bush, issues that developed in the Middle East warranted actions, but under the radar. A very small secret agency was developed that only a few individuals are aware of in Washington, even now. We're stealth enough that the congress doesn't know we exist; only the president, his national security advisor, and the heads of the CIA and FBI. It's the International Terrorism Agency, consisting of less than 50 people worldwide. Most of our members are ex-special forces and seal team members. We're quite good at getting shit done, if you'll pardon my French."

Frank raised a questioning finger into the air, a deep crease burrowed between his brows. His eyes looked far away.

"How…where does…"

"We were put in place to handle specific problems exactly like this," interjected Brett. Frank's arm dropped slowly, his expression full of puzzlement. "When the ITA is put in place to complete a mission, it's shoot first, collect whatever intel might be available, and disappear. No one will ever hear about us. I won't sugarcoat it: once verified from the bottom up on this list, these folks will be eliminated. Usually once the process begins and the first few are eliminated, word gets out and the higher-ups realize if they don't stop with their plan, they'll be next. I've already placed our members in locations where some of these folks may be in hiding, though we weren't given specific names until now. We had a good idea who some might be." Brett picked up his mug and took a sip of coffee. Only then did they notice his forearms were huge, like the branches of a towering tree. "I'm sure you're all aware that you never met me."

"As the ex-assistant director of the NSA, it's just remarkable to me this has been able to be kept so quiet," noted James quietly, as if speaking too loudly would reveal the secret to the world.

"It's actually pretty simple," said Brett. "We aren't located in Washington, but in a surrounding state under the guise of a defense supplier to the DOD. Our members live in their own home-states and travel as needed."

"Remarkable," muttered James, leaning in.

"We'll inform Mr. Gardelli the pope is in good hands," said Frank.

Little did the men know that just a few months prior, Brett and his agency had stopped what could have been a terrorist act far more massive than 9/11. ISIS and other terrorist groups want to eliminate Christianity and cause panic, and their goal with this attack was to kill as many people as possible at a University of Notre Dame football game. They couldn't commandeer commercial planes, so they used small private planes; three Cessna 340 twin engine prop planes, to be exact.

The planes would each carry a 900-pound payload of explosives directed to the target from three private airports all within 150 miles of South Bend, Indiana. There were enough small airports with private hangars in the region that keeping this under the radar was easy. The group of eight had been coordinating their plan for almost two years. They made sure not to rent hangars in close proximity of each other or too close to rental timelines, and the planes were each purchased under individual company names as recreational aircraft. There would have been thousands of fatalities if they were successful, and who knows how many injuries. Their plan was almost perfect.

They rented a private T hangar at the Gary International Airport. The hangars are connected in lines and face each other in a corridor layout. One day as they were removing two seats from their plane, another pilot was taxiing his plane by their hangar. The group tried to quickly cover the seats with a tarp, but the taxiing pilot noticed one of the seats and the concern on the terrorist's faces. He gave a casual wave and went on his way. The next day, he drove to the Gary police department to report what he'd seen. The police went through their registration application and noticed the company renting the hangar had no business background whatsoever.

These concerns led to calls to the local FBI office for further investigation. This single pilot being proactive saved thousands of lives. The FBI put an immediate plan in place, easily tracking the terrorists. A group of international terror experts reviewed the information coming in from Washington, and a plan was set to monitor the hangar and the two individuals registered to the hangar. Local and national offices would now begin an investigation into other airports and any hangar registrations that may have happened within the past two years. They came up with five other potential registrations requiring additional investigation. In two days the list was narrowed down to just three, all of whom had the same type of plane, LLCs with similar registration, and nonconforming names. No one was sure what the exact plan was, but it was plain to see there was going to be an attack.

It was time to break into one of the hangars and find out what was being altered in the planes. The hangars had alarm systems and cameras in place, but it was a non-issue, as any of these devices could be put to sleep for a small amount of time. Three FBI specialists broke into the hangar, where they discovered a few bugs in place that they were able to temporarily disable. Once in the plane, what they discovered was hair-raising. All but the pilot seat had been removed to eliminate any extra weight and leave more open space for cargo. Behind the pilot seat were a number of large plastic boxes, along with 20 drum tanks. This was a bomb with wings. Whatever they were planning would cause serious human damage. Something had to stop this, and soon.

The deputy director of the FBI was flown into Gary to discuss the findings. If the FBI was to move ahead, proper paperwork would have to be filed with the DOJ, which would take at least 48 hours—too long when unknown numbers of lives are at risk. Instead, the decision was made to allow the president and his national security advisor move forward in their own ways. The president contacted Brett Patterson directly and put his team in play. Within six hours, 20 ITA members were diverted to three locations where the planes were stored and the terrorists were located.

They learned the attack at Notre Dame would be that Saturday with a stadium full of 81,000 fans against UCLA. As both teams were ranked in the top five, the television audience would be one of the largest of the year. The ITA team was in place by 10:00 a.m. Tuesday, fully geared. A review of responsibilities, layout of living locations and exact whereabouts of the terrorists was reviewed. By midnight, all eight terrorists were eliminated and the planes removed from their hangars. The ITA completed their plan and disappeared in less than 24 hours without a trace.

Two days after Brett's visit to Detroit, plans were in place and the first group of six ITA members were sent to a coordination point just outside Rome. Within six hours they'd be taking their first actions against the terrorists looking to eliminate the pope. The three assassins were staying at individual locations in the city of Marino, located approximately 12 miles southeast of Rome. The city, with a population of 38,000, was big enough that someone could live there relatively anonymously. The suicide mission would take place the next day as the pope's motorcade was heading to mass services at the Basilica of Santa Maria del Popolo, a charismatic church constructed in 1477. It stood near the north end of the famous Piazza del Popolo, a relatively small open court.

The plan was to drive in two cars and a van from three different directions, each loaded with explosives to be tripped simultaneously surrounding the motorcade. The vehicles were being kept inside a warehouse in Rome, their explosives installed by two outside parties. These two terrorists were being tracked by the ITA and the Enigma GPS system, a new technology capable of tracking individuals by DNA. Their DNA was collected from utensils used as they ate around town. The goal of the ITA was to eliminate the three suicide terrorists at the same time. The whole process would take fewer than three minutes, and the deaths would take place just after 1:00 a.m. at the terrorists' rental apartments, no questions asked. The bodies would be removed in individual vans and disposed of immediately. Simultaneously, four other ITA members were in place to eliminate the two terrorists who had installed the explosives in the vehicles. These two terrorists, separated from each other, would be tracked to their respective living quarters and eliminated.

The first was killed in the bathroom of his apartment. Two ITA members picked the lock and entered the main living space, where they found a man asleep on the sofa, television illuminating him in flashes of blue and white. When the men closed the door behind them, the soft click startled the sleeper awake, and he scrambled in a daze to the bathroom, where he closed and locked the door. The agents didn't even exchange a glance; it was too easy, like a rat in a trap. Agent Two broke the door open with an easy bump, and Agent One stepped inside and slipped a black mask over the head of the man who squatted in the shower whimpering a jumble of pleas for his life. Using a silencer, the man was shot once in the heart. He was quietly pulled from the bathroom, out a back door, and into a van. The entire process took less than two minutes.

Meanwhile, the second explosive-installer was putting up a bit more of a fight, throwing mostly-missed punches and kicks in the direction of the agents. Bored, Agent Three twisted him into an easy headlock, and Agent Four administered a quick shot of tylapenthenal, instantly disabling the combatant. He was loaded into a van and driven to the nearest alley, where Agent Four shot him in the head and left him there for authorities to find. Brett and his team wanted terrorists who were overseeing the pope's assassination from the Middle East to understand they were not safe no matter where they might be. The message was clear.

For now, the pope was safe. A preventative plan for

the future would be put in place using the other U.S. agencies and international intel services in Europe and the Middle East. All anyone knew was that an attempt to assassinate the pope had been eliminated. Only the president, his national security advisor, and William Beauchamp were aware of the details of the completed mission. The ITA members left Italy on individual flights back to their homes in the States, and word to the Middle East had come in loud and clear: You're next.

XXI

John Sr. was a good man. He worked long, hard hours to support his family, and he boasted an enduring love for Bernice and his four sons.

John Sr. and Bernice met at an organized dance on the west side of Detroit in 1939. Bernice, being the oldest of six children, was forced to quit school at 13 to help support her family. John was the oldest of five sons. Both were brought up during the Great Depression and never took anything for granted. At the dance that cold December night, Bernice needed a ride home for herself and her two sisters. John and his brothers had a car, so Bernice smiled, danced, and eventually scored the ride. Little did they know they would fall so deeply in love. 14 months after that ride, they were married and shared a bond most couples today can only pray for.

John was at his studio Wednesday afternoon working on another painting. Soft jazz rolled in the background; he found it helped him concentrate. This was the largest piece he'd ever worked on. The 6' X 8' painting was an animated piece depicting various characterizations of historic individuals. Around 2:00 p.m., his phone rang through the music, shattering his focus. The number was his uncle Tony, which was strange. Uncle Tony never called.

A Change of Faith

"Hi Unc, how are you?"

"John, you have to get to the hospital right away. It's your dad. He was just rushed there from home."

John's brush froze over the canvas. "What happened?"

"Your mom just called me and asked me to run over. She'd just called an ambulance. By the time I got there the ambulance had him loaded up. He's unconscious. John, it's not good...you'd better hurry."

The brush, loaded with yellow paint, fell onto the canvas. "I'm out the door."

Tears of worry running down his cheeks, John tried calling Bob, the road blurring in front of him. Bob picked up the phone, but John couldn't make himself speak.

"Bro, it's Dad," was all John could get out.

"What's wrong? What's going on?"

John took a deep breath. "He's being rushed to the hospital, he's not conscious. Can you call Larry and I'll call Frank?"

"Yep. How's mom getting there?"

"Uncle Tony's taking her. See you in a few."

As he was driving, John let his mind slip back to days when he and his brothers would watch his dad and all the uncles playing croquet in their backyard. There were more arguments than shots made as they played until they couldn't see anything, not even each other. Sunday mornings Dad would drive John and his brothers to the bar before church to scrub the booths, barstools and counters with Murphy's Soap before they were allowed a scoop of cherry ice cream. Then there was Thanksgiving, when the Detroit Lions would play at Briggs Stadium. They'd attend the game in freezing weather before going home to a huge turkey dinner with all the relatives.

As John neared the hospital, time stopped. It didn't matter what day it was or what was happening in the world around him. He was about to lose the family anchor. He finally remembered to call Maria.

"Baby." He choked on the words.

"John, what is it?" Her voice was colored with panic. He pictured her at her desk having a normal day, papers scattered around her. "What's happening?"

"It's my dad, he's...not good. I'm heading to the

hospital."

"I'm leaving work now. I'll see you in 30 minutes."

Entering the emergency room, John saw his mother, Bob and Frank. They sat huddled in chairs, his mom with her head in her hands. She looked up. "Mom," he said, grateful to see her face. But as he got closer, he could see that her face was reddened and crumpled, her eyes wet.

"Your father...he's no longer with us," she said sternly, her voice broken.

"What do you mean?" John asked, the words rolling right off his brain.

"He's gone!" she cried. Frank wrapped an arm around her narrow shoulders, and she leaned against him and wept.

John stood and watched the scene numbly. It was as if he were watching through a thick pane of glass. The four hugged in an awkward clump of tall men and a brand-new widow. The man known as Dad at home and Honest John at the bar was gone. Forever.

Larry arrived, and then other members of the family, and then Maria. Everyone sat in the corner of a private room talking about what happened. They knew Dad wasn't in very good health, so this wasn't a total surprise, but the fact he was no longer with them and they couldn't say goodbye was still soul-shattering. Stories began to circulate within the room about Honest John's granite personality and all the times he would take John to the furnace room for a rear end belt licking whenever he brought home his report card. Seems John wasn't the class scholar. Story after story was told, the hospital staff coming and going to offer their condolences. The next few days and months would be difficult, but with all the love around, life would go on.

John went to his parents' house with Maria and his brothers. No matter how many friends and family members stopped by, the house felt totally empty to him. Sitting up in his childhood bedroom, which had since become a sort of storage room, John stared at the door, listening to the muffled conversation filtering up through the floor. It had only been a few hours...how long would it feel this way? What was he supposed to do? Lost, he dialed a familiar number.

"Charlotte, it's my dad. He's...no longer with us."

"Oh, no," Charlotte breathed on the other end of the line, "what happened?" John gave an overview of the day's events, finally falling into tears. "John, what can I do? Ask me anything."

Maria tapped on the bedroom door. "John?"

"I'm on the phone," he called.

"Oh. Okay." He heard Maria's footsteps patter away.

"Well," he said to Charlotte, "we were discussing the funeral, and although my parents have their own local parish, my father truly loved The Sweetest Heart of Mary. He considered you a daughter. We'd like to have the funeral there with you presiding over the service. If you'd do that."

"Of course, I'd consider it an honor. Please give your mom and brothers a hug for me, and anything else I can do, just ask. Your father is in everyone's prayers, he was so loved by so many people, John. Truly. My heart breaks for you."

"Thanks, Charlotte. Call you tomorrow."

"John?" Maria again. The door cracked open. "I was trying to tell you that your cousin was here."

"Sorry."

"Well…he's about to leave…"

"Will you give me a break please, Maria?" John blinked, startled by his own snappiness. He opened his mouth to apologize, but Maria had eased the door back closed and was gone. He let his head fall in his hands, and he wept.

It was 10:00 p.m. when the house began to clear. Larry said he'd spend the night with Mom. John, giving his mother a very long hug, finally left with Maria. The whole drive felt oddly surreal. Once back at his studio, he picked up a pen and wrote:

Best Friends
The pain I feel within must have been designed to leave me with self-pity. I have no anger, and there is no bitterness, but a loss; a temporary loss of motivation, a permanent loss of a dear friend.
With a smile and the strength I depended on, he taught me. We learned how to balance a checkbook, plant a tree and hit a ball off a tee. But more than that, he showed me how to care for my family and friends. He made me notice people not by sight, but by inherent love. He always believed in me and gave me the freedom to be my own self. He showed me how to celebrate life as though every day

was a holiday and how to smell the roses. I was fortunate to have this man as my friend and blessed to have him as my father. I only hope one day I may be able to fill such a large shoe in such an unassuming way.

Maria read what he'd written, tears spilling down her cheeks.

"I'm sorry I snapped at you," John said softly. It was nearing midnight, and they were both tired beyond words. "You didn't deserve that."

Maria shook her head. "Honey, we've all lost loved ones, but the love you had for your dad was deep. I understand. It's okay."

John leaned his head on Maria's shoulder as she held the paper out in front of her to read it over again.

A day passed and John drove to see Charlotte. As their eyes met, Charlotte began to cry a little. She gave John a warm hug.

"John, I can't tell you how sorry I am…"

"Thanks," he said. For the first time in his life, he realized condolences don't actually make the pain go away. At all. The words, though true and well-intentioned, are hollow.

"How's your mom doing?" she asked.

"She's a strong woman, and she's got a lot of support." He nodded, more to himself than to her. "She'll be okay. Everyone has to live through these times, and it's not easy, so we're just focusing on the wonderful memories." He looked at her, "Is there a chance we could have the service here day after tomorrow?"

"I've already cleared the schedule for you and your family. The church will be prepared and mass will be conducted by Father Williams and myself."

"Thank you. You really are a sweetheart."

Charlotte smiled. "I'll see you in the next couple of days."

Charlotte was itching to tell John her news about an opportunity she's just heard about from the archbishop, but she knew it wasn't the right time. The church and its accounting methods in Rome were in complete disarray and required new systems with four international auditing firms quoting the project. The cost would be tens of millions of dollars, and someone with the skillset to interview and review the four quotes was being requested. The pope wanted Charlotte in Rome for the process. It could take up to two years. It was an extremely important and flattering opportunity, and it's not like she could ever say no to the pope. She'd wait until things settled down after the funeral, she decided, and offer to take John and Maria to dinner and give them the news.

As Charlotte performed the funeral services, the cathedral was full with family and friends. During Charlotte's homily, she thought about her own father. During the couple of days it took to review Honest John's life and accomplishments, people left the church shaking hands, hugging, smiling and offering warm wishes. A modest man, Honest John would have been embarrassed to hear how people spoke about him. God bless you, Pops, John thought as he left the church. We'll miss you.

XXII

The Catholic Church and its operations had been a mystery since its inception, and by no accident. The Vatican Bank, founded in 1942 with approximately eight billion dollars in assets today, had been riddled with corruption since its initiation. Many accounts opened and maintained at the bank were held by wealthy Italian businessmen hiding assets to avoid income taxes. Income statements from dioceses around the world were consistent with fraud and lost funds commonplace. The 1.1 billion members of the international Church regularly made donations but rarely asked where they were being spent.

In the U.S. alone, during the flood of sex abuse cases by priests, tens of millions of dollars were used for legal expenses and settlements. Since his days as an archbishop in Columbia, the pope was aware of the financial issues often buried by the College of Cardinals. They thought that outside their own little chambers, it was no one's business how the Church operated financially. Pope Peter Paul, on the other hand, was committed to making changes to create a system capable of providing more transparent financial statements. This would take years, as audits would have to be capable of reviewing 2,988 ecclesiastical jurisdictions, including 640 archdioceses and 2,206 dioceses. This would require accounting packages that could adapt to various reporting procedures and still interact with a core accounting system in Rome.

A Change of Faith

No one, and this probably included authorities at the Vatican, really knew what the Catholic Church was worth. With its cash assets, corporate investments, properties, artwork and the Vatican Apostolic Library, started in 1450, the Church could be worth 90 billion dollars, probably much more. The library alone had 75,000 codices, books printed on wooden sheets, and 1.1 million books total, 8,500 of which were handwritten masterpieces from the early 15th century.

The cardinals from those earlier centuries, when Pope Peter was serving as the church's first pope from 32-67 A.D., were often hidden from any accountability. By the fifth century, the popes elected to office were often more involved in European politics than they were with the Church and Catholic religion. The internal attitude was that public issues could always be swept under the carpet. Unfortunately, many cardinals still believe the public and even members of the Church shouldn't be allowed to see any financial information.

With this old attitude in place over the past 20 centuries, making these changes would require a sense of stubbornness from the pope and his allies. Bringing individuals into the fold with experience in accounting and operations along with a social media marketing strategy would be required. Charlotte was asked to report to Rome by May, giving her three months to find her replacement at The Sweetest Heart of Mary. Fortunately, she already had a priest ready to step in.

Charlotte walked towards the coffee shop, a cold March wind tossing her hair over her shoulders. She was going to have dinner soon with John and Maria, but since it had been a while since she last had a cup of coffee with just John, they'd planned to meet alone after mass. When she arrived, John was already there, sitting with two cups of coffee and two muffins. He smiled and stood when he saw her, and they shared a hug and kisses on each cheek. As she sat down across from him, Charlotte was suddenly grateful that Maria had come into John's life; otherwise, she may have spent her whole life wondering if she should leave the priesthood to be with him. Maria kept the boundaries of friendship in place for John and Charlotte.

"Well, how're you?" asked Charlotte. "How's your mom?"

"She's doing as well as she can under the circumstances. Takes time to adjust, and some people never do. But as she always tells us, she'll keep moving forward until the end."

Charlotte smiled. "Good."

"The service was beautiful, and your homily was perfect. Thank you."

"You're welcome. It's a reality-check. Makes me realize sometime in the future I'll have similar things happening in my own life. Hard to avoid."

John smiled sadly, then picked his mug up with renewed fervor, shaking aside the topic. "So! How are things going at the church?"

Charlotte's eyes flashed something that John couldn't quite place. "I didn't want to bring this up at the funeral, but I've been requested by the archbishop and pope to go to Rome and work on some new accounting and operation auditing proposals. The archbishop seems to have convinced the pope I know what I'm doing when it comes to numbers. He'd like my opinion on some of the issues with the Vatican's accounting procedures."

John stared blankly. "What? Charlotte, that's huge! You'll be reporting directly to the pope! You might need a manager…should I call Michael?"

Charlotte laughed, relaxing. She was grateful for his encouraging response. But she didn't know why she'd assumed it would be anything but. "It's overwhelming to think I'll be putting in place an accounting package responsible for the entire Catholic Church. I'm spending the next two days with the archbishop reviewing his methods in the Detroit archdiocese to see if any of his balance sheet programs could be expanded to handle locations internationally. I'm hoping I'm only in Rome for two years. I'll miss the interaction with the parishioners. It's a catch-22; how many people wouldn't kill for this new position, and yet I love what I'm doing now."

"Well, they know in Rome you've been blessed with a unique talent, and your education and career background as an auditor in one of the big three firms makes you look even better." John looked across the table at Charlotte picking the chocolate chips out of a muffin with her fingertips. Two years without her would be a long time. "I can't wait to come and visit you," he said.

Charlotte placed the chocolate chips on her tongue. "Enough about me. What's happening in your career? How's Maria?"

"Your news tops mine yet again, but things have been better than I ever imagined they would be. James has been in contact with the Bovier Gallery, one of the top five galleries in New York. They want five of my pieces for a September exhibit. They've contracted six of what they consider the most exciting new talents from around the world. I'm 44 years old—new talent my ass!" John laughed in spite of himself, meeting Charlotte's eyes. "Who would have thought you and I'd end up where we are?"

Charlotte chuckled lightly. "Life's a funny thing."

"James said my pieces would be listed in the $50,000 price range," John said, rolling his eyes. "Jesus. I can't even wrap my head around that one. But as far as Maria goes, between you and me, I'll be proposing soon. She's in her early 30s, and if we want to start a family it's best we get moving. Maybe I can twist your arm to perform the ceremony!"

Charlotte laughed and smiled in a blur of congratulations that social norms demanded of her, but inside she felt a little pain in her heart. Yes, it was her choice to enter the priesthood and it was her choice to remain, but all the bible study and prayer in the world couldn't numb her to the flutter John made her feel year after year. And now he was planning children with another woman. Children. Permanent children, forever, who would never belong to Charlotte.

"Maria is a very lucky woman," she managed, looking outside for fear of betraying her thoughts.

She knew future visits with John would be more infrequent and under very different circumstances. She wondered if they'd ever get coffee alone together again.

The next day Charlotte visited the archbishop's office to begin her operational review of the Detroit archdiocese. The archbishop, who normally kept his emotions in check, was visibly excited to show Charlotte how the diocese operates.

The reputation of the Detroit archdiocese had always impressed the accounting offices in Rome, and eventually the pope himself. Everyone respected how things in Detroit were coordinated. So when the archbishop recommended Charlotte for the position in Rome, she was one up on anyone else on the list.

"Over the past 15 years we've put accounting procedures in place with expansion in mind. Our systems have the ability to incorporate not only our parishes, but those of all the dioceses in the U.S. We've put severe checks and balances in place. Take your time looking over the procedures. We'll review your findings before you head to Rome."

Charlotte nodded, slightly overwhelmed by the workload in front of her. "Got it."

The archbishop began to leave her, then hesitated. "Charlotte…I can't tell you how proud I am. You'll be deeply missed." Charlotte opened her mouth to respond, but the archbishop held up a finger. "Let me say this, Charlotte. I'm retiring in two years and have had conversations with his holiness about my replacement. He is aware of who I have in mind, and he doesn't seem opposed."

It became obvious to Charlotte the archbishop had an inside track with the pope. His mystery trips to Rome were more than just visiting friends and sitting in meetings with other senior representatives of the church. In fact, he and the pope had enjoyed more than one game of dominos together while they discussed church issues, Charlotte's potential promotion being one of them.

"A conversation for another time," he said. "Just something to think about."

XXIII

John had been through a lot over the years, but nothing requiring as much thought and commitment as this.

Maria was everything he could hope for in a potential wife and future mother of his children. She was not only a beautiful woman, but also the warmest person he'd ever met. She had a great compassion for people, volunteering regularly at a number of charities and hospitals in the Detroit area. Though John's reputation frequently got him invited to charity and social events, he always tried to make Maria the center of attention while she tried to revert the focus back onto him. It was a sort of game between the two, especially at some of the artificial cocktail parties they'd prefer not to attend. They would rather be in the kitchen at home with close friends than at a party with dozens of fakers.

The real challenge to this whole proposal thing was to figure out a unique and fun location. They traveled to the British Virgin Islands frequently to sail, and it would certainly be a great place to pop the question, but it seemed like a location where many others may got engaged. Too conventional. Where else? Somewhere in Detroit? Of course—Mackinac Island! It was a small island between the upper and lower peninsula of Michigan requiring a short ferry ride from Mackinaw [R1] City. Famous for its fudge, the island didn't allow any motor vehicles, the only means of transportation being bikes and horse-drawn carriages. Mackinac was home to the Grand Hotel, one of the most beautiful hotels in the world, overlooking the straits of Mackinac, an area dividing Great Lakes Huron and Michigan. It also connected the northern peninsula of Michigan to the southern with the Mackinac Bridge, a five-mile structure most beautiful at night. The hotel was known for the world's longest porch, scattered with rocking chairs and friendly staff.

Early June would be pre-tourist season, so John booked a trip at the Grand for a couple of weekdays. Next, he wanted to be proper and ask Tony Gardelli for his daughter's hand. They met for lunch at Whispers Pub located just outside the Eastern Market. The pub got its name many years ago because the area's politicians and mafia members would meet there for discrete lunches. It was now owned by a couple of young men who kept the interior in its original state. The pub was full of booths with very high backs to keep conversations private.

"Mr. Gardelli!" John said, plastering on his most gentlemanly smile.

"John, it's time you call me Tony." They shook hands, and John sat down. Tony smiled. "Relax, son. I think I have a good idea why we're here."

"Maria is an amazing woman," John blurted out. "You and your wife have to be extremely proud." Tony thought about putting John out of his misery, but he was quite enjoying the show. "Over the past couple years, we've fallen in love, and more importantly we appreciate who we each are as individuals. I'm sure you never envisioned your daughter with an artist, hoping more for a doctor or a lawyer. Yes, I'm an artist. It's funny even to me to think I make my living painting pictures, and for some insane reason, my paintings have become valuable to collectors. Who would have thought I could ever ask for tens of thousands for one painting? But I do, and there's a waiting list. I guess what I'm saying, sir, is I'm capable of supporting your daughter, and hopefully a family. With that said, I'm...I'm asking permission to marry your daughter. I promise to take very, very good care of her."

John understood he was speaking to Tony Gardelli, and if he wasn't the perfect husband, he could become walleye bait in the Detroit River.

Tony folded his hands. "I respect you inviting me

here, and I certainly knew this moment would come." Tony had a very firm face and a very distinct voice. "Did Maria's mom and I have bigger expectations than her meeting an artist? Of course we did. Did we hope for an Italian son-in-law? Yes. And did we hope for someone we could trust with our baby? Yes. So, am I concerned about you and my daughter getting married? No, not really!"

John's tongue stuck somewhere down in his throat, Tony bellowed a deep laugh and stood to give him a rough, squeezing hug. "My son, we're thrilled to have you as part of our family. We welcome not only you into our home, but your entire family. You're good people."

Here John was with Tony Gardelli, who may have saved the pope's life a few months earlier. This man had more connections and quiet power than most business executives and politicians combined, and now he was going to be John's father-in-law. Life was unreal.

John and Maria were finally going to have dinner with Charlotte. They picked her up and headed over to Peter's Steakhouse. This would probably be Charlotte's last chance to go out before she left for Rome. As she sidled into the back of the car, John could immediately sense she was nervous. Was it because the three of them were together, or was it because she was leaving soon? Whatever the reason, John was good at breaking nerves.

"Just to let you know," he said, eyeing her in the rearview with a devious smile, "we all booked tickets to Rome with you. We couldn't let you do this alone!"

"What?" Charlotte asked.

John laughed. Maria slapped his arm.

"Are you pulling my leg?" she said.

"Yes," John laughed, "but don't be surprised if we show up sometime in the near future. We'll give you plenty of heads-up when we do. Don't worry."

"Not worried at all, I'd love that. Just let me get myself situated. A woman monsignor in Rome looking over accounting procedures is going to have its barriers for sure. I'm expecting a certain amount of hostility."

"Well, you have plenty of experience dealing with

that," Maria said over her shoulder.

The three enjoyed their dinner together. A couple of bottles of Italian wine were opened as they talked, laughed, and even shared a few tears knowing that with Charlotte gone, the coffee shop meetings would have to wait.

"Charlotte, I can't tell you how much we both love and respect you," John said as they parked outside Charlotte's home, moonlight striping the asphalt through the trees. "What you'll be doing at the Vatican will be huge, but you'll be so missed here. You're very special."

Monsignor Kotlinski smiled, wrapped her arms around him and Maria both, and went inside to pack for the biggest step of her life. She was going to Rome.

XXIV

As her flight took off from the Detroit Metro Airport, Charlotte felt like a little girl. She looked out the window and watched the clouds stretch through the sky like cotton candy.

It's so funny how life can be taking you in one direction one day, and then all of a sudden the street sign says turn right. She was going to Rome and being asked by the papal office to make recommendations for a system that had been in place for hundreds of years! Not so long ago she was falling in love with a young aspiring artist in the city.

As she fell asleep, she dreamt about taking a journey through space where there were no hardships and no pain, a perfect world of silence and being. Even in the dream, she knew that wouldn't be the case where she was heading. But she pretended it was.

After the plane landed in Rome and she waited at the carousel for her bags, she was met by an American priest who had been at the Vatican for six years. He appeared to be in his mid-thirties and was quite handsome.

"Monsignor Kotlinski, I'm Father Simon," he said with a warm smile. "I've been assigned to you and your office during your term here. Let me get your bags—a car is outside waiting."

"Thank you, Father." She handed him a duffel bag. "If

we're going to be working together on a daily basis, let's call each other by our first names. I'm Charlotte."

"Right, Charlotte. My name's John." Charlotte laughed, and he asked, "Is that a funny name?"

"Not at all. Just reminds me of a very good friend."

As they loaded up their car and began the drive to the Vatican, Charlotte and John got to know each other, though John was already quite aware of Charlotte and her history. Everyone at the Vatican knew she was coming. John was from St. Petersburg, Florida where he was raised by two highly religious parents, both schoolteachers in the Pinellas County district. He majored in mathematics and then attended the University of Central Florida, where he majored in accounting. He would be the perfect assistant for her.

With the Vatican's 136 departments, each of which tried to keep its operations private, and members of the cardinals curia trying to keep financials away from the public eye, it was going to be an operational and political challenge, so she needed all the help she could get. The pope's prime minister, Cardinal Brava, was against bringing in any audit firms capable of putting in place appropriate accounting systems. Charlotte feared he'd send her straight home.

As the car entered the north gates of the Vatican, Father Simon looked to her and said, "Monsignor Kotlinski, the holy father is waiting to see you."

"What?" Charlotte looked down at her clothes, wrinkled from the long flight. "I'm not the least bit presentable to see the pontiff." She at least had to put on some lipstick before any meetings.

John laughed. "You have an hour to freshen up before your meeting. Quite a way to start your stay, eh, Monsignor?"

He showed her to her room overlooking some of the Vatican's gardens. The room wasn't overly large, but it did have something not many were provided with: its own bathroom. As expected, the rooms were all stark, with simple walls and a small cross hanging. Charlotte hadn't slept well on the flight and she could feel the weight of her eyelids as she rifled through her suitcase. Maybe after she got cleaned up she could close her eyes for just five minutes...

A Change of Faith

Father Simon was prompt in knocking at her door exactly 45 minutes later. "The pontiff is ready to meet with you."

Charlotte had barely finished fixing her hair. She took a breath and closed her eyes. What am I doing here? she asked herself, anxiety rising in her chest as they walked together to the pope's private quarters. The apostolic palace was the official residence of the pope, also known as the papal palace, or as insiders call it, the Palace Of Sixtus V. The building contained the papal apartments, various offices of the Catholic Church and the holy see, a number of museums, and the Vatican library, which included the Sistine chapel. Though construction of the palace could be tracked back to the 15th century, construction of the current building began in 1589, with ongoing additions continuing into the 20th century.

Charlotte was led through an endless maze of ornate hallways, each magnificent in décor with renaissance paintings lining both sides. Windows were all at least eight feet high, some overlooking St. Peter's Square. Finally they arrived at the office the pope used for his personal meetings. Charlotte was seated before he arrived. She was expecting an ornate room with similar décor to that she saw during her walk, but looking around her, she saw the room was purposely stark, with little furniture or decor. Pope Peter Paul was a believer in keeping things as ordinary as possible. He didn't think himself better than any other priest, and he wanted whoever he was meeting to feel as comfortable as possible. He made it a point to eat at the cafeteria, and never alone. One day in an elevator, a young priest entered, stunned.

"Your holy father!" he stammered, starstruck.

The pope smiled. "Your holy son!"

A man dressed in black with tails entered and announced to Charlotte, "His holiness." Though the Pope would have preferred to just walk in, there were some traditions that simply couldn't be broken.

"Your holiness," said Charlotte, standing as he entered. He smiled warmly and all the anxiety in her dissipated.

"Please my dear monsignor, relax. We have much to do." He took a seat behind the desk. "And I'd like to get it all done before I might be gone. I admire how you've been able to handle your position as the first female monsignor of the church. To be quite frank, I'm not too sure your job hasn't been more challenging than mine. I know you're aware of the attempts made on my life. I greatly appreciate what has been done to protect me. But remember, it's not about my own life, but what could have happened if a new pope was elected. Please, when you speak to your friends, give them my thanks once again."

Charlotte could feel her heart pounding in her ribs. "Your holiness, I'll certainly pass along your thanks. It's truly an honor being here and having you consider me for this assignment. And you're right, there are mountains of work to be done."

"Charlotte…" The pope shook his head sadly. "You have no idea what really has to be done, and the barriers we will encounter. There are those who will do whatever they can to keep you away from their departments, and cardinals who will be most resentful of you. I have a small team in place you'll be part of, and offices have been set aside to help you complete your evaluation process of the different proposals. Don't be afraid of the resentment, just know your back will be covered, as they say in America."

"Thank you, your holiness," said Charlotte, nodding. She was quite familiar with resentment. "I promise I'll do everything to make sure we keep our goals in line. I'm sure the team you've assembled feels the same way."

The pope smiled. "You must be tired. Go rest and spend the next couple of days enjoying the Vatican's grounds. Soon you will be very busy and your head will be nailed to the grindstone. God bless you!"

Charlotte rose and kissed the sacred papal ring. The pope's smile gave her comfort, as if he were a long-lost friend.

XXV

It was the beginning of May, and John was coordinating the details of his proposal. He'd already booked the Grand Hotel for a couple of days in June and asked Maria to see if she could get time off work. Though Tony rolled his eyes when she came to ask him for the vacation time, he granted her request with a heart full of pride.

The car ride would take about four hours, giving the couple plenty of time to talk and enjoy each other's company, something relatively rare between their busy careers. In Mackinaw City, they boarded the ferry and headed to the island. The ride took 20 minutes, and once there, the horse carriages would pick up their bags and take them up to the hotel. As expected, once walking off the ferry, the fresh aroma of fudge and horseshit floated by. Fortunately, being a Monday, the hotel and island were quiet.

John had nothing scheduled for the day. He just wanted to relax with Maria, walk the streets of the island and have dinner at the hotel's jockey club, a small but well-appointed dining room finished in dark mahogany and green leather chairs and booths. Their stay would be in the lilac suite, which had a marvelous view of the straits of Mackinac. Somewhere in Time, starring Jane Seymour and Christopher Reeve, was filmed at the hotel in 1981. The place felt like a historical monument.

John and Maria meandered about the hotel lounge

meeting visitors from various states, even a couple from Ireland. The next day would be big. John enjoyed a Petoskey stone gin martini both shaken and stirred, which helped soothe his nerves. But as he began to understand what tomorrow would bring, he realized he might need two drinks that night.

The next morning, strolling down to the restaurant for breakfast, John received a call from Michael. "Hey Michael, what's going on this wonderful Tuesday morning?"

"Did James get in touch with you?"

"No…why do I hear something different in your voice?"

Michael was probably supposed to let James break the news, but he couldn't keep a secret. "The Bovier Gallery called yesterday and made a decision about exhibiting your work." John's heart dropped. "They're eliminating the fall exhibit for the six artists and want you to have a one-man exhibit."

His mouth fell open. Maria pulled on his arm, worried. "Honey, what is it? Is everything okay? What'd he say?"

"It's…it's the Bovier Gallery in New York, baby. They want me to have a one-man exhibition. Michael, when were they talking about having this show?"

"They were still considering this fall. Do you have enough work to exhibit?"

"I don't know. Let me call you later, I'm at breakfast now. Thanks, Michael."

Maria could see the excitement and apprehension in John's face. "Baby, that's amazing news, isn't it?"

"It is, but I need enough work to support such a show…guess this summer just got very busy. Be careful what you ask for, right?"

After breakfast they walked down a slightly sloped road to the main part of town, where they rented two bikes and pedaled the seven-mile meandering road along the water. It was a beautiful early summer day requiring just light sweaters. They slowly rode past a number of old Victorian homes and Fort Mackinac, a stoic white structure constructed in the late 1700s by British troops providing safety to residents from French military boats sailing through the straits.

About two miles out of town, John stopped to check out a view from some of the limestone rock structures. As he walked around and Maria waited on her bike, he finally called to her. "Maria, come on up and let's take a few photos." Maria wasn't big on walking up a makeshift path, but she agreed. Turning a small bend, she heard the sound of a violin. In front of her was a table set with beautiful china, a chef standing by.

"John, what the heck is this?" she asked, laughing.

As the violin played and the chef popped a bottle of Dom Perignon, John eased to one knee and said the magic words. "Maria Gardelli, there are a few times in life when you feel something very special happen. When I first saw you at Brady's, something inside me said I better not let this opportunity go. Baby, I can't let this opportunity go. So I'm asking you now: will you marry me?"

Maria couldn't stop giggling, her hands covering her mouth. "John Adams, you stinker. Of course I will!"

John stood, and they kissed deeply. Looking over the waters, they enjoyed a personal meal with soft music, candles, flowers, wonderful whitefish and a grand bottle of Dom Perignon.

"I love you so, so much," Maria said dreamily, her chin in her hand. "I can't wait to get married."

"Me too, baby."

"Oh my god, I have to call my parents," she said suddenly, pulling her phone out of her purse. "Do they have any idea?"

John smiled. "I met with your father to ask him for his approval." He placed his hand over her phone, lowering it to the table. "Let's take our time and enjoy this moment. The view is wonderful."

The next day was as if they were on their first date all over again, smiling and giggling uncontrollably as they enjoyed the beautiful island. Maria called her parents and tried to give them grief about keeping a secret from her, but she was just too excited and happy to play any other part.

With a one-man exhibit in September, John had a lot

of work ahead of him. More than ever before. He had 11 pieces, and the gallery wanted 20. But he didn't want to paint just for an exhibit. A very good friend once told him, "John, paint for yourself!" He decided to guarantee the 11 he had and provide more only if he liked what he painted. If the gallery found that offer unacceptable, then he would have to pass on the opportunity altogether. People would think he was crazy, but he knew Charlotte would approve.

XXVI

Monsignor Kotlinski had been at the Vatican for four months. The experience made the politics in Washington D.C. look like kindergarten. Reviewing and interviewing a potential auditing firm was the easy part, but putting up with the internal politics was miserable. The church had hundreds of people working at the Vatican, and cardinals and their staffs were putting up walls wherever they could. They didn't want change. Charlotte constantly had doors slammed in her face. In fact, she and her staff turned it into a game of wits: who would be today's problem, and how would they handle it?

A percentage of the cardinals were still bitter that women were allowed to become priests, but because that vote happened years ago, many of these cardinals had passed away, and new appointees were more progressive in their thinking. Charlotte was looked at as a rock star by some, and a very unwanted change by others. With so many new women who were going to be ordained beginning this year, it would be all but impossible to retract the law.

Beyond the financial issues, some strange things were happening. Within a couple of months there had been two mysterious deaths of young priests from Columbia who both seemed to be quite healthy people. A tight monitoring system was put in place to make sure the three cardinals who'd been removed from their offices weren't involved. The best bet was from the Middle East and Iran once again. But did the terrorist group that wanted the pope assassinated have any help? There were certainly those determined to eliminate Pope Peter Paul, but how far would they go, and how? Because of the significance of the issue, the only people made aware of the probable murders were the pope and his two chiefs of staff. The deaths were being publicized as accidental, but that story wouldn't hold forever.

The relationship between the Italian mafia and the papal office had always been significant. The head of Vatican security had a direct contact in Rome when problems had to be investigated and issues resolved. Don Gianetti was a lifelong police officer and was appointed Chief of Security overseeing all Vatican security. His uncle, Geno Garza, was well-connected with the mafia in Rome and in the Casamonicci family, a crime family that had been operating for almost 100 years. There were approximately 45 crime families operating in the greater region of Rome, and the Casamoniccis were one of the three most powerful.

An additional problem now was that the Mafia Capitale, which consisted of crooked politicians, city employees and a variety of unscrupulous businessmen, had been in collusion with far-right terrorist groups. This group skimmed millions of dollars each year from municipal projects and ruled with an iron fist. These groups, though they outwardly got along, had little trust in one another and rarely agreed to meet to negotiate their income streams.

As Don Gianetti began his investigation a month earlier following the two deaths, he'd narrowed down the search to a couple of suspicious employees working directly in the Vatican. One was a priest from Turkey assigned to the deputy secretary general's office who had been working there for the past 16 months. He was known to disappear weekly to various locations around Rome for hours at a time. The Vatican security office began tracking his meetings and discovered he was showing up at the same location every time with another man who worked at the Vatican and was employed by the auditor's office. When the security office requested background checks with Europol (European Police Office), which handled serious organized crime and terrorism, they discovered both men spent six months in Syria three years previous to their employment.

These reports created grave concern. The men both had significant positions, giving them access to many people and much potentially harmful information that could ultimately lead to more deaths. It would be important to investigate these men to find contacts and hopefully the higher-ups who were making these deadly decisions. A plan would be put in place to investigate the men, but it would require some help.

The pope's senior officer, Bishop Sanchez, was the only one notified of the situation. He would keep the pope informed as information was gathered. Monsignor Kotlinski, now a personal advisor to the pope's office, was being considered to aid in the investigation, since one of the two suspicious players worked in the auditor's office.

As for Don Gianetti, he was being quiet. He knew the information his extended contacts were beginning to turn up wasn't good. Apparently the deaths of the two Colombian priests was a smokescreen for a plan to eliminate the pope himself. Nothing Charlotte had been involved with since her ordination would compare to the events now developing in the papal offices. If the pope was in fact assassinated, his replacement would likely put an end to female priests and install ordinances leading to changes in Catholicism that would skew the true meaning of the Bible. Don had to decide if he would require outside help. This of course meant the possibility of information leakage as each new security contact could be a potential source of unwanted threats. He had to be careful who he brought into the loop.

Charlotte, along with her small staff, continued to work on their review of the Vatican's accounting procedures. It made procedures in the pentagon look like math 101. Political roadblocks were everywhere, and a consistent accounting formula would take years to implement. Nobody could ever figure out the finances and balance sheets of the Catholic Church because, unlike an audited public company, the Church never wanted to know—until now. Charlotte and her team would complete their review over the next three months and submit their recommendations to the papal office. Once the selected auditors were under contract, she would spend the next year coordinating the reviews.

Security at the papal office was doubled; few could be

trusted. Fortunately, Don Gianetti got through and was able to meet with his holiness to discuss the assassination rumors. His sources were reliable and indicated there were people at the top of the Church ready to implement the process of voting for a new pope. Certain cardinals, bishops and staff members were prepared to make a new papal election happen quickly; a preselected cardinal was already identified. In response, Pope Peter Paul recommended to Don that he bring NSA Director William Beauchamp into the loop; he trusted his abilities. He also wanted someone more intimate with all the suspects, someone he could trust as much as he trusted Bishop Sanchez.

The next morning Archbishop Morley received a surprise call from the papal office asking him to set aside some time for a call with Peter Paul. The pope trusted Archbishop Morley and openly discussed the assassination plot one detail at a time.

"I'd like you to be a part of my team on this," the pope said, "and I want to add another resource, too—someone qualified to coordinate with Don a strategy to track down and expose those who want me eliminated. Someone intimate with the American security resources."

The archbishop knew exactly who Peter Paul was talking about. The next day, Monsignor Kotlinski would be meeting again with the pope.

XXVII

As John and Maria coordinated their upcoming wedding, they both found it hard to keep from smiling all the time.

"What are you so happy about?" people asked Maria at work. "Did I miss the joke?"

She'd reach up to touch her cheeks, surprised to find she had in fact been smiling. Actually, the sides of her face hurt. At night as she leaned into John on the sofa, bridal magazines and fabric swatches encircling them, Maria's head and heart felt full of bubbles, full of love. There were only a few minor setbacks in the planning process: first, they didn't want to wait until after John's New York exhibition in the fall to have the wedding. They weren't getting any younger, and they wanted to start a family. Secondly, they wanted a small wedding, an idea that would be ludicrous to Maria's traditional Italian parents, who'd prefer a large wedding and an even larger reception. As a sort of compromise, John and Maria decided to have a small ceremony somewhere outside the Midwest and let the parents have the reception whenever and wherever they'd like. Now to break the news to the Gardellis!

Maria approached her dad at work and took a deep breath. It's my wedding, she reminded herself sternly.

"Dad," she said tentatively, "John and I were discussing wedding plans and have a suggestion we hope you and Mom will agree to. John's fall exhibition is very important to his career and our future; he has six paintings to complete before the show—"

Tony lifted his hand gently to stop her. "Don't worry —Mom and I have spoken about it. Your ceremony is your choice, but yes, we would like to coordinate a reception at the yacht club where we can invite family and friends. Where are you thinking about having the ceremony?"

"Eloping to Vegas would be easiest," she began, to which she saw something inside her father's eyes catch fire. "But we couldn't get ourselves to do that," she added quickly. "We found a small island in the Florida Keys we thought would be perfect. It has a resort where guests can stay."

"Have you settled on a date?"

"The island is available next month on the third weekend, giving us five weeks to coordinate everything. I hope you both understand."

"Of course, honey. After John's show we'll have a larger reception at the yacht club."

Maria smiled. She knew it was frustrating for her parents to see her stray from tradition. "Thanks, Dad. You're the best."

The next morning Pope Peter Paul called Monsignor Kotlinski to his office. Charlotte had met with the pope a few times now and was beginning to feel more comfortable in his presence, as intimidating as these meetings could be. The pope was officially introduced, and Charlotte stood up.

"Sit, Monsignor Kotlinski," Pope Peter Paul began. He folded his hands on his desk and searched for the right words. "We've had a short history together that I guess we could consider quite colorful and at the same time quite stressful, no?"

She nodded. "Absolutely."

"Well, we still have events taking place that require some more help. I've been working with our security teams and am satisfied with their work. But after what I've been exposed to, I've decided to bring in some outside resources to expand our investigations and hopefully put to bed this little problem."

"Your holiness, if I may... why am I here? What can I

offer to help take care of whatever the issue may be?"

"Monsignor, you have one of the suspects working in your office. You also happen to know intimately some of the Americans I'd like to bring onboard for help. In order to give you the control required to demand help both internally and externally, we have to change your title. Today I am making the decision to elevate you to a bishop of the Church. You would be highly considered for this position once Bishop Foley retires, so we're just stepping up the inevitable. It's an unusually expedient promotion, but, such are the times we live in."

"Your holiness," Charlotte stammered, caught off guard, "I'm not sure what to say. Your enemies will become even angrier when this news spreads."

"Oh, we're counting on that," said the pope with a small smile. "We believe it will expedite their plan to eliminate me. With proper people and monitoring methods in place, we think we can expose all the conspirators sooner than later. I'm not as concerned about my own life as much as I am about their plans. Now go—we'll all begin working together immediately. And congratulations, Bishop Kotlinski."

"Thank you, your holiness. This is quite a unique way of receiving a promotion." The pope chuckled as Charlotte left the room.

Unlike her promotion to Monsignor, which brought excitement and joy, this conversation left Charlotte with mixed emotions. She knew she should be happy, but knowing the game plan of the papal office, she was left in a bittersweet mood. She worried for the pope's safety. She considered calling home to share the news of her promotion, but it was still very early in Michigan. Anyway, how would she explain the promotion? Should she wait until after speaking with the papal PR office and getting their point of view? Charlotte was finding herself becoming more and more famous, no matter how she tried to remain anonymous. Not only was the pope's safety at risk, she thought, but with all her publicity, those who killed the other vicars would be easily motivated to take her life. A sudden panic swept over her. Was she in danger, too?

In a rented room on the other side of Rome stood a

man gazing intensely into a mirror. He was in his mid-40s with a lean body, a shaved head that was once blonde, and very cold green eyes. Though his "profession" was an IT engineer, in reality he was a for-hire assassin. A client had recently retained his services to eliminate the new female bishop in Rome. Over the past few years he had already taken the lives of Vicars Anderson and McPherson. Killing someone was just a job; he bore no emotion when it came to taking a life. In fact, he took pride in his skills. He rarely left evidence at the scene of the murder unless he wanted to put the authorities on edge.

How would he end the life of the newly appointed Bishop? He was supposed to make the killing impactful, with a message to all other female priests or women thinking about becoming one. He was excited about the opportunity, as most of his crimes were done very quietly. Finding her somewhere in the immediate Vatican area would certainly leave that message.

In the distance he heard the loud clamor of church bells. A sense of peace washed over him as he closed his eyes, reaching into his pocket and taking out a long switchblade. The sound of the bells was euphoric. He moved to the window, brushing aside the curtain so he could look out on Rome in all her beauty, her narrow streets spreading every which way like the blood vessels of a dry eye. So many alleys and dead ends. So many dark places to stumble down and become lost.

As the church bells tolled, he pictured Bishop Kotlinski in the next room, getting ready to go out for her evening espresso before an all-nighter at work.

The sun close to setting, he went and pressed his ear against the wall: yes, she was almost ready, a zipper running up her coat. Several minutes ago he had heard the pipes creaking with water as she showered. Then came the familiar sound of the blow dryer and her frustration as it blew the circuit. He heard the circuit panel opening, a switch turning, and her muttering something in English as the lights came back on. Now, the door was opening. There were footsteps in the hall.

He already had on his coat.

He waited until the footsteps disappeared, then ducked out of his room and went in the opposite stairwell, clutching the knife in his pocket. He flipped his hood up and opened the door, a wash of failing sunlight hitting his eyes as he stepped onto the cobblestone street in a convergence of noise: the bells, motorbikes, beeping cars, and footsteps on stone.

His eyes scanned the crowd, quickly settling on the lone woman walking defiantly across the street. He followed her, careful to remain just far enough away. Sometimes he lost sight of her, but she always resurfaced. She went down one side street, then another, and the church bells grew louder.

The man branched right, quickly jogging the distance around the building and entering a narrow alleyway behind a butcher's shop. The sun setting, the bells now screaming, he quietly took off his shoes and socks, opened his switchblade, and crouched in the shadows beside a trash can.

Footsteps emerged. Charlotte was walking down the alley. The bells were so close and so loud he barely heard her. But she was there, walking past without noticing him, flipping her hair to one side. His feet padding the naked stone behind her, he crept up noiselessly, the knife gripped in his hand. She craned her head as if she sensed his presence: then he lightly held a shock of her hair and slashed the knife.

Charlotte felt a slight tug and her heart stopped. She whipped around, but there was no one in the alley. No one but her. Feeling disturbed, she quickened her pace, all but jogging out of the alley. She felt a sense of dread propelling her. When she reached the street, she looked back. No one was there.

Hiding in the darkness, the man held a piece of her hair. His body was trembling with the thrill of it all. He quickly put on his socks and shoes and went back to his apartment building. Using a Bogota rake, he easily picked the lock to Charlotte's door. He went inside for the fifth time in so many days, closing his eyes and breathing her sweet scent. He laid the hair on her nightstand where she was sure to find it. Then he went back to his room, standing at the window and opening his switchblade repeatedly. Waiting, dreaming, planning.

XXVIII

Don Gianetti was asked to contact the office of William Beauchamp and ask for his support in exposing those who wanted to kill the pope. The NSA had a vast database of terrorists, which could immediately be made available to his offices. William would bring in Brett Patterson and the ITA without anyone's knowledge. Individuals would be detected, interviews (more direct then waterboarding) would take place, and elimination would ensue. The NSA, along with Don's contacts among mafia families, secured a secret surveillance system throughout Rome.

"Little time to celebrate your promotion, eh?" Bishop Kotlinski's colleague said with a smile as they flipped through tables of paperwork. It was nearing midnight, the dim orange overhead lights doing little to keep the two lively.

"Celebration is a luxury reserved for the idle," Charlotte replied flatly, plastering on a smile of her own. But it wasn't real. She felt utterly scared, though she didn't know why. It was like someone was watching her every move. She felt undressed, vulnerable. Only hours ago she had been in an alley where she could swear she heard footsteps. But when she looked around, no one was there. Was she imagining things now?

The audit review proposals were now taking place,

and a decision was soon to be made on which firm to retain. It would take two years for the initial implementation, and at least two more of installations and procedures. This system had to incorporate across the globe a very tasking objective.

"No rest for the wicked," the man replied vaguely. Charlotte tried for a moment to make sense of his comment, but quickly dismissed it as idle chit-chat designed simply to fill the quiet space between them.

The man was an IT consultant, but he'd graciously offered his time to help her go through paperwork. He was an expert at finding things, he'd told her.

At one in the morning, after they'd finally finished and were putting on their coats, the man offered to walk her home. She looked at him, with his strange green eyes, his shaved head. There was something off about the man. Something strange. He seemed overly eager. She decided whatever the reason, this wasn't someone she wanted to be around after hours.

"I'm fine," she said. "Thanks though."

"You sure?" he smiled, his eyes darting to the window behind her. "All sorts of scary things out there. Never know what you might stumble upon."

"I appreciate it, but really, I'm fine. Have yourself a great night."

"You as well, Bishop Kotlinski." She felt his eyes on her as she left the room.

She was being too paranoid, she thought. He was just a nice man who wanted to walk her home. Why had she acted like that? Since her promotion last week, all she could see were bogeymen and monsters hiding in every shadow.

Back in her room, she hung her coat and went to the bathroom, splashing cold water on her face. Then she put on her robe and went to the kitchenette, putting on the kettle for some hot tea before bed. Getting in bed with a book, she switched on the light. Her heart stopped.

As the kettle boiled, she spotted a shock of dark hair. She felt the back of her head.

The kettle screamed.

William, Brett and James flew into Rome to meet with Don and his three contacts. In all, there were seven attending the meeting.

"Gentlemen," Don began, standing. He was a brute of a man, but short, like a small powerful bear with black hair everywhere but on his head. He had soft, pudgy cheeks and bright eyes which radiated cunning. He introduced each participant and gave a brief overview of their positions. When he introduced his three contacts, their summaries were quite brief—but everyone understood their capabilities.

"It's a pleasure to be here working with you, however unfortunate the circumstances," said William. "When Don first contacted us about participating in this problem, we were a bit hesitant... but with the blessing of the president, we're here to help in any way possible. We've confirmed that a plan to eliminate the pope is being coordinated out of areas in Iraq. We have a good idea who the ultimate lead is, and possibly his location. Our goal is to eliminate not only him, but his captains and lieutenants at the same time, hopefully leaving a message for anyone else who might be having similar thoughts.

"This isn't about the murder of a pope, it's about having one of their own elected, giving radicals more influence on decisions being made in the Catholic faith. There's a cardinal in place who's been groomed for this position and will begin a complete twist on the Catholic faith if elected. We believe we have less than two weeks."

Everyone began to chime in, and information was soon crossing paths across the table, the volume rising in the room. Don sat back and smiled, surprised by the professionalism and the amount of information the government agents had. The hour-long meeting went to three, and everyone agreed to meet again in two days. There was much to discuss.

Though James was tired from the travel and the extended meeting, he was anxious to see the new bishop from Detroit. He contacted her office and set up a dinner with her that evening. At 7:30 they met at the main dining room. Charlotte now had a driver to take her to meetings. She was dressed in a long green skirt with a dark sweater accentuating her hair and eyes. She didn't look like any bishop James would ever meet again.

"James," she said, smiling as she extended her hand.

A Change of Faith

"I can't tell you how wonderful it is to see you! How are you? We have tons to catch up on. Please, tell me everything about everyone."

James could see the loneliness in her eyes and tried to make his voice as chipper as possible for her sake. "Charlotte…" he beamed, then, confused, "or should I say Bishop Kotlinski? Congratulations!" He gave her a bear hug. "I tell ya, you're one hell of a woman. Bishop? Everyone back home is so proud of you. When you get back there's going to be a giant party waiting for you."

They took their seats at a corner table. James ordered a bottle of Valpollecci wine accompanied by a small cheese plate. He knew what Charlotte really wanted was an update on John, his exhibition in New York, and of course Maria, but James first filled her in on the condition of Archbishop Morley, who'd spent the last six days at Henry Ford Hospital for a heart condition. "He's feeling good, but I wouldn't be surprised if he requests an early retirement. I think if you can wrap up your work here you'd be considered for his position. Unless this position at the Vatican is something you'd prefer to keep… forever?"

Charlotte blushed. Again, she felt out of her depth, like she'd been thrust into a world she didn't really know. "The experience here is something you dream about when you're putting those long hours in at the seminary," she began, searching for the right words. "But I would love to go home. I can't tell you how nice it is to reconnect. It feels like home came to Rome for one night, so… thank you. But there are issues going on with the pontiff. Some of them right in my own department."

James looked down, saddened the conversation took this turn. But he knew it had to. "We're here to see if we can't find a way to put that exact problem aside. Without going into detail, I can tell you there aren't any resources not being used to help him. Things will be happening shortly, but for now, let's just try and catch up, yeah? How about I give you an update on our favorite neighborhood artist?" Charlotte brightened at that, so he went on, "Over the past 18 months he seems to have become one of the hottest international talents."

All thoughts of assassination plots and homesickness and political turmoil and fear dissolved, and in spite of herself,

Charlotte broke into a beaming grin. "He's doing well, then?"

"Better than well. His exhibition in New York was an absolute sensation. He exhibited 15 paintings and sold three before the exhibit even opened. It was a sellout, Charlotte. The phones are ringing from all over the world asking for his work. His paintings were selling for 50 thousand dollars at that show. 50. I'm not even sure where the limit is anymore. My friend Patricia from the International Arts Magazine pulled me aside and said she hasn't seen something like this since Jackson Pollock. Can you believe it? Jackson Pollock, Charlotte."

"Wow," she said, warmth swelling in her chest. She was so fiercely happy for John. But there was something else, too. Was it a sin to love someone and be a bishop? "I saw he and Maria had their wedding down in the Keys with just close friends and family. No big Italian wedding? Give me the scoop!" she demanded, flawlessly playing the part of interested friend.

"John would have wanted you to perform the services," James said slowly, but they both knew it would have been a dagger in her heart. "The ceremony was simple with about 40 guests. A steel drum band played, and of course with Maria's family the archbishop of the Miami Diocese was flown in to perform the ceremony. The reception was relaxing, just what you'd expected from John and Maria. Of course, the Gardellis insisted on having a much larger formal reception at the Grossest Pointe Yacht Club, where 500 of their friends were invited. John sucked it up for the day, but he would've preferred hanging with his buddies on the pontoon, no doubt. Maria was stunning," James added.

"I'm sure she was!" said Charlotte, forcing a tight smile.

"They also bought a house," James said.

She frowned. "Wow. Really?"

James nodded. "An older Tudor in the East English Village not far from the Eastern Market. It's a canal-front four-bedroom, but it'll require some TLC."

"Wow," mused Charlotte. Stop saying wow, she scolded herself. "So they got rid of the studio?"

James shook his head. "They couldn't—too much history. Plus John finds peace painting there. Tony's offered to install proper security systems in each location since John's newfound fame."

"And now they can begin a family?"

"Well, you wouldn't marry a beautiful Italian woman without thinking about a family!"

Little did James and Charlotte know, Maria was already three months pregnant.

After they finished their meal, James escorted Charlotte to the front door of the hotel where her ride was waiting for her. She left feeling happy and melancholy at the same time. The man she could have been with was now married and leading his own life; it hurt. It shouldn't have, but it did.

"Do you need any help, Bishop?" Charlotte's driver asked over his shoulder. Charlotte sat upright, lost in the darkness. Had she fallen asleep or just switched her mind off?

"Oh, I'm sorry, George. I didn't realize we'd arrived." She began gathering her things from the seat beside her, slinging her purse over her shoulder.

"Is everything alright, Bishop?" George asked after a pregnant pause.

Charlotte opened the door and hesitated, the cool night air rushing in against her legs. "Sort of, but not really at all, no. Thank you, George."

She closed the door and headed up the cobblestone path, the crunch of tires on gravel starting up and then growing faint behind her. A security guard greeted her at the door. She had told her superiors about the stalking episode. They'd immediately moved her to another apartment in a safer neighborhood and installed a guard. She smiled at him in greeting. Then they walked together up to her apartment, where he waited outside the door.

She looked out the window, thinking vaguely of John. Then a memory occurred to her. A terrible memory of a man in a crowd with blond hair and deep green eyes. Staring at her. She had seen that face before, just the other day.

Dear, God, she thought.

She picked up her phone and dialed.

XXIX

William's heart banged against his chest as he dialed James' number first, then Brett's. Before the meeting with Don and the rest of the group later that day, he wanted an emergency conference with only James and Brett. As the two arrived at William's hotel, his eyes, stern and afraid, immediately alarmed his guests.

"What?" James asked, his nerves rising as he and Brett sat down. William remained standing, pacing tiny laps back and forth between two kitchen chairs.

"Guys, overnight I received a concerning call," he said. "Apparently when Pope Peter Paul was in Detroit, after mass at Sweetest Heart of Mary, Charlotte told one of the secret service agents she noticed a man there who gave her the chills. Once the pope went home, Charlotte was asked to come in and review the people in attendance. As the congregation left, she noticed a man who was just about to put his sunglasses on. This is the same guy who's recently been appointed to Charlotte's team at the Vatican. Coincidence? Then she says the other day she was being stalked. She now believes it was him."

"Bill," interrupted Brett, speaking slowly, "I hope you're not going in the direction I think you are."

"I'm afraid I am. His name is Brian Stevens, and though quite legitimate on paper, he has moments when we're completely unable to identify where he's been. He didn't show up to work today, we assume because somehow he knows she knows. Two weeks ago, Interpol identified him under an alias coming into Rome. I'm afraid this is our man, the same one responsible for the deaths of Vicars Anderson and McPherson. I'm not sure how much time we have to find him, but Bishop Kotlinski's life is at risk. Great risk."

James and Brett watched intently as William continued his pacing.

"The two weeks we thought we had is now condensed to days. I'll be notifying Don this morning about the situation and have more security placed around Charlotte. Brett, is this something I can put you and your group on for now?"

"Glad to take care of it," Brett said harshly, an air of darkness falling over the room. "Got eight team members already in town, four more coming today. We'd be more than happy to take out a crumb like this. We'll work with the security groups and begin a surveillance. Knowing this type of personality, he'll want to kill in a location that'll relate to the Church, I'd guess somewhere in the Vatican. I'll round up my troops within the hour."

William stopped walking and looked at him sternly. "Hurry."

That afternoon the entire group, save for Brett, met for the second time and began a full dig into the potential members of the assassination group, including the two already in the Vatican offices. An initial list of six individuals currently in Rome were the lead prospects, with almost 20 outside the country coordinating the assassination plans.

"There's also someone new," William said to the group, laying down a sheet of paper containing the information. "This individual mysteriously showed up from Turkey just yesterday. I recommend he be eliminated quickly; he's a known radical assassin."

Without hesitation, Sergio Francus from the Pessitti family lifted his hand. "We will take care of the issue," he said, his face and voice entirely calm.

Charlotte kept focused as much as possible. If she

wasn't elbow deep in her work, she was worrying about the pope's safety, and quite frankly, her own. The accounting proposals were submitted and reviewed, and a decision would be made that week. On their way out of the office, Charlotte's colleague turned to her and smiled. Unlike Charlotte, he was relieved to have the work finished.

"Almost vacation time, eh, Bishop?" he said sleepily. Once a decision was made, Charlotte was planning a two-week vacation back home to visit her family, friends and parishes. And if she happened to see John, so be it.

Their footsteps padded through the empty marble halls, moonlight slicing in through a high stained-glass window as two guards followed at her elbow. Charlotte followed the beam of light up to the window, which depicted Jesus nailed upon the cross, his head hanging down.

"Almost time," she agreed.

But she was thinking of something else entirely.

Located just steps from the Vatican stood the Hearth Hotel, where Brian Stevens checked in the morning after his brush with Bishop Kotlinski. He immediately went for an extended walk into St. Peters, facility map in hand.

Lost among the sea of tourists, Stevens had little interest in any of the normal art exhibits like Michelangelo's Pieta or the Bernini main altar. Instead, he snapped photos of doorways, signage and exit points. While he appeared a normal visitor taking photos of normal attractions, he was plotting the details of a horrific plan. He was quite the actor, nodding and smiling at friendly faces in the crowd, dark glasses concealing his eyes. He'd even gone out and bought a new pair of white New Balance sneakers that he felt would make him appear more… fatherly. Harmless. Boring. They were also excellent for running, and he knew he'd be doing a great deal of that in the hours ahead.

He looked down at his new shoes, suddenly conscious of how outrageously white they were. They'd be sure to attract some attention. He glanced around in search of some dirt to shuffle through, but all the roads were cobblestone. Fountains trickled into concrete basins. Flowers grew in high wooden window boxes. No dirt. He bit his lower lip, looking around.

"Hey, mister!"

Brian froze. Here it was. All his years of flawless work, and these damn white shoes would be his demise.

"Mind taking a picture?"

A round, sunburned man held a camera towards Stevens, who smiled and took it. A woman in a straw hat and two smallish boys grinned at him, waiting. "Of course," he said, but he sounded annoyed.

As he brought his eye to the viewfinder and looked out at the family, he noticed the man's shoes, identical to his own: New Balance sneakers, white as snow. Stevens smiled wide.

Click.

Encouraged, he continued his stroll through the city. His plan was to find an appropriate time and place where he could find Bishop Kotlinski and complete his contract. He was informed she would be leaving on a vacation within the next few days, so time was limited. He knew she had a normal routine but was specifically interested in what she did when the doors were closed and security a bit laxer. His little incident had worked perfectly: after initiating the scare, Charlotte had moved to a new place, this one right within the confines of the Vatican. It made for a very public execution; the very kind he was ordered to commit.

It was now Tuesday, and if things went according to plan, Thursday evening would be Charlotte's last. She would be asked to attend a revision audit review at 7:00 p.m. at the central auditor's office. In most cases, these offices were quite empty, all the help gone for the day. The office was just off one of the main corridors which led to the Sistine Chapel. The hallway was quite ornate, lined with renaissance paintings from Caravaggio, Giotto, Titian and Raphael, tall vaulted ceilings trimmed in dark mahogany and gold leaf. It would be the perfect location to display his work. He knew two guards now accompanied her at all times, but they wouldn't be a problem. He would knock on the door dressed as a cardinal. In his robes would be a drawn gun, as well as numerous knives, each serving a different purpose.

It would be embarrassingly easy. It always was.

That evening William received a call from Sergio Francus of the Pessitti Family. He asked to see him immediately about Bishop Kotlinski. William requested Brett join him since it would be his team assigned to take care of the issue. The three met at an espresso café located on a quiet side street not far from the hotel.

"Mr. Beauchamp," Sergio said hastily, "Bishop Kotlinski's life will be taken Thursday night in the Vatican."

"What?" William gasped, impressed Sergio and his connections found out so quickly. "Are you certain?"

Sergio nodded.

"Sergio, we have to put a plan in place to prevent this. Tell us what you know."

"We planted someone with the people involved. He learned they have a plan Thursday night with Charlotte, ending with the assassination of the pope next week. Our first goal is to save Bishop Kotlinski. They want to exhibit her remains in the hallway leading to the Sistine chapel."

William and Brett exchanged an uncomfortable glance. Words like "next week" and "remains" made this all very real, and they were suddenly feeling the pressure more than ever before. Like so many Christians brutally killed in the Middle East and elsewhere, now these murderers wanted to exhibit their violence in the holiest hallways of the Catholic faith.

"What will you gentlemen be having?" a tall, dark waiter asked as he approached the table, pen waiting on his paper.

"Nothing, nothing, go," Brett said hurriedly, waving the man away. He rushed off, disgruntled. Brett spoke quietly. "Sergio, we know who the assassin is. We were able to track his identity via our contacts in Washington. But do we know where he's staying?"

"We know exactly where he is, down to his room number. We recommend he be eliminated Thursday. Tomorrow you must set up surveillance." Sergio gave them the hotel name and room number.

Afterwards, Brett went to work organizing the next day's surveillance mission with eight ITA members. Under normal circumstances something like this would only require two or maybe four team members, but because of the killer's portfolio, they knew he would be attentive and skeptical of everything around him. If something out of place caught his attention, he'd have multiple exit routes. The ITA members had to make sure they had all potential exit routes covered. The goal would be to capture him, but they knew from experience someone like Brian Stevens would rather be killed than caught.

The next day all eight members took positions around the Hearth Hotel at every exit point, with two across the street monitoring Brian's room. At 10:00 a.m. Stevens left the front door of the hotel and headed on a short walk up a side street. Everyone watched closely, weapons aimed and ready, as he slipped into a doorway of a nondescript apartment building. While he was being monitored and the doors to the apartment watched, two ITA members slipped into his room through an exterior window and installed two bug cameras before sneaking back out. They knew that Stevens, being a professional, would have a device monitoring his door in case it was opened.

After 40 minutes, Stevens left the apartment and headed back to his room. With a high-caliber rifle, the members could easily have taken aim and eliminated their assassin, but once word got out, red flags would go up with all the other perpetrators, and the probability of catching them would drop dramatically. They were going to wait until Thursday, unless he made an attempt on the bishop's life before then.

Sergio and his two friends from the other families then had another meeting with William and James.

"Gentlemen," he said, "we're about to identify the list of people wanting to take the pope's life. You're aware of the three cardinals from the past who began the problem. The extended list consists of nine individuals directly involved, two of the existing cardinals and two new ones. The two new cardinals are Cardinal Rhône from Zambia and Cardinal Berdigon from Turkey. It's Berdigon who would likely be the newly elected pope. The others are the two priests already located in the Vatican, two captains in the palace guard, and finally our friend in charge of Vatican security, Don Gianetti himself.

"It's Gianetti and the two palace captains of the guard who have arranged to have Bishop Kotlinski arrive at her fictitious meeting. Why are these insiders involved? Money, too much money to refuse. The cardinals would have their new pope elected, and the other cardinals would request a revote on the religious rules declining female priests. We feel that all involved should be taken in tomorrow. We'll have a couple of talkers once they're arrested."

William's heart was racing. "Gentlemen," he said, dazed by the overload of information, "if this is all true, especially about Don Gianetti—"

"Excuse me, William," interrupted Sergio as he slid three photos across the table, "these photos were taken today at a small apartment building near St. Peters. As you will notice, the first photo is our murderer, Mr. Stevens, leaving the apartment at 10:45. Shortly after that are another two photos of Don Gianetti leaving the same building."

"Well, I only have one question."

"Of course, William."

"Would you consider taking a pay cut and joining the NSA?"

They all smiled for a moment.

"Gentlemen, I have to inform the president of this," said Sergio, and the smiles fell away. "Because we know of the men involved and their locations in Iraq and Syria, I'm sure he'll want them eliminated with drone strikes at the same time our actions take place. This will become an international news event. We'll make sure to have the appropriate Italian law enforcement in place to take full credit for the arrests and ongoing surveillance. Our goal will be to complete the actions and leave town immediately. Of course, none of us have ever met."

"Of course," they echoed.

"So it is done," Sergio said.

The men nodded. But they did not feel it was done. It hadn't even begun.

XXX

The next morning all involved gathered, including NSA department members, Interpol, ITA and two of William's old friends from the Italian Internal Information and Security Agency. Italian law enforcement is known to be corrupt, but William trusted his two old friends. They'd give everyone a way to disappear as they took credit for the operation and became the focus of the press.

At exactly 1:00, each person was found and arrested. The process was quite easy, as none of the conspirators, including Don Gianetti, were the least bit suspicious. Cardinals Rhône and Berdigon happened to be at lunch together and put up the most resistance; after all, they were cardinals of the Catholic Church, untouchable.

"This is hilarious! A joke!" Rhône shouted as he was dragged from his chair and forced to his knees.

"You will not touch me! Sikismek!" Berdigon yelled furiously, yanking his arm away from the officers as they reached for him. Cutlery clattered to the floor in the ruckus, bystanders taking notice, bringing their children close and holding their phones up to catch the scene on video.

Rhône and Berdigon looked good in handcuffs as they were led away in front of their fellow cardinals, finally silent.

At the same time, the rest of the conspirators were found and arrested simultaneously. And three drone strikes were dispatched in Iraq and Syria, missiles colliding against known headquarters of the plot's lieutenants, whose presence in the buildings was confirmed via satellite monitoring. On the black and white screens relaying the drones' feed, the only thing that could be seen were billows of white smoke and crumbling buildings with scatterings of fire.

The buzz hit the city quickly, the streets clearing as families grew nervous for their safety. Still, there was one more person who would put up the biggest fight. Brian Stevens would not hesitate to take hostages.

At exactly 1:00, Brett, along with three of his men, worked their way up to the third floor of the hotel as quietly as they could, careful with their heavy boots on the marble stairs. Two more men stayed in the lobby, each watching the stairwell and elevator, as well as one outside the building and two across the street with their rifles concealed but ready.

As Brett approached the door and leaned in to listen against it, rapid shots came ringing through. Stunned, he staggered back, and he and his men ducked and covered instinctively, dropping to the carpeted hallway. As he lifted his head from the floor, Brett noticed a camera set up in the corner a few feet away from him. "Shit!"

The door flew open, and as a pair of running feet flashed by Brett's face, a smoke bomb deployed, filling the hall with a thick white haze, the automatic firing continuing all the while. Stevens worked his way down the hall in the smoke. Dazed by the surprise attack and lost in smoke, Brett grabbed his walkie talkie to notify the team members downstairs and across the street. "He's on the move!" he yelled, choking. "Go! Go!"

Slamming through the stairwell, Stevens encountered two members on the first level waiting for him. He continued rapid firing down the stairwell as he walked. The members leapt through a door, taking cover, and Stevens cursed loudly, running down the stairs. He fired shots wildly behind him, aiming at nothing in particular but keeping up the appearance of retaliation. Bits of drywall crumbled to the floor. Screams erupted outside as people heard the shooting and ran.

Brett followed Stevens silently, hoping to be somewhat veiled by the smoke. Stopping at the emergency exit, the assassin took another smoke bomb from his coat, engaged it, and opened the door and thrust it outside. Brett knew his men would dare not shoot in the smoke.

"Damn it!" he muttered into his radio. "Hold your fire, I'm right behind him. Watch where he goes."

"Roger."

The assassin slipped out of the doorway into a cloud of smoke. Using it to his advantage, he crouched alongside the building until he found an open window. He opened it, slipped inside, then sprinted through the room into the hall, heading for the other side of the building.

Brett's radio crackled. "We can't see him!"

"Got him. He's back in the building moving to the south side. Reconvene there now. I'm switching off my radio."

Gripping his firearm, Brett moved swiftly through the room, his eyes darting everywhere at once. Screams erupted down the hallway on his right. A woman burst out of a room and ran away crying. A window shattered and Brett heard a heavy thump as something landed outside. Crunching glass. Another thump.

He raced to the door, extending his gun as he made his way into the room, quickly checking every corner before proceeding to the window, where he saw Stevens sprinting through the busy Rome streets, pushing people who got in his way. He whipped around, spotted Brett in the window and opened fire until his clip was empty. He threw down his gun and continued running.

A bullet embedded in his shoulder, Brett stumbled to the wall, turning on his radio. "He's gone," he said. "We've lost control. Notify the local police. Seal off the exits for a mile radius. Contact the guards on the pope and bishop. Do it now!"

Charlotte was boiling tea in her apartment when she heard a loud thump! from outside her door. On her desk, her phone started ringing.

Ring... ring!

But she didn't pick it up. She frowned at the sudden silence outside, puzzled. "Eduardo?" she called, moving closer to the door. There was no answer. She put her ear to the door. "Eduardo, are you there?"

Nothing. But there was a shadow through the crack under the door. Someone was standing there. She backed away, slowly. The door handle jiggled. Locked. Someone pounded on the door. Kicked it. The door bent inward. Charlotte rushed to her nightstand just as the door burst open with a spray of splinters. The green-eyed man stepped forward, sweating, haggard. In his hand was a long thin knife, bloodied. Behind him was the crumpled form of Eduardo on the ground. He was not breathing.

"What do you want?" Charlotte said, panicked.

"You know," he grunted, stepping forward and raising the knife.

Charlotte took something from her nightstand drawer. A gun. She held it in front of her, trembling.

The man stopped for a moment, surprise washing over his face. Then he smiled. "You wouldn't," he said. He walked forward.

Two shots rang out, and Brian Stevens crumpled to the ground.

The phone was still ringing. In shock, Charlotte went and picked it up. "Charlotte! He's coming for you. He's…"

"Dead," she said, her voice muffled. "I just… I just shot him."

William paused. "Are you hurt?"

"No, but Eduardo is dead. I don't know about Marco. I don't… God help me."

"He already has," William said. "We'll be right there. Keep the gun aimed at the door and don't let anyone in until you hear my voice. I'm coming."

Fifteen minutes later William announced his arrival. There were police outside the door, but they had been ordered to remain there to make sure no one came near Charlotte's apartment. Marco had run up the moment he heard the shots fired. Apparently, Stevens had climbed up a fire escape, broken into an apartment and then found his way to Charlotte's floor. If she hadn't been carrying a gun, she'd be dead.

Charlotte didn't cry as they led her away. "Pope Peter Paul," she muttered. "Is he okay?"

A Change of Faith

"He is," William said, covering her face with his coat as a crowd of onlookers and media snapped pictures. It would be all over the world news in a matter of minutes.

She hesitated before they reached the car. "Is it over?"

William put a hand on her shoulder. "Yes," he said. "It's over."

Charlotte melted in his arms as a wave of relief flooded over her. "Thank God," she said. "Thank God."

As local police arrived, Brett brushed drywall from his hair. He identified himself as American Secret Service and exited the building, his muscles aching and shoulder pounding from the impact of the bullet. He'd been shot before, on occasion much worse than this. He'd survive.

"Sir, wait!" an officer called after him, but he continued on. Once he felt he was far enough away, he glanced over his shoulder to see his team members staggering out of the building behind him, seemingly unharmed. He smiled to himself and ruffled more dust from his hair. He had received word: Stevens was dead. Bishop Kotlinski was okay. It would go down as an assassination attempt gone sideways. Italian law enforcement took full credit for the nine arrests at the Vatican and for attending to the scene at the hotel to apprehend Stevens. Soon, news would spread throughout the world about the alleged plot to kill the pope. Italian authorities would become international heroes. Within a few months, all nine involved in the plot would be sentenced to prison.

One of his agents caught up to him. "Sir, are you all right?"

"Yeah," Brett said, smiling. "I'm doing just fine."

Epilogue

John soon found himself the father of a baby girl, Alka, named after his grandmother. He was settling into his new home with Maria, adjusting to marriage, parenting, and his fame, which he still couldn't quite accept. Though his success still hadn't set in, he realized his life would be very different going forward. Thank God for his friends, especially Michael. When they came to his little studio for their monthly dinners, he was still just John Adams, and his work was still just "interesting."

Charlotte was finally reappointed to Detroit by the pope, this time as Archbishop Kotlinski in charge of the entire diocese. She was something of a superstar, what with her title and her surviving an assassination attempt. Women were now entering the seminaries in multiples, and Catholicism was "cool" again. So much had happened since her first days in the seminary. Her parents both passed away, and her sister Shawne was married with two babies. The downtown Detroit churches she oversaw were prospering, as was the city itself, and her soup kitchen was still being operated on a daily basis.

One Saturday morning in the crisp fall, Charlotte spontaneously decided she wanted a few fresh goods from the Eastern Market. She'd prepare a lovely dinner for one, she decided. Pulling on her peacoat and woolen hat with her jeans and black boots, she drove down to the market. As Archbishop of Detroit, she was pulled in many directions every day, and sometimes it was nice to get away for a few minutes and just be Charlotte again. Roaming through the vegetable booths enjoying the cool air, a friendly old voice whispered in her ear, "Hey, ma'am. Want some asparagus?"

Charlotte's mouth fell open with a breathy laugh, her eyes filled with tears. For some reason, she was afraid to turn around. "I… I believe I have all the vegetables I need for the day, thank you very much," she said. Silence. "But a cup of coffee sure would taste good." Then she turned and faced those bright blue eyes she hadn't seen in so long.

"Hey, I'm John Adams," he said, smiling. The smile felt like home. "And you are…?"

Charlotte's heart swelled so full that she placed a hand on her chest, certain for a moment that it would burst. "My name's Charlotte Kotlinski," she said. "Please try and remember it."

They hugged hard, arms tight around shoulders and waists. Then side-by-side, they made their way to the Eastern Market coffee shop, where two raggedy chairs in the corner sat empty, waiting for a pair of old friends to fill them.

END

Made in the USA
Middletown, DE
20 September 2018